Someone to Watch OVER ME

BOOK 3 IN THE WOUNDED HEARTS SERIES

DEBBIE CROMACK

Printed in the United States of America

Book Cover & Interior Formatting: Qamber Designs
(https://www.qamberdesignsandmedia.com/)
Developmental Editor: Susan Staudinger (https://www.stylisticediting.com/)
Copy Editor: Kat Wyeth (https://katsliteraryservices.com/)
Proofreader: Ellison Lane (https://katsliteraryservices.com/)

The publisher is not responsible for websites (or their content) that are not owned by the publisher.

ISBN 979-8-9864008-1-5 (pbk.)
ISBN 979-8-9864008-0-8 (eBook)

This book is dedicated to those who are following your dreams of
becoming a published author.
The road may get challenging.
Those who you thought would support you, may not.
There may be days you feel like you have no idea what you're doing.
You may feel lonely sometimes, even isolated.
Know you're never alone.
The book community is filled with kind and supportive people.
Just reach out.
And never, EVER, give up.
You've got this!
Sending you my love, encouragement, and lots of hugs.

VISUAL RECOMMENDATION - PINTEREST

Get a glimpse into the world of Angelo and Lucia in Someone to Watch Over Me: https://www.pinterest.com/debbiecromackauthor/someone-to-watch-over-me/

PLAYLIST

Also on Spotify: https://open.spotify.com/playlist/6AUdAWXtqI5jp0pBPTTfo9?si=5600789e592643a0

Prologue – "I found" by Amber Run

Chapter 1 – "I Think I Love Him (Kean Dysso Remix)" by Antonia and "anything 4 u" by LANY

Chapter 2 – "i'm yours" by Isabel LaRosa and "Falling" by Besomorph, N3WPORT & Meo

Chapter 3 – "Teardrop" by Massive Attack

Chapter 4 – "Tequila (Live in Aspen)" by Music Love Travel

Chapter 5 – "Maybe Tomorrow" by Stereophonics

Chapter 6 – "Silverline" by Omido

Chapter 7 – "Faded" by Alan Walker

Chapter 8 – "Lift Me Up" by Mree

Chapter 9 – "Photograph" by Ed Sheeran

Chapter 10 – "Lay It On Me" by Kyler England

Chapter 11 – "Drops" by Jungle

Chapter 12 – "I Knew I Loved You" by Music Love Travel

Chapter 13 – "Waiting for the Stars" by Jordan Soulman and "Ruin My Life" by Zara Larsson

Chapter 14 – "Lost in the Fire" by The Weeknd and "Carry You (feat. Fleurie)" by Ruelle

TRIGGER WARNINGS

This book contains some things that may be triggers for some readers. Those things include miscarriage and the passing of a grandparent.

PROLOGUE

—

Angelo

Watching someone you love get their heart broken time after time and not being able to take away their pain is crippling. Yet, this is exactly what I've chosen to do.

When I was ten years old, my dad shared with me a piece of life-knowledge that I took to heart. He told me that your first love is never your last love. So now I suffer as I watch her get her heart broken and wait for the time to be right and for her to be ready for me.

And through my suffering, I try to remember the joy that will come when she's finally ready. This is my plan and what I've chosen to endure because I've been in love with Lucia since the day she was born.

One thing my dad didn't share with me is that plans can change in the blink of an eye. And nothing could've prepared me for the obliteration of my heart.

1

Angelo

I'm supposed to protect her, like a big brother should. I'm not supposed to fall in love with her.

I was two years old when I fell in love with Lucia Cipriani. I've known her since the day she was brought home from the hospital. Our parents are best friends. We've grown up just blocks apart and our families spend a lot of time together on weekends and even vacation together sometimes.

We've gone to the same schools our entire lives. Though she's two years behind me, she's always been smarter than me, just one of the things I admire about her. I've taken to being a big-brother figure and watching out for her, which frustrates her sometimes. It's the role I've assumed. One, because I *am* protective of her, and two, because both our dads expect it of me, and they've told me so. She's so damn pretty too, with a body any guy would masturbate to, including me — a fact she'll never find out about. Her physical appearance draws attention from a lot of guys — a lot of dirtbags.

I graduate from UCLA in a couple weeks and tonight's frat party is an epic celebration so far. Drinking with my friends, playing pool, and dancing sweaty bodies-smashed-against-sweaty bodies in the dimly lit basement. The floor and walls vibrate to the pounding music as the stench of stale beer and pot wafts through the air.

Then *she* walks in.

My Lucia...but not mine. I didn't know she was coming.

Though she's been here a lot, she's never come to a party. At least she's with her roommate-slash-best friend, Prisha. Neither of them are party girls, quite the opposite, in fact. I wouldn't have had so much to drink if I knew I'd basically be on bodyguard duty tonight.

The theme of the party is, "boxer shorts and lingerie." Seeing my white dress shirt on her, now I know why she borrowed it. Thank God she's wearing it over her lingerie. Only two of the buttons are closed at her chest, and the boxers, also mine — little thief — cover her butt and tops of her thighs. Her long legs are accentuated by black stiletto heels. *Jesus, I want to know what she's wearing underneath my clothes.*

Trying not to ruin her night by stalking over and telling her to leave, I tuck into the hallway with the burnt-out light bulb, watching her like a hawk as drunk, hormone-raging turkey vultures sniff out her virginity and circle around her and Prisha like they're prey. She shouldn't be in a place like this. My jaw tight, I grit my teeth, ready to pounce if any of them so much as thinks about touching her.

One of my sleazeball frat brothers, Joe, enters the circle and hands them each a beer. He's not necessarily a bad guy, he's just a man-whore, and *not* someone I want hanging around Lucia. With her still here two more years after I'm gone, I have no idea how I'm going to protect her from assholes like him. Irritation pounds at my temples to the thump of the music as I tilt my plastic cup into my mouth, letting the beer slide down my throat while keeping my eyes on Lucia.

The girls spot me, exchanging words as they look at me and back at each other.

Lucia

"Never?" Prisha's voice rises as her dark brown eyes widen in disbelief.

"No, never. We don't think about each other that way." My heart sinks a little. The statement is a complete lie on my end. I say it to convince myself, knowing the effort is pointless. "Angelo just

—" I shrug, "doesn't see me that way. He looks at me like I'm his little sister and that's all." He thinks he's being sly, tucked into the shadow of the hallway. But I feel his protective eyes watching me.

Outwardly, I'd always expressed my frustration with his need to protect me, but inside, I wondered if he intimidated any guy who even thought about asking me out because maybe he wanted me to be his and he was waiting for me to be old enough to tell me. That naïve thinking was of a hopeful, pitiful little girl. I know that now.

I've been waiting twenty years for him to tell me he feels something more for me than just friendship. As we've gotten older, my innocent childhood crush turned, shifted, morphed into a deep love that intertwined with heated lust once my hormones finally kicked in. But as long as I've waited and hoped, there's never been any indication that he feels anything close to the need and desire I feel. It's painfully obvious that he doesn't feel the same way about me as I feel about him. *Felt about him.*

"Well, maybe it's time you show him you're not so little anymore. Day-um." Brushing her ink-black hair over her shoulder, she shamelessly roves her eyes up and down his body of sculpted muscles that are accentuated by the dim lighting of the shadowy hallway. "I know I'd be all over his fine ass." She snaps her fingers with a tilt of her head.

"Prisha." A laugh slips out of my numbing mouth.

She's not the only girl who swoons over him. His dark, Italian features and lean, muscular body have always captured gawking glares from girls.

Before we came to the party, Prisha and I had several glasses of wine followed by a few shots of Chocolate Cinnamon Toast Crunch and the effects are kicking in. I briefly look over at Angelo, catching a glimpse of his perfect chest and abs hiding beneath his open, black, collared shirt. I've seen his body plenty through the years and his dedication to working out since he came to college is evident in his mouthwatering physique.

"I'm serious. He's so damn hot. If you two didn't have this weird relationship, I'd get after what's behind those black boxers." She spouts a playful roaring sound, making me laugh. "I don't see him with anyone." Swiveling her head from side to side, she continues the motion through her wiggling body. "Let's just test him and see what happens."

"What do you mean?" I ask, lifting my heels alternately from the sticky floor.

"I mean," she says, taking a gulp of her beer then handing it to me to hold. Her eyes focused and twinkling with mischief, she unbuttons the two buttons on his shirt I'm wearing. "Let's test him…and see." She winks at me and opens the shirt a little.

"What are you doing? I don't think this is a good idea. Maybe we should go home," I say, sensing eyes surrounding me like a pack of wolves as my head grows dizzier.

"Not yet. I want you to walk over there and lean against the wall next to him. See what his reaction is." She cocks her head in his direction.

"I can tell you what his reaction will be. He'll cover me up and tell me to go the hell home." I know Angelo. When he looks at me, he sees a ten-year-old girl with pigtails, not a fully-developed woman. It's a truth I've cried about many a night. It took a long time, but I finally let go of my crush on him when he came to college. *At least that's what I keep telling myself.*

"Go on," she says, nudging me. "I'll be watching and I'll tell you what *I* see."

I sigh and decide to appease her so she'll let it go. Tossing back the rest of my beer, I hand her both of our cups. Though it's pointless, I turn and start walking toward him. His dark hair is a little longer on top and perfectly disheveled. The scruff dusting across his jaw is hours past a five o'clock shadow, making him even sexier.

Each step toward him sends sensations through me that I shouldn't be feeling but can't stop. His gaze travels up my body and I practically hear his thoughts, *"Put some clothes on and go home."*

When his brown eyes lock onto mine, they level me, sending butterflies flitting in my stomach.

Angelo

Lord, have mercy on me. She's a tall, straight shot of silky-smooth tequila. Every step of her heels onto the concrete floor sends a shock straight to my balls. As I watch her beautiful breasts bounce behind her black lace bra, I'm wishing I was wearing jeans instead of boxer shorts. *Think of disgusting shit.*

"This isn't quite your scene," I say as she approaches me. "Didn't expect to see you here." Resting my arm on the wall, I try not to seem as drunk as I am.

She leans her back against the wall, standing close to me. "Prisha and I were bored. I couldn't study anymore. We knew you guys were having a party so we thought we'd stop by."

I turn myself to face her, trying to block the view of her hot body from ogling, testosterone-filled, thirsty glares, and put my palms on the wall on either side of her. "You had to pick the boxer shorts and lingerie party to come to, huh?" It's taking all my willpower not to glance down at her full, succulent breasts. Instead, I bore my gaze into her hazelnut eyes.

"Yeah, why?" she asks, her tone bordering belligerence.

I fucking cave, glancing down at her breasts then forcing my eyes to return to hers. "Do you want a sweatshirt from my room?" It comes out more like a command than an actual question that would imply she has a choice. I'm not trying to be an asshole. I'm simply trying to prevent her goddess-like body from being visually defiled by every guy in the room.

Her eyes darken, darting back and forth between mine as I take a deep, heavy breath…trying not to visually defile her myself.

She heaves a disgruntled sigh. "You can't protect me from everyone forever," she says, a hint of venom rides her tongue as her eyebrow raises and she sasses her head from side to side.

I lower my face, inches from hers. "Wanna bet?" Provoking her,

I raise an eyebrow right back at her.

It's rare for her to drink much and I can tell she's had plenty. Shit, if her sassiness isn't turning up the heat of the air between us. A line dents her brow as her chest rises and falls with hot breaths that sweep across my lips. *What I'd do for just a taste.*

She's a wicked temptation who's becoming harder to resist. *Fuck. Get a grip on your drunk ass.*

She growls at me, frustration steaming from her ears. When she tries to duck under my arm, I scoop her up and throw her over my shoulder, causing laughter, hoots, and howls from the surrounding sea of bodies.

With eyes on us, I start walking up the stairs as she pounds on my back, yelling, "Put me down!" So feisty.

I head straight for my room, close the door, and put her on her feet, holding her until she's steady in her heels.

"What's wrong with you?" she shouts. "No guy on this entire campus will come near me because of you." Eyes squinched together and pointing her finger into my bare chest, she takes a step toward me like she's ready to rumble and it's so damn cute. "You're *not* my brother and you're *not* my boyfriend." I can't tell if her voice is laced with anger or hurt…or both. Then she softens. "You're my best friend, Ang." Her yearning eyes are killing me.

I say nothing. Hunger boils my blood. It's taking every ounce of restraint to not throw her sexy ass on my bed and put my mouth on every part of her body I've wanted to taste for as long as I can remember. I keep my secret hidden. Hidden under layers of steel. I can't let her know until the time is right.

Throwing both arms in the air, she growls again and tries to get past me. I reach out my arm and stop her, pinning her against the wall.

Startled, she looks up at me from between my arms. So… fucking…beautiful. Her long dark waves hug the sides of her luscious breasts as her eyes spit daggers at me from beneath thick lashes.

We stare at each other, breathing the same air. The dulled pounding of music filling our ears.

"Why do you put me on this pedestal so no one can reach me?" Her feistiness shifts to confusion, grasping for answers. Answers I'm not willing to confess. She belongs on a pedestal. There's not a single guy on this campus, or anywhere for that matter, who's worthy of her.

"None of the guys you pick are good enough for you."

Fury returns to her as she puts her hands on my chest and pushes me away. "No one is, Angelo, according to you! Who *is* good enough for me?" she blasts, getting up in my face, glaring at me. "*You?*"

The question smashes me in the face. Nope, not even me. My heart fists in my chest, pounding.

I step back to prevent myself from grabbing her and kissing her. "You've had too much to drink. I'm not letting you go back down there dressed like this and drunk."

She slams her arms by her sides. "You can't stop me," she fumes, making another attempt to leave.

Without much effort, I grab her again and toss her onto my bed. "You'll stay here tonight so I can look after you. I'm not letting you near those vultures. Take off your shoes and get under the covers."

She squints her eyes, resigning to the fact that she's lost this battle. "You're infuriating. You know that?" Standing up, she starts taking off my boxers.

I quickly look away, wanting to watch every move she makes as she takes my clothes off of her body. Listening for the sound of my sheets, I wait. Trying to distract myself from picturing her, I stare at the painting of the flaming guitar on my wall. Dad gave it to me on my thirteenth birthday. It's my favorite piece of art. And it's also a reminder that'll I'll never be anywhere near as musically talented as him.

"Are you in?"

"I'm in, bully."

I take off my shirt and shoes, and shut off the light before getting into the bed, turning my back to her. Wanting to do the exact opposite, and knowing that's a bad idea. She's been in my bed plenty of times, usually crying on my chest about some jerk who stood her up or getting a B on an exam. This is uncomfortably different, I've never been drunk with my self-control compromised.

Her soft hand is on my shoulder, tugging me.

I lie on my back, gazing at her beautiful, moonlight-kissed face, restraining myself and trying to ignore the flames licking my dick. *Give me willpower.*

"I'm sorry." She makes a pout with her lips. "I *am* drunk. I shouldn't have come here. But, Ang, you're not going to be here next year to protect me from *the vultures.* You have to let me stand on my own two feet and trust that I can take care of myself when you're not here."

Not being near her and not knowing what's happening in her daily life is going to kill me. It's not her I don't trust. It's asshole guys who only see her beautiful face and want her body. She thinks they like her, she falls for them, then they show their true colors when she won't let them fuck her, and she's left brokenhearted. Watching her hurt tears me up.

I blow a puff of air and roll my eyes up. "It's gonna be hard not being here and wondering if you're okay." The thought's been plaguing me for months. Agitation tightens my chest at how helpless I'm going to feel.

"Will you do me a favor?" The sweetness of her voice is an elixir, a drug of temptation that gives me a rush like nothing else.

"Anything." I would literally do anything for this girl.

She lifts up then throws her leg over my body and sits up, straddling me. My shirt slides off one of her shoulders as she rests her hands on my stomach, heating my skin with her touch. *Holy fuck.* Lust shrieks through my body. Desire pounds, relentless, matching the thumping of the music filtering up from the basement. I can't stop my dick from hardening. Resisting the urge to grab her hips, I grab my pillow above my head, sinking my fingers deep into the stuffing.

"Will you make love to me?" The purity in her eyes stabs my heart.

Anything except this.

"What?" *The fuck!* I clench my hands harder into the pillow as tension burns in every muscle. I've only fantasized it a million times.

Here she is, asking me to do it. The truth is, I've always wanted to be her first. But no. I'm holding out to be her last. And we're not doing it like this. Not with her drunk and not in a frat house.

"I know you've had sex with other girls already." A tug at the corner of her delicious mouth rides the line of fear and seduction.

"Lucia, fucking no." It flies out with an edge of anger I wasn't able to filter in my hazy head. A mix of confusion and craving twists inside me as hot blood swarms my veins. I swivel my head once to each side, reinforcing my clipped words.

She winces, shattering me. "Why? Am I not pretty enough or sexy enough or...good enough?" Those pained, hazelnut doe-eyes search mine frantically.

Instinct rushes my hands to her hips and I grip tightly. "Stop it. Don't say that." She's all of those and *so* much more. She's fucking perfection.

"Please, Ang. I don't want my first time to be with some guy I barely know. I want it to be with someone I trust. Someone I know won't hurt me...or my heart." Her pleading eyes test my willpower, tempting me. Naïve seductress. She's devastation drenched in innocence.

My best friend is sitting on top of me as my uncontrollable hard-on presses against the thin lace fabric of the panties covering her virgin lips and she's begging me to fuck her.

This girl is going to destroy me someday.

2

Lucia

I first found out about Angelo having sex from Jenny Simpkins. I overheard her talking to some friends at the café. She couldn't see me so didn't know I was listening when she started talking about having sex with him. I was sick to my stomach and ran out of there so fast before I could hear any more. I vividly remember that ache in my chest. It was unlike anything I'd ever felt before. It hurt far worse than when I found out about the first girl he kissed. It was supposed to be me. I'd wanted to be his first kiss, the first girl he made love to, and the girl he married.

Turns out, I'm not his first anything…and I never will be.

You'd think after all this time I'd realize that nothing more than friendship will ever exist between us. Yet, my heart can't seem to figure that out. It's holding on to a hopeless fantasy, refusing to let go.

My heart pounds so fast and loud in my chest, it's echoing in my ears. I can't believe I just asked him to take my virginity. Who did I think I was kidding? I'm not over my crush on him. I don't know that I ever will be. Though I'm not his first, I want him to be *my* first. And right now, my desire is in overdrive, consuming my thoughts and my body.

I've spent years only being able to admire his beautiful body, desperately craving to touch it. Finally feeling his heating skin beneath my fingertips, I want to touch every muscular inch of him and let my hands roam his entire body.

His hard-on grows beneath me. That has to mean he feels *something* for me, doesn't it? Or is he hard just because I happen to be female and he's drunk? My breathing is audible as I stare down at him waiting...

With his hands gripped tightly around my waist, he tugs me down as he pushes his pelvis up into me. Two quick gasps accompany a flurry of tingles that blaze the surface of my skin. A low growl rumbles deep in his throat as he repeats the motion, hungry eyes matching his increasing breaths.

Since I have no idea what I'm doing, I let my body respond, spreading my knees a bit wider, pushing down harder.

"Fuck." The word breathes out of him in a lust-filled whisper as his eyes close. He tilts back his head, veins bulge along the sides of his neck.

Before I can take another breath, his eyes fly open and he lifts me off him, flipping me onto my back and pinning me beneath him. Holding my wrists on either side of my head, he hovers his upper body above me. Moonlight streams through the window, casting a glow across his face and the peaks of his chest. His lower body is snug between my thighs where the tip of his head is perched at my entrance, thin fabric the only barrier between us. My breaths are so rapid, I think I might be hyperventilating.

He bends his elbows, bringing his face close, our noses almost touching, our lips a breath apart. My entire body ignites with need at the thought of what his lips will feel like against mine. To kiss him the way I've longed to kiss him for so many years. Though I'm nervous and terrified, I'm ready to give myself to him.

He doesn't kiss me. He stares at me with his moody brown eyes, his gaze moving from my eyes to my mouth and back again. Hot, heavy breaths sweep across my heating skin. When I lift my face toward his, desperate for his lips on mine, he pushes his upper body back up, causing his hard-on to push slightly into my wet lips behind my panties.

"Fuck." While his earlier expression was laced with a hint of surrender, this one is jagged with anger. A growl strangles in his throat as he releases my wrists and pushes himself off me and onto his knees. Thrusting his hands into his dark hair, he releases an exasperated sigh then flips onto his back.

Why did he stop?

After two slow, loud, deep breaths, he speaks. "No, Lucia. I can't do this."

My anticipation vanishes, replaced by the pain of unrequited desire. The heat scorching the air between us seconds ago has turned to frosty condensation that instantly cools the surface of my skin and stabs my heart like an ice pick. As fast as I can move my hands, I tug his shirt around me as if covering myself is going to magically erase every emotion that's raging through me and I'm sure are plastered all over my face.

I bite the side of my tongue to keep from letting any tears escape. "Can't or won't?" I challenge. Will he answer me honestly?

He lifts up and sits on the edge of the bed with his back toward me. In the dull moonlight, I watch his head drop between his shoulders.

"Get some sleep," he says, defeat lingering on each word. With a sigh, he gets out of the bed. "I'll be right back. Don't leave. You know I'll just find you and bring you back. You'll stay here tonight." Every word is heavy and delivered like he's fighting exhaustion. "I'll keep you safe." This last, low utterance sounds more like a mantra.

Rejection splinters my heart. Embarrassment winds through my veins. If I wasn't so buzzed and tired, I'd run out of here. As soon as he walks out the door, the tears building behind my eyes flood out as my body hunches and my shoulders jerk to the rhythm of my sobs. That's the last thing I remember as the thumping music from below me fades in my ears and I fall asleep.

⪢⪡

The sun sears through the window like a beam shooting directly onto my aching eyelids. I close my mouth and move my tongue around, trying to bring some moisture to the arid canyon. Squinting, I force my eyes open which only intensifies the throbbing in my head. As I sit up in Angelo's bed, it only takes a couple seconds for the memory of last night to pummel forward in my thoughts. I'm a gnarled mess of emotions that I don't have the energy to process right now.

Angelo's not in the bed, so I don't know if he even came back in to sleep. What I *do* know is that I've got to get out of here. I put on his boxers I wore last night, take off his shirt, grab one of his sweatshirts, and put it on. *Shoot, I don't have the best shoes for sneaking out and running home.*

I slide into my heels and, very gingerly, put only the ball of my foot onto each step down the wooden staircase, careful not to let the heel touch and announce me. As I get closer to the bottom, I hear voices coming through the kitchen doorway.

"Damn, Ang, you still didn't hit that?" Joe blurts crassly.

"Fuck you, Joe. Have some respect. Lucia's not like the chicks you bang and drop. Besides, you know she's like a sister to me."

His last words pierce my core. I miss the bottom step, landing hard on my heel that twists beneath me, sending pain shooting through my ankle and up my leg.

"Ow!" hurls out of me as I drop with a thud to the ground. So much for quietly sneaking out.

Angelo barrels through the doorway and rushes to me. "Are you okay?" he asks, helping me to my feet.

"I'm fine," I seethe. "Leave me alone," I blast, my face hot as I glare at him. Ripping my arm free from his grip, I hobble as fast as I can toward the door, pain continuing to sting. I force open the old, warped, wooden door and head for my apartment.

"Lucia, wait!" he calls out.

With the pain in my ankle, there's no way I can outwalk him. If I had sneakers on, I'd run through the pain. Within seconds, he's by my side, grabbing my arm.

"Lucia, stop. You're hurt. Do you want me to take you to the hospital?"

I keep walking. "No. It's not broken. If it was, I wouldn't be able to walk at all. I just twisted it. I'm fine. Please just leave me alone."

"Lucia, come on. Please don't be upset."

I stop and face him, heat crawling up my neck, balancing on one foot and a toe. "Upset? I'm humiliated, Ang. Yes, okay, I was drunk. I shouldn't have done and said those things. I still meant what I said. I'm going to lose my virginity someday. And I hope I'm smart enough to wait for someone I care about to lose it to. But," I can't stop my lower lip from quivering, "but, I know whoever it is will probably still end up breaking my heart. And with you, I would've been safe."

He takes my shoulders in his hands and lowers his head for our eyes to meet. "No, Lucia. You wouldn't have been safe with me." His voice tender, he gently shakes his head, holding my gaze. The muscles along his jaw flex. "I'm not safe for you that way. I have to protect you."

My boiling blood flares, a raging storm brewing inside me. "In case you missed it, I'm a grown woman and I don't need someone to watch over me! Least of all, *you*!" On the last word, I crane my neck up so I'm in his face.

"Watching over you *is* my responsibility. And I can't protect you if I…if I —" His eyes dart back and forth between mine then sweep down to my lips before returning to my eyes.

"If you what, Angelo?" Adrenaline surges through my core and out to each limb. *Tell me you love me. Tell me you want me the way I want you.*

"If I were to have feelings for you," he grits out, his fingers pressing into my arms.

"Do you?" I beg, softening, hoping. "Other than our friendship, do you have feelings for me?" I search his face, praying for him to feel something for me.

The muscles in his jaw tighten again as his nostrils flare and my question floats between us. "Lucia, you have to understand. My role in your life is limited to protecting you and making sure you're safe."

"And that's it? That's all?" I challenge.

Hovering above me, nostrils still flaring, his darkening eyes bore into me. "Our entire lives, it's been expected of me to be your protector. And that means I can't have feelings for you." His chest heaves so close to my face, passion twists between our heating bodies.

The conflict in his eyes screams louder than his contrasting words, revealing everything they're not saying. His jaw hard, his eyes feral. Is it possible to want to punch someone and kiss them with every fiber of your being all at the same time? It must be because that's exactly how I feel right now. A stone statue, I stand silent, awaiting his response.

Longing etches lines between his brows as his silence meets mine, answering me.

Well, I guess that's it. He feels *nothing* for me. Nothing other than I'm like an annoying little sister he feels he has to protect. Whatever minuscule thing he might've felt that revealed itself in his eyes during those few seconds, vanishes in an instant. Acid swirls in my stomach, mixing with last night's alcohol. I might vomit. Instead, I blast him with violent words I rarely ever use and *never* thought I'd say to him, but they fly out of my mouth, directly from my wounded heart. "Fuck you! I hate you!"

Yanking my shoulders from his grip, I turn and shuffle-walk in my heels as pain shoots through my ankle.

In seconds, he's in front of me and squats down. "Get on my back."

"No." I don't want his help. I don't need his help.

He turns his head back to look up at me. "I'm not asking you. I'm telling you," he commands. "Stop being stubborn and get on my back."

Though I vehemently do *not* want to, my ankle really hurts. Giving in, I climb onto his back and he walks to my apartment. Neither of us says another word. My teeth clench in annoyance the entire way.

When we enter the kitchen, Prisha's making breakfast. "Well, look what the cat dragged in." I'm not in the mood for her insinuations or her sass. This mess is kind of her fault.

He lowers down for me to climb off. I hobble straight to my

bedroom, hearing them on my way.

"What the hell happened?" Prisha asks, losing her sassy tone.

"I'd better let her tell you. Make sure she ices her ankle, okay?"

I step out of my shoes, crawl onto my bed, and bury my face into my pillow, letting the tears flow.

About ten minutes later, there's a knock on my door. I don't answer. Prisha comes in anyway. When she opens the door, I turn myself over and sit up, crossing one leg under me and leaving my injured ankle resting. She's carrying a tray with scrambled eggs, bacon, toast, and my favorite Pooh Bear mug filled with coffee. We've been friends since elementary school so it's tough to stay mad at her, especially since she's the most badass friend a girl could have.

She places the tray in the middle of the bed and joins me, sitting cross-legged in front of me. "Wanna talk about it?" she asks, her soft tone comforting me.

I blow a long sigh and look up at the ceiling before picking up my coffee mug and meeting her eyes. "Well." I half-smile, swallowing the lump in my throat. Looking down into the coffee I'm holding with both hands, I squeeze together my puffy eyes, then look back up at her. "We have our answer." I push a smile to my lips as a tear leaves my eye. "He doesn't have any feelings for me." Sadness tugs down the corners of my mouth as I shake my head.

Prisha's mouth mirrors mine as she reaches her honey-brown-skinned hand out to rest on my wrist. "I'm sorry. And I'm sorry I encouraged you to basically throw yourself at him."

I shake my head. "It's okay. I've wondered for years if he ever felt anything for me. And with him graduating this year and going out into the world, I know it's going to change our relationship. If you hadn't pushed me, I wouldn't have done it, and I'd always wonder." I look down, running a thumb up and down the side of my mug. "As much as it sucks, at least now I know."

She squeezes my wrist, quirks her lips, and then lets go. "What happened anyway? I have to admit, when you didn't come home, I actually got excited and thought you two finally gave in and got together."

"Ugh," I groan. "I was mortified. He insisted I stay over so he could watch over me and I completely threw myself at him." I drop my head into my palm then look back up at her. "I sat on top of him, both of us in our underwear, and asked him to make love to me."

At my confession, I can still feel the heat of his skin beneath my fingers and the way his hard body pressed into mine, lighting me on fire with a need I'd never experienced before. My body's never reacted to a guy's touch the way it did to Angelo's. Even now, after his rejection, I yearn to feel his skin press against mine.

Her eyes widen as she gasps and her hand flies to her mouth. "W-what did he say?"

"Well, of course, he said no. Then he flipped me over and was, like, right —" I motion between my legs, bugging out my eyes, "there. And —" I exhale.

"Yeah?" Overly excited anticipation pitches her voice. Her eyes are even wider now.

"And I was inches away from kissing him." The last time our lips will ever be that close. My heart sinks.

"You were? What happened then?" She looks like she's going to burst.

"Then, he jumped out of the bed." I fling my hand through the air.

"He *did*?" Her voice raises two octaves.

"He did. I wanted to disappear. I was so embarrassed."

She tilts her head. "No. Don't be embarrassed."

"How can I not be? I'm such a fool." I drop my head in defeat.

"You're not a fool. You're in love."

"Not anymore. He'll never see me the way I see him. When I came down this morning, I overheard him confirming to Joe that he only sees me like a sister." I shrug. "So, that's it. I have to realize that what I have — had — was a childhood crush and now it's over, for good." If only my heart would latch onto this concept.

Her shoulders slump as her lips turn down again. "Maybe it's for the best. The love of your life is out there. He's getting ready for you." Unfolding her legs, she grabs a piece of bacon, and gets off the bed. "In the meantime, you're going to live your life and date some guys. And when it's time to lose your virginity, you'll know." She winks and takes a bite of the bacon. "Mm, I left the curry powder out of the eggs. Figured your stomach might not do well with it after all that alcohol." She walks out of my room, still talking. "I'm gonna grab an ice pack for your ankle."

I chuckle. Seriously, I can't stay mad at her. Ultimately, I made the choice to strut my half-naked self over to him. And now, I know exactly how he feels.

My heart is crushed.

3

Angelo

Torturing myself on my walk back to the frat house, I replay every moment of last night and this morning in my head. I wanted Lucia so badly last night. I can't even believe I had the willpower to stop. When my dick popped through the fly of my boxers, it took everything in me not to slide her panties aside and plunge into her. But that's not how I want it to be, fast and sloppy with both of us drunk. When I make love to her for the first time, it's going to be slow and romantic with both of us being completely ready for each other.

I've never lied to her before. My stomach twisted when I lied to her about my feelings. But what was I supposed to say? "Uh, yes, I love you and I want to marry you and have babies with you and grow old with you." I need to let her experience life and other guys. Though the thought of her with other guys sickens me, it's only fair. I never want her to have regrets.

Everything's about to change and, I admit, I'm kind of freaked out. In two weeks, I graduate, then we have our combined family vacation for a week, and then I move into my condo and start my adult life with my adult job. I don't know when I'm going to see Lucia once I'm out on my own. She's always been only minutes away and part of my daily life. Waiting at least two years for her to graduate and be ready for me is going to be so freaking hard.

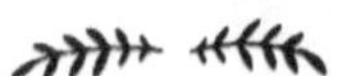

My graduation celebration was small, comprised only of my family, Lucia's family, and a couple close friends. Lucia gave me the cold shoulder all night, only offering a cordial congratulatory — and stiff — hug in front of our families. Not even a gift. Not that I need one. She's just a very thoughtful gift-giver and it's surprising that she wouldn't get me anything for graduation. I've kept every gift she's ever given me.

She's still mad at me. Who knows what our vacation's going to be like. I can't stand having her mad at me.

Ever since I got my license, I'd drive Lucia and my little sister, Bella, to our family vacation spot. Our parents rent the same, huge house in San Francisco every year and we'd have a blast driving up in the "kids only" car. Lucia would call me the night before we left and we'd talk about the fun things we were going to do and how excited we were for vacation.

This year, no phone call. And she's decided to drive up with her parents. I was hoping this would be the best vacation before I head off into full adulthood and responsibilities. Now it's going to be clouded and murky. My heart is heavy, conflicted.

Groggy from a restless night, I pack up the car with Bella and we head out. I'd promised to stop at her favorite place for snacks, Beachwood Market, on our way up north. Her stomach full with a breakfast sandwich and coffee, she excitedly tells me about the colleges she's applying to. She's so artistically talented, it blows my mind. While eighty-five percent of my attention is on her, the other fifteen percent is thinking about Lucia.

"Earth to Angelo." Bella leans over, waving her hand in front of my face. "Are you even listening to me?" She puts her elbow on the center console, rests her chin on her knuckles, and looks up at me with a pout on her lips.

"I'm sorry, Bells. Yeah, I'm listening. I'm just, uh, you know, paying attention to the traffic."

She looks around us. "You mean the *two* other cars on the road that are nowhere near us?" Her sarcasm is playful, but I do feel bad for not fully paying attention to her.

"Safety first. I have precious cargo in here." I look down at her and smile. It's going to be tough being hours away from her too. As far as little sisters go, Bella's the best. She's one of the most tenacious people I know and has a huge heart. She also has a confidence that I often wish I had more of in myself.

"Come on. Spill it. You've been cranky the last couple weeks. Did you and Lucia have a fight? Why isn't she with us?" Always curious and so perceptive.

"No, uh, we didn't have a fight. A lot's changing, that's all. And my mind's preoccupied." I avoid her question about why Lucia isn't with us. "I'm so proud of you. You're going to have your pick of schools."

"Thanks Ang." Sitting back into her seat, she's quiet for a moment. "It's gonna be weird not having you around as much. I kinda liked that, even though you lived on campus, and in that disgusting frat house, you still came home a few times a month."

"Yes, the frat house was gross, but you know how clean my room was. And I'm not moving to Alaska. I won't be *that* far away." I give her shoulder a little shove.

"I know." She looks over at me, a slant to her lips. "It's just gonna be weird. You're going to meet all kinds of new people and you'll be doing things with them. And, I know that's what happens. You gotta go be an adult and start creating your life." She shrugs. "Still, I'm gonna miss my big brother." The sadness in her eyes tugs at my heart.

"Hey. Bells. I'll always be just a phone call away, okay?" I pat her thigh. "And you can come visit me."

That Bella-smile lights up her face. "I'll come decorate your condo for Christmas," she says, her words practically bouncing out of her as the sparkle returns to her eyes.

"You better." I give her a big smile. For as long as I can remember, every Christmas, Bella brings a few decorations to my room so I'll have "Christmas magic" around me. She even did it at the frat house. "Now, tell me more about your schools. Are you leaning toward one more than the others yet?"

She launches back into talking about the colleges she wants to attend. She's always been a go-getter. Highly organized, motivated, and knows what she wants. I have no doubt that my little Bells is going to pave her way to the success she wants.

She's so much like Lucia in that way. Lucia knew in fifth grade that she wanted to be a teacher. She's incredibly smart and great with kids. I'd have failed a couple classes if it wasn't for her tutoring me. And now she's on her way to being an elementary school teacher. She's going to be amazing with those kids.

When Bella and I arrive at the house, everyone else is already there. We bring our bags to our rooms and go to the kitchen to help put away groceries. The grocery run is top priority upon arrival.

"Lucia!" Bella squeals, running to Lucia and wrapping her arms around her. "I feel like it's been so long since I've seen you in person."

"I know." They release. "Have you grown since I last saw you?" A warm chuckle accompanies her feigned question. I'm left wishing I was the one making her laugh. I've missed the sound of her laughter.

"Probably," my mom says. "She's growing like a weed. I think she's going to be tall like her dad and brother." Mom loads the regular milk and almond milk into the fridge.

"How'd you do on your test?" Lucia asks Bella as she grabs the Oreos and sets them on the edge of the kitchen island.

"I think I aced it, thanks to you. Thanks again for jumping on Zoom with me."

"Anytime." Lucia smiles. Her smile is another thing I've missed. She hasn't even looked at me since I walked into the kitchen.

"I don't know why we have to learn all this stuff. I'm never gonna use it." Bella complains.

"I know it feels like you won't, but you never know. Foundational stuff can be more useful than you think it'll ever be." Lucia has a way of softly and subtly convincing my stubborn sister to see things from a rational perspective.

"I'm just going to trust that you're right." She gives her a side-eye paired with a smile.

"Go throw on your suit. Meet you at the pool?" Lucia nods and grabs the bag of Oreos.

"Be right out." Bella turns and heads toward her room.

Before going out to the pool, Lucia's hazelnut eyes land directly on mine for a split second before she looks away. I can't stand it when she's mad at me.

Mom must've felt the air chill as well. She walks over to me and hands me a bag of chips. "You two okay?" she asks, a hush in her voice.

"Yeah, yeah. We're good," I lie. "I, uh, I'm going to go take a walk on the beach before dinner. Pizza tonight?"

"Yup," Aunt Candi interjects. "Don't be too long. I'm going to order in half an hour so it'll be here in about an hour."

"Hey, Aunt Candi." I walk over and give her a hug. She and Mom have been friends since they were kids. So, even though we're not related by blood, we're all so close, we're like one big family and I've always considered her and Enzo my aunt and uncle. "Okay, I won't be long. I just want to stretch my legs after that drive."

I change into my swim trunks and a T-shirt and go out to the pool where the girls are.

"Anyone want to go for a walk on the beach?" I ask, pulling my shirt off over my head and tossing it onto Lucia's feet where she's lying on a lounge chair, looking sexy as hell in her white string bikini. Will she join me? Or is she going to make this whole vacation uncomfortable?

"I'm good here," she says, taking a bite of an Oreo.

"Me too." Bella chimes in.

This is going to suck.

4

Lucia

I'm not sure how I'm going to make it through this week. Yes, Angelo flat out rejected me. Yes, my heart is broken. And yes, I don't want to be anywhere near him right now. None of these truths change the reality that I'll always be in love with him *and* my entire body ignites with desire at the sight of him. Two facts I'll have to learn how to ignore, though I have no clue how I'm going to do that.

It's good he's not going to be close by once he moves into his condo next week. Maybe I'll figure out a way to get over him once he's not around as much. He's trying so hard to make things normal between us, but it's all still too fresh for me. I'm going to do my best to avoid him without being blatantly rude. Being near him, knowing how I feel, knowing how he *doesn't* feel, it just hurts.

Since this is a week where we're basically together all the time, it's going to be tough avoiding him. And having to look at him and be close to him when he's half-naked most of the time is going to have me flustered. Ugh, this week is going to be so hard.

Most nights, we start a fire out on the back deck after dinner and listen to music on Spotify or gather around Uncle Nicco, Dad, and Angelo as they play and sing. Angelo is incredibly talented, just like his dad. I'll never understand why he didn't pursue a career in music.

Now that we're older, our parents let us drink a little as long as we stay at the house. These nights are some of my favorite memories.

We always have pizza the first night we arrive. After we've

cleaned up the kitchen, we head out to the deck. Now that Bella's seventeen, she's even allowed to have one glass of wine.

Dad and Uncle Nicco make up music together while Mom and Aunt Destiny bring out some snacks and drinks to us. Bella and I get a glass of red wine and sit on the edge of the hot tub, dunking our legs into the warm bubbles. Angelo's pulled a chair to the edge of the deck and he's drinking a beer as he stares out into the ocean, the setting sun making him a silhouette against the sky. Each time I glance at him, my emotions wrestle inside me like a storm without mercy.

"Are you and Angelo mad at each other?" Bella asks.

Clearly, we're not very good at hiding the tension between us.

"No." Mad isn't the word I'd use. I don't know that there's a word to describe what happened and, even if there was, I'm certainly not telling his little sister. "We're not mad at each other. I think it's just a weird time of transition, you know? With him moving out on his own, it changes things. For all of us, really. Even for our parents."

"Yeah, he and I were talking about that on the drive up. We missed having you in our car." She takes a sip of wine, looking at me from over the rim of the glass like she knows there's something I'm not telling her.

"I missed you guys too." I do my best to remove the twisting emotions from my voice and my facial expression. "I felt like I hadn't spent much time with my parents recently because I've been studying so much. So I wanted to drive up with them." I lie, swishing my legs through the hot, frothy water. I couldn't bear being in the car with Angelo for hours after his rejection and me still licking my wounds.

My thoughts drift mindlessly with the whir of babbling bubbles as I graze my fingers up and down the side of my glass. Angelo didn't do anything wrong. He wasn't mean to me. And it's not like he led me on. All he really did was make it *very* clear that he sees me like a sister and that's all our relationship will ever be. If I continue to stay mad at him, this whole vacation's going to suck. I suppose it's time to get over myself with what happened between us.

Mom and Aunt Destiny join us at the hot tub, bringing over more wine and some snacks. Angelo joins Dad and Uncle Nicco as they fiddle around on their instruments, creating background music for us. It's a nice night of catching up with each other.

After a few hours, the parents go inside along with Bella. Angelo grabs a beer and sits next to me at the hot tub.

"Nice night," he says, grabbing a bottle of wine and pouring a little into my glass.

"Yeah. It's nice to be all together."

He takes a swig of his beer, hangs his head, then looks at me. "I don't like it when you're mad at me." That look in his eyes brings me back to our childhood. Brother and sister by a created family and the best of friends. We didn't fight a lot, but every now and then we'd have a disagreement. I'd dig in my heels and brood. He was usually the first to make peace and it always started with the sweet charm in his eyes and, "I don't like it when you're mad at me."

My woeful heart flinches as I catch that childlike gleam in his eyes. "I don't like being mad at you." In that moment, I decide to release my hurt and embarrassment. I've missed my best friend.

"Are we gonna be okay?" he asks, not bringing any details into the conversation.

"Yeah." I take a slow sip of wine. "We're gonna be okay." I meet his gaze and smile, with an ache in my heart. *How do you stop loving someone you've loved your entire life?*

The rest of the week is filled with some of our favorite activities and traditions including making s'mores, getting ice cream at Swensen's ice cream parlor, and watching the sun sink into the ocean every night. We even try a few new things like a day trip to tour the giant redwoods.

Though things mostly return to normal between us, something's different — shifted. Every time we're near each other, my skin warms. Every time our eyes meet, I have to take a deep breath. Every time we accidentally touch, my heart races. And every time I lie alone in bed, I'm assaulted by memories of that night, unable to erase the feel of Angelo's hard, sexy body pressed against mine.

When will it all fade?

By the end of the week, I've locked away those feelings. They're not gone, they're just banished to a prison cell I want to forget about. It's taken some time, but Angelo and I have settled back into our comfortable friendship which makes me happy. It's our last night here and we're relaxing on the back deck with the usual: drinks, snacks, fire pit going, and music filling the air. We dance like fools until a slow song comes on. Dad takes Mom in his arms. Uncle Nicco does the same with Aunt Destiny. My heart warms at how in love they still are. Angelo grabs Bella and twirls her around as she laughs. Sipping my wine, I wallow in the joy flowing through me.

The music shifts the mood and dancing subsides as the night grows late. Everyone's gone inside to bed except me and Angelo. He gets the bottle of Casa Dragones Joven tequila, along with two shot glasses, and brings them to the steps that head to the beach where I'm still sitting.

"I'll be right back," I say, then get up and hurry to my room to get his graduation gift.

When I return to the steps, he has the two shot glasses filled.

"Here." I sit next to him on the top step. "I didn't get a chance to give this to you earlier. It's your graduation present." I was still mad at him and immersed in my embarrassment when we had his party that it didn't feel right to give it to him then.

A broad smile spreads across his face, revealing his gratitude. "What's this?"

"Open it. Card first." Anticipation swirls in my stomach.

Warm, golden light from the fire pit cascades out, providing enough light for him to see. He opens the card and reads it out loud. "Angelo. Congratulations on your graduation. This is to help remind you that you can accomplish anything you set your mind to. When the day feels tough, look at this and remember that you can conquer the world. Love, Lucia." He looks at me and smiles as he rips open the paper. When he sees the picture in the frame, his eyes widen and his jaw lowers.

Satisfaction sends goosebumps across my skin.

Looking at me, he shakes his head as a smile returns to his face. "Where…did you get this? How? I —" He shakes his head again, with his mouth open.

I laugh. "Your mom had it."

"Oh, my God." He runs a hand through his hair. "I remember this. I never thought we'd have this old go-kart ready in time for the race. Dad spent *hours* on it with us." Throwing back his head, he laughs then looks down at the picture again, rubbing his thumb along the side of the frame. "Is this how old we were? We look like babies. Check out the smile on my dad's face." He stares at it quietly for a moment. It almost looks like a mist coats his eyes.

My heart warms with how pleased he seems.

"Lucia, this — this is —" He shrugs. "Incredible. Thank you so much. I love it." His words hit my ears with heartfelt emotion.

"I thought you could put it in your new place." I swallow. *Please don't forget me. I'm going to miss you.*

"I'm going to put it in my bedroom." He hands me a shot. "This has been the best vacation." He holds out his glass.

I clink his with mine. He tosses back the whole thing at once and I follow him. *Whoowh!*

He pours two more shots. "Let's take this one a little slower," he says, handing me one. "I don't want to have to hold your hair back while you puke." He chuckles.

"Yeah, we've both had a few tonight." My tipsiness is bordering being drunk and I'm enjoying the ease of our rekindled friendship.

We sip the shots, reminiscing and sharing the highlights of the week, enjoying the new memories we've made. "Photograph" by Ed Sheeran fills the air.

"I didn't get to dance with you earlier," he says, standing and holding out his hand, his hushed tone unintentionally seducing me.

Silently, I take his hand and stand up, slightly dizzy from lots of wine and a couple shots of tequila. With both of us barefoot, the bottom of his chin is level with the top of my forehead.

Looping his arm around my waist, he pulls me against his body. I suck in a breath, trying to temper how good it feels to be in his arms. It's both safe and arousing. As I weave my arm around his muscular back, he cups my other hand in his and tucks our clasped hands into his chest. The low, faint hum in his throat trickles over my skin as he moves our entwined bodies to the cadence of the music.

I rest my head on his chest, tilting my nose toward his neck and inhaling his mild scent of cocoa butter, jojoba, and cedarwood into my lungs. My nerve endings ignite and I exhale to calm myself. "I'm going to miss having you around next year," I say, unable to keep the sadness from creeping into my voice.

"I'm going to miss being able to keep an eye on you." His deep timbre vibrates against my chest which tightens from the intensity of his words.

I lift my head to look up at him. "I'm guessing you've put Joe in charge of that?"

"If any guy is giving you a hard time, Joe can kick his ass. Just don't get too chummy with him." His tone emits a warning.

"I thought you guys were friends."

"We're frat brothers, but I wouldn't go so far as to say we're friends. The guy's a man-whore when it comes to women. I just don't want you getting too friendly with him, okay?"

"Tequila" by Music Travel Love comes through the speakers, saturating the air with seduction.

"Always my protector." While the fact has frustrated me for much of my life, there's a part of me that's grateful he was always there, watching out for me.

I'll never forget the time I had my first French kiss and Prisha blurted it out in front of him. It was one of the rare times I'd actually been mad at her. I'd been waiting years for Angelo to kiss me. He was supposed to be my first kiss.

I was always behind the other girls when it came to boys. By my sophomore year in high school, I still hadn't French kissed anyone. One day during a study hall period, I was helping Loren Danzis with his math homework in a back corner of the library. When we were done, he leaned over and kissed me. Then he stuck his tongue in my mouth. I wasn't prepared for it. His tongue was fat and slobbery and gross. Thankfully it was quick because I was about to push him off me.

Of course, I had to tell Prisha what happened and then she blabbed about it in the car on the way home from school. Angelo always gave us and Bella a ride home.

"Guess who finally had her first French kiss?" Prisha asked Bella with a sing-song insinuation in her tone.

As soon as she said it, the look in Angelo's eyes as he glared at me in the passenger seat made my stomach drop.

Pulling my gaze from his, I turned in my seat, bugging my eyes out at her and frowning so hard, my entire face tensed. Bella squealed with excitement.

Angelo shot daggers at Prisha through the rearview mirror. "Really Prisha?" Annoyance coated his tone.

"What was it like? Did it feel good? Were you all tingly?" Bella's overzealous questions spat out of her.

I looked back at her and shook my head. "No, it didn't feel good and he didn't even ask if he could. A boy should always ask." Though she was old enough to understand about boys and kissing, I agreed that the discussion was inappropriate, especially given that Angelo was in the car. I did my best to un-romanticize it for her impressionable mind.

Steam billowed out of Angelo's ears as he glanced at me. "Bella, close your ears. This conversation *isn't* for you." He gave her a stern look through the rearview mirror. "Close them, *now*," he instructed.

She grumbled and stuck her fingers in her ears then peered out the window with a huff.

"Someone kissed you? And didn't ask? Who was it?" The urgency in his questioning told me he disapproved. "Who kissed you, Lucia?" he demanded, almost wincing when he looked over at me, knuckles turning white as he gripped the steering wheel. It was as if he was hurt that someone other than him had kissed me. Which almost made me think that he actually cared. But I knew better.

"Why do *you* care?" I asked, snidely.

"Because it sounds like some disrespectful asshole forced himself on your lips and if that's the case, I'm going to have to set him straight." His words held a threat, like if I'd told him, he would've found Loren and punched him.

It was the first time I'd witnessed his protectiveness turn angry. That's not in his nature.

"Hmh, someone sounds jealous," Prisha provoked.

The fire in his eyes as he stared at her in the mirror was enough to shut her up.

"It doesn't matter who it was. It was awful and it'll never happen again. At least not with him."

The conversation was over, but his tension combusted the air in the car. He shifted in his seat, pressing one hand into his thigh and gripping the steering wheel tightly with the other. His expression was a strange mix of relief, irritation, and hurt.

I'll always remember that look on his face.

Returning from the memory, I tease him. "Maybe now guys won't be terrified to ask me out."

"Hey." He lifts my chin. "A couple idiots did and they landed you on my chest, sobbing." He jokes back, then softens. "You have to be careful, Luc. There's a lot of dirtbags out there." The firelight glows on his face as he releases my hand to his hard chest. My fingers on his soft T-shirt, I feel his heart beating. It's so fast. Beating as fast as mine is. As fast as it always beats whenever he's near me. He runs his thumb along my jaw sending a chill chasing over my flesh. We've danced together before, but it's never felt this intimate. And he's never put my hand on him. Being this close to him, body-to-body, is unbearable. His tender eyes volley between mine. "Most of them won't see past what's on the outside to your beautiful heart." He takes a long inhale and lets it out.

My heart thrashes in my chest as my pulse thumps...*boom-boom, boom-boom*. Without my permission, my eyes shift to his lips. I was supposed to banish this desire. The alcohol has dulled my ability to control its riot. I'm desperate for his kiss, for him.

"And what an incredible person you are." His arm tightens against my lower back as his breath heats my lips. "They won't see what I see."

My breaths are audible as my heart slams against my ribs.

He lowers his head, placing his lips on mine, a sensation I've dreamed about — craved — for years. Hot, intense, soft, sensual, powerful. Lightning-energy bolts through my relinquishing body. Our chemistry is explosive. Undeniable. A growling sound rumbles in his chest as he slides his hand to cradle my head. He lifts his lips from mine, leaving me breathless, wanting.

When he looks at me, wolf-like hunger invades his tender gaze as his breaths pant out. Conflict washes his face as he slams his lips back on mine, the warm air from his nostrils sweeps across my cheek as he holds me against his body. With the tip of his tongue, he parts my lips, magnifying my intoxication.

Both of his hands grip tighter, but his mouth softens, like he's restraining himself. Pleasure swarms me, raising prickly bumps all over my body. He slides his confident tongue into my mouth, his hard-on begging against my stomach. I love the way he feels. I want him. I want him so badly I can't think straight.

A moan fills my throat as he slides deeper into my mouth with his tongue. Accepting him in, I surrender to my desire and let go. I wrap my arms around his neck, lost in euphoria as our tongues seduce each other. The pleasure is more potent than anything my imagination had conjured all these years.

Every whimper I can't hold back drives his mouth. His breaths grow louder as he probes more aggressively, consuming me. Just as I'm melting beneath him, he pulls away abruptly, grunting. Holding both of my shoulders in his hands, he's panting, eyes frantic across my face.

"Lucia. Fuck. I'm sorry. I — I shouldn't have done that." He pants. "I'm — I'm so fucking sorry." His eyes oscillate between mine, frenzied breaths heaving out.

My heart races wildly. My head's in a haze. "What? Why?" Confusion tangles my thoughts, twisting my emotions.

He rips his hands from my arms like my skin is burning them. "Go inside." He points to the house and drops his head toward the ground.

"Why?" Desperation fills me. "I don't understand. What's going on?" I beg, my stomach churning.

"Now Lucia," he demands, pointing again, his gaze searing me.

"What did I do?" Passion evades, taken over by fear. Fiery tears burn behind my eyes.

"Nothing," he says, frustration lacing his tone as he rubs his hands over his hair. A growl roils in his throat. "I'm sorry. This is my fault." His brow snarled, he shakes his head, glaring at me. "Lucia, *go.*" His words singe with a mix of remorse and a potent anger that I don't know if it's directed at me or himself.

Rejection slaps me across the face as a tear stings my skin on its journey down my cheek. I turn and run to my room, flopping onto my bed.

Confusion wrecks me.

He kissed me.

Angelo kissed *me.*

Passion detonated the moment our lips touched as if he wanted me just as much as I've wanted him.

As if love was the undercurrent of his passion.

Then he shoved me away and dismissed me like he regretted that it happened at all.

This pain cuts deep below the surface of my skin, all the way to my heart.

5

Angelo

What the fuck is wrong with me? What did I just do? *I kissed Lucia.*

I held her in my arms and kissed her as if she was *mine* to kiss. I put my lips on hers and pressed my dick into her, allowing her to feel what she does to me. I claimed her mouth in a way a big brother shouldn't and I loved every hot second of it.

And she kissed me back like she needed my kiss to breathe. So addictive.

The way she tasted…*fuck*. For years I've imagined what her mouth would taste like. Now I know…silky-smooth tequila and sweet honey. Her taste will haunt me. And now that I've tasted her, I want her even more.

My head spins. I've had too much to drink. But my senses aren't numbed, they're heightened, acute. I still taste her on my lips. Feel her in my arms. Smell her sweet coconut that's lingering in my nose. Instead of dousing my desire like I should have, I kissed her and fueled it. I want her so badly. A forbidden fruit I crave like a drug. And I'm scared shitless that I just ruined everything by not being able to control myself.

My Lucia. In my arms. No one watching us. My guard compromised by tequila. Her looking up at me with those big hazelnut eyes. Desire heated my blood. I weakened. I cracked. Now I have no idea what to do.

Did I just destroy our friendship?

Guilt stirring inside me, I go to my room, directly across the hall from hers. A dim light spills from under her door. Her muffled, whimpered cries fill my ears, echoing in my head. My heart sinks, heavy in my chest. I've hurt her…again.

We'd finally gotten back to being us, or at least it felt like it. This time I crossed the line. I'm not sure she'll ever forgive me. Shame and despair join the guilt as I toss and turn in my bed.

Morning announces itself with blinding sunshine beating my eyelids. When I go out to the kitchen for breakfast, Lucia and her family are already gone. I shovel the eggs, bacon, and toast Mom cooked for me into my mouth, then pack my bags and help my parents tidy and clean up before we leave.

Thankfully, Bella has no idea what happened so I'm not bombarded by questions on the long ride home. Tomorrow, I'll pack up my things and Mom, Dad, and Bella will help me move to my condo that's a few hours away. I'll have the rest of the week to settle in and buy some things for my new place before I start my job.

Hah. My job that my dad helped me get with his connections. A job I never would've gotten on my own merit. A job I don't really want but took because it's stable.

Lucia loves her parents. One thing she didn't much care for growing up was their constant coming and going for their careers. It's not that she ever felt neglected or not loved. It's just that one of them was often gone. They scheduled their jobs to make sure one of them was always home with her. While she appreciated that, she's always wanted a stable lifestyle with a stable partner.

So, here I am, about to be an accountant and build a stable lifestyle for a girl who may never want to speak to me again.

As soon as we get home, instead of packing, I text my best friend, Tony, and see if he wants to grab a beer. He's the only person in the world who knows how I truly feel about Lucia. I need his advice because my thoughts are chaotic.

We meet up for hoops before going to Brew Works. It's a casual place with good food, great beer, and not so loud that you can't hear each other. Grabbing a high-top table, we order beers and wings, and I get right to it.

"I think I really screwed up with Lucia," I admit, looking down to where I'm rubbing my thumbs against each other above my laced fingers.

"What do you mean you screwed up? How?" He leans forward with an incredulous expression like he can't imagine the possibility.

"I had a few too many shots of tequila and I…kissed her."

My confession sends him back in his seat. "Whoa. Okay, I didn't see that coming." He rests his elbows on the table, clasping his hands. "What happened after you kissed her?"

"Well, I —" I shrug. "I stopped. I apologized and told her to go inside the house." Pangs of remorse dart inside me.

"Ooo." He grimaces. "Bet *that* didn't go over well."

"No, it didn't. I'm afraid I really fucked up and she's never going to want to speak to me again." The thought toils my insides.

"Ang. You've been in love with her your entire life. And you're building your life around her. What about what *you* want? I mean, I know your grand plan, but maybe this wrench is a reality check. You know? Maybe this is your chance to do something with your music. You're so damn good, man. I'm sure your dad would hook you up."

The waiter drops off our beers and wings.

I take a swig of my beer, feeling so unsettled. "Lucia's always telling me I should pursue my music. She's so supportive and encouraging. But it's not stable work. And you know I don't want to lean on my dad and his connections for that. It's bad enough I needed him to help me get this freaking accounting job. Plus, you know what it's been like for me, living in the shadow of his fame. I'd never live up to the public's expectations of his son. I'd be afraid to fail him." My shoulders sag under the weight of this conversation. I wanted to talk to him so I could figure out what to do and feel better.

This isn't helping and I feel worse. Though, in fairness, it's not his responsibility to fix this. He's always been there for me and I for him. Guy's a great friend.

"Okay, so don't lean on him. You're so good, you'll make it on your own," he says, grabbing a wing. "All I'm saying is you owe it to yourself to at least let your talent be seen more widely." Popping the wing in his mouth, he sucks off the meat and drops the bone to his plate.

I blow a sigh of frustration. "Right now, I'm lucky I have a job. I'm not going to let my dad down by walking away from this opportunity. I at least need to give it a shot. The money's good and maybe it won't be so bad." I grab a wing, suck off the meat, and go for another. "What the hell do I do about Lucia?"

"Look, you two have been friends forever. There's no way she's never speaking to you again. Things were gonna change anyway with you moving. This'll give her a chance to cool off. How'd you leave things?" Without wiping wing sauce from his fingers, he grabs his beer and takes a gulp.

"That's the thing. We didn't. I haven't seen or heard from her since I kissed her." It was so hard to stop kissing her. The memory of our passionate kiss intensifies the heat of the wings, creating beads of sweat on my forehead. Trying to cool things down, I take a long drink of beer.

"Do you just want to get it over with and ask her to marry you?"

His question stuns me and I almost choke on my beer. "No. No way. It's not time. She's not ready. I need to let her live a little first, date more assholes."

He cocks his head. "And what're you going to do if she falls hard for one of those assholes?"

I shake my head. I know her. "She's fallen for them before. She's young and somewhat naïve, but she's not stupid. It doesn't take her long to see them for who they are."

Resting his arms on the table, he glares at me and shakes his head. "Then why don't you tell her how you feel about her and save both of you from all the what-if bullshit?"

I pull my lips in, pondering his question, feeding my doubt. "Honestly? I'm scared she might not feel the same way. Then I've laid it out there and made things awkward and risk ruining our friendship, if I haven't already. Plus, there's our families. It would just be a mess."

"But she asked you to take her virginity. Isn't there a chance she feels the same way?" He picks up a piece of celery and takes a crunchy bite.

"That was only because she sees me as being *safe* because we're friends. I think it's best if I just give her some space. And, somewhere down the road, I hope to hell she feels the same way. I want forever with her."

He takes a gulp of his beer. "Well, in the meantime, I suggest you live a little too. We're young. You're going to be meeting tons of new people. Go date some girls, party, and get it all out of your system so *you're* ready for her. You don't want her to have regrets. So, no regrets for you either."

I don't want anyone else. I want Lucia.

"Thanks, man. I appreciate you coming out tonight and talking through this with me."

"Any time. But I'm not sure I helped."

"You did." I nod, doing my best to validate his input. "I just needed your help to get my thoughts clear." Except they're anything but.

I resolve to give her some space. Yet, all I want to do is hold her in my arms and tell her I'm sorry I hurt her.

Tomorrow, I move away. And I don't know when I'll see her again.

The fact crushes me.

6

Lucia

"I can't believe we graduate in a month," Prisha says, applying a dark burgundy lipstick to her full lips in our bathroom mirror. "We're going to make tonight the best night ever!" Squealing, she turns and throws her arms around me.

Though we're not big into parties, we were invited to a party at Angelo's old fraternity house. Angelo. My heart aches when I think of him. We haven't seen each other or spoken since the night he kissed me two years ago. He vanished from my life. Hasn't even come home for the holidays. Always claims work is too busy, or so Aunt Destiny tells me. Something makes me think it's because he doesn't want to see me.

The rest of that summer, I painfully replayed our kiss over and over in my head. Why did he kiss me? Why did he stop? Did I do something wrong? Why did he throw away twenty years of friendship? Every limb, every organ, every piece of my soul hurt…and still does.

His silence broke my heart — shattered me.

The void since he's been gone has scarred my heart forever. We were the best of friends our entire lives and he walked away from our friendship…from *me*. Him vanishing and never looking back is the worst pain I've ever felt. *Indescribable.*

When school started again, I threw myself even more into my studies, anything I could do to distract myself from thinking about him. The nights were the toughest. I cried every night for months.

Prisha worried I was depressed. I wasn't. I was broken and empty. Her friendship helped me put my broken pieces back together and figure out how to fill myself up. But my heart will never be whole again.

The pain is now a dull ache, but it's still there. A reminder of my unrequited love and the loss of my very best friend.

I zip up my black leather boots, we down shots of Goldschläger, and head out to the party. Since Joe invited us, we weave through the crowd to find him and thank him for the invitation.

"Hey, ladies. Glad you could make it." Joe hugs each of us, giving me a peck on the cheek. Though Angelo warned me to stay away from him, he's been pretty nice to me and Prisha these past couple years. "Stay here, I'll be right back."

Swallowed up by dancing bodies, he returns with two beers, handing one to each of us.

We take them and thank him, then he's off again, greeting people like he's the host of the party.

Prisha and I find a few of our friends and dance to the pounding music, making occasional beer runs. I catch Joe's eyes on me more than a few times. Maybe tonight's the night. Maybe I'm ready. I'm the only person of all my friends who still hasn't lost her virginity.

I always hoped Angelo would be my first. I wanted him to be my only and forever. I saved myself for him. But he made it perfectly clear that he doesn't want anything more than my friendship. And now, we don't even have that.

Desperate to rid myself of my infatuation with Angelo, I pointlessly forced myself to date, through high school and into college. A guy would show me some attention and I'd think, maybe he's the one who'll finally help me get over my crush on Angelo. A couple times, I even thought, maybe he's *the one*. It only ever took four or five dates for them to reveal what they were truly after. Once I told them I wasn't going to have sex with them, they were gone faster than I could blink.

I'd be left with a broken heart and a shattered perception of dating, men, and love. I'd run to Angleo and cry, and he'd console me and make me feel like I mattered. All our lives, the silly things he'd indulge in with me because he cared made me feel special… important. No one could ever measure up to Angelo. I'm not sure I'll ever meet anyone who does.

Thankfully, as I've gotten older, I've gotten wiser. It takes much less time for me to detect a guy's sexometer and I move on before they can hurt my heart. Still, there's always a little sting in the realization that they're not actually interested in *me*.

Though I'm not dying to have sex, curiosity has bitten me. I've kissed guys and fooled around, but I've still never taken the plunge and gone all the way. According to my friends, sex is amazing.

Angelo will always have my heart, but it's time I move on and stop living in the hope that we could ever have a life together. I know now, that'll never happen.

Sorrow biting me and alcohol starting to swim through my veins, I feel like being reckless. While it's not in my nature, I could use a little escape from the norm.

Joe's become a friend. I know he's a man-whore, but he'd probably be someone safe for me to do it with since it would be purely physical — for both of us. No feelings or emotions to complicate things. And I'd make sure he wears a condom.

My underarms are dewy. I need just a little more to drink before I'm ready. I grab another beer and head over to talk to him as Angelo's warning ghosts through my thoughts. I shake my head, trying to shake out Angelo's voice. I can do this. But how do I ask Joe to have sex with me?

"Hey, Joe. Great party." We have nothing in common and that's all I could come up with to say, given the state of my nerves.

"Yeah. You ladies having fun?"

"Absolutely." I take a huge swallow of my beer. "So, uh, what room did you end up with here anyway?" I ask, hoping he can't hear my vocal cords vibrating as I try to force nonchalance into my voice.

A mischievous grin spreads across his face. "Why? You wanna see it?" His eyebrows rise above his beady eyes.

"Yeah, okay." *Am I ready for this?*

His grin drops as his eyes darken. "Okay," he says, tilting his head toward the stairs. "Come on."

I catch Prisha's gaze as I follow him. Her brow furrows and I shoot back a nod with a smile that I'm okay.

Joe heads up to the third floor. The music from the basement fades, taken over by thumping beats from the room two doors down. He opens the door to his room…Angelo's old room…allowing me to pass him on the way in. As he closes the door, the latching click of metal against metal magnifies in my head. Flicking on the light, he joins me in the center of the room and spreads out his arms.

"This is it." A hint of arrogance rides his words as an ostentatious smile smears across his face.

I'm in his lair.

I gaze around the room. *Some lair.* Beer bottles and open pizza boxes litter the tops of his desk and dresser as mustiness and pot suffocate the air. Random clothes and shoes are strewn around. This is a far cry from how neat and clean Angelo kept it. *Stop thinking about him.*

"It's nice." I lie. Nerves rattle throughout my body.

He steps in toward me, close, and hovers above me. "What are you doing in here, Lucia?" His voice is low and scary, carrying a whisper of evil.

I'm not going to pass out. I'm going to do this. It's nothing. All my friends have done it. It's pathetic that I haven't yet. Joe and I are friends. It'll be okay.

My mind is void of words to answer him, so I stretch up and kiss him. Taking my shoulders in his hands, he pushes me back, releasing a sinister chuckle that fills the room.

He cocks his head to the side. "What are you doing here?" His words come out stronger, demanding, sin slick on his tongue.

"What do you think I'm doing here?" I step in to kiss him again, my insides quivering.

He holds me back and looks around the room. "Is this a joke?" His eyes narrow to slits. "Is Angelo going to jump out of my closet and beat the shit out of me?"

The mention of his name jars me. I shut out my emotions. "No. Angelo is *not* here," I insist. His presence haunts the walls like his protective eyes are watching me. I soften. "I — I don't want to be a virgin anymore."

A wicked laugh barrels out of him as he holds my shoulders. His pupils expand to the size of his irises, making his eyes look entirely black. "Are you sure you know what you're asking for, baby girl?" A gluttonous grin smears his expression as the air sucks out of the room, leaving a cool hollowness.

I halt a gasp, trying to hold onto courage. "Yes," I say, barely getting the word out.

"'Cause I don't want this turning into some kind of rape situation." He drills his blackened eyes through me. "If we do this, you tell me if you want me to stop and I will."

"Okay. I will." Every cell in my body shudders.

"Well then, why don't you start by sucking me off, baby girl," he says, unbuckling his belt and unzipping his jeans then nudging me to my knees with one hand while holding the back of my head with the other.

I fumble with his dick, trying not to think about how many other mouths and vaginas it's been in. Pushing the thought from my mind, I put his dick in my mouth and slide my lips down toward the base.

He groans as I move my head back. "Yeah, baby girl. That's it."

All I can think about is Angelo. Squeezing my eyes shut, I struggle to get him out of my head.

Before I can slide back down, Joe wraps my hair around his hand and shoves himself into my mouth while yanking my head forward. He repeats the motion, fast, before I can even take a breath. And again.

"That's it, baby. Take all of me."

Practically choking, I push him hard. He lets go and I drop to sit on the floor, coughing and gasping for air.

He hurls a perverse laugh. "You okay?" he finally asks, though it doesn't seem like he actually cares whether or not I am.

"Yes," I say, attempting to temper my coughing.

"A little too much for ya, huh?" He smirks down at me.

Cocky bastard. "I, uh, I just don't really know what I'm doing."

He holds out his hand to help me up. "I'll take care of you." A phrase that should provide a sense of safety somehow has the exact opposite effect, sending an icy chill through me.

Without taking his hand, I stand up.

"Come here." He nods toward his bed as he walks backwards to it, keeping his gaze on me.

I follow as silence falls stagnant, my heart pounding.

He sits on his bed and pats his hand on the mattress. "Do you want a drink to settle your nerves?"

"No. I'm not nervous and I don't want any more to drink." Truth be told, I'm an absolute wreck.

"You still wanna do this?" he asks as he stands up, kicks off his shoes, and strips off his jeans and underwear.

"Yes." I swallow. Nothing else comes out. I know I'm scared, but everyone probably is their first time.

"Okay then. Get undressed. I wanna see what's under your clothes." He tilts his chin up, scanning my body with his eyes.

I'd imagined my first time being with Angelo. It was going to be sweet and passionate and romantic. This is awkward and creepy and detached.

I stand and step out of my shoes then remove my clothes, setting them on a nearby chair, while he takes off his shirt and socks.

"Get on the bed. Let me have a look at you," he directs. His piggish gaze rakes over my naked body as I lie exposed on the bed with my legs together and my arms by my sides. "Fuckin' shit you got body." He licks his lips then opens the top drawer of his nightstand and pulls out a condom. Ripping the packet open, he slides it on and gets onto the bed.

"Are you ready? 'Cause I sure as fuck am." He looks down at his erection with a smug smirk.

I suck in a breath and nod.

He spreads my legs with his hands and kneels between my thighs. There's no kissing. No touching. Which is perfectly fine because I don't want to kiss him and I don't want his hands all over me.

Leaning his body to hover over me, he shoves his dick into me. In that instant, Angelo's pained face pops into my head, filling me with sadness and regret. Tears burn behind my eyes as my heart wilts with an agonizing ache. I gasp then hold my breath as Joe moves in and out of me. Though I think the condom is lubricated, his movements hurt a little. He quickly picks up speed, thrusting in and out as he stares down at me with a gorging gaze. I wait for something. I don't know what though. Shouldn't I *feel* something?

"Fuck yeah, baby. Shit, I'm gonna come so fucking fast with you. You're so fucking tight, baby."

And with two more pounding pumps, he moans and shakes.

I feel *nothing*. Nothing but disgust.

"Angelo doesn't know what he fucking missed out on," he says with a callous laugh as he pulls out of me and rolls onto his back, panting.

The mention of Angelo's name chastens me again. Remorse smothers my heart as I hold my composure, ready to unravel any second.

The whole thing lasted about fifteen minutes from when I entered the room to when I left and was the most awful experience of my life. Escaping his room, I run to the bathroom, clean myself up, and go find Prisha in the basement.

"Are you ready to go?" I ask, unable to stop my voice from rattling.

Her gaze sweeps across my face. "Hey, are you okay? What's wrong?" She doesn't need more than a glance at me to know something's not right.

I shove back tears, choking a swallow. "I just wanna go." I'm about to lose it.

Prisha knows me so well, she immediately feels my unease. Grabbing my hand, she leads us through the crowd of dancing, drunken bodies and out the door.

Once we're outside, the cool night air strikes me, burning my lungs.

"Luc, what happened? You're not okay." Concern weighs down her tone as she matches her strides with my hurried steps.

"Ugh. I just want to go home." Acid churns in my stomach. I'm physically nauseous about what I just did. Thankfully our apartment isn't far from the frat house.

"You don't sound good. And you look worse."

I release a loud exhale. "I had sex with Joe," I blurt, the words reverberating in my head.

She stops and turns to me. "*What?*" The question hurls out, laced with anger.

I stop and face her, shame billowing inside me.

Her eyes search my face. "Lucia," she says calmly. "Did he rape you?"

"No, no." I shake my head. "He didn't. Not at all. I went to his room specifically to do it. It was all me."

"You did? Why?" Intensity pulls her brows together.

"Because." I throw my arms up, shuffling my feet beneath me. "Because I'm the only person I know who hasn't and I…just…I don't know, Prish. I wanted to just *do it*. Get it over with. And, and, it was awful. So fucking awful. I have no idea what everyone's going on about."

The corners of her lips draw down and she pulls me in for a hug. "Oh, Lucia." She squeezes me and sways, comforting me. Then she releases me. Her lips pull into a thin line as one eyebrow drops. "The first time usually is." Her chuckle eases my tension for a brief moment. "Come on. Let's go home, eat cookies, and talk about it."

Within ten minutes, we're in our pajamas, sitting cross-legged on the sofa, eating her homemade nankhatai cookies.

"Okay, tell me what happened. And *Joe?* Really?" The disbelief in her voice is a reminder of my very poor decisions tonight.

I drop my head back, hunching my shoulders as I let out a disgusted groan. "I know. *I know.* I just figured that he'd be a safe choice. And I know he sleeps around which is why I made sure he wore a condom."

"So, how did this all go down?"

"I got it in my head that I didn't want to be a virgin anymore. And I figured I'd choose Joe because at least neither of us would have any feelings about it afterwards, you know?"

"Well, that's a given. Definitely on his part. I don't think the guy has any feelings for anyone."

"So, I chugged a beer and asked him to take me to his room. Which, by the way, is Angelo's old room." I slunk my shoulders, leaning forward. "Anyway, when we got there, I kissed him. He thought it was a joke and asked if Angelo was going to jump out and punch him." I chuckle and so does she. "I told him it wasn't a joke and that I didn't want to be a virgin anymore." I suck air in between my teeth and voluntarily shiver. "You should've seen his face when I said that."

Her face squishes like she'd eaten a sour candy. "I'm sure he *loved* knowing he was the one taking your virginity. Smug bastard." She sticks out her tongue in repulsion. "Then what?"

"He strongly encouraged me to suck his dick, which I did. That didn't last long before he rolled on the condom and stuck himself in me." I cringe. "It did *not* feel good at all. It hurt, like you said it would. The things he said to me were so crude. Nothing about it was romantic or passionate. And he kept calling me 'baby girl' — I guess with screwing so many girls, he calls them that so he doesn't have to remember their names."

"Ugh." She sighs. "It sounds absolutely awful. I'm so sorry your first time had to be *that*." She makes an expression of pure disdain, then softens. "Especially since you probably wanted your first time to be with Angelo." Her lip twists to the side as compassion floats on her words.

My heart pricks. I drop my head, tossing a cookie into my mouth. "Yeah, well, that Cinderella-dream died when he ended our friendship." Heaviness sags my chest.

"I take it you still haven't heard from him?"

"Nope. Nothing." Though I refuse to go back to that dark place of emptiness, my heart still mourns him.

7

—

Angelo

On the way to my bed, I pass my bookshelf. The picture Lucia gave me for graduation catches my eye. I stop and stare at it, a void scrapes the depth of my heart. Every time I went to text or call her after that night, the pain in her eyes flashed through my head, destroying me.

Days passed. Then weeks. I didn't know what to say. How to erase the pain I'd caused. Now years are gone. I walked away. That's on me.

I screwed up big time. So fucking afraid that the timing wasn't right. That she wouldn't feel the same way about me as I feel about her. Making the decision for her that she was too young and needed to experience other relationships in order to be ready to take on forever with me. In trying so damn hard to solidify that, all I ended up doing was pushing her away. Not only did I lose the love of my life, I lost my best friend.

If I had the chance to go back and change things, I'd do it all differently. I wouldn't be such an idiot. I'd tell her how I feel. How much I love her. That she's the reason my heart beats every day. That I don't want to live another day without her. Now, I've lived endless days without her. It's agony.

Can I even repair the damage I've done? Would she forgive me? Not knowing kills me.

Without Lucia, my life is aimless. I'm in a job I got for her so I could provide her security and stability. And now, she's not even in my life. It's an okay job and the pay's good, but it's not what I want to do for the rest of my life.

I fuel my true passion by playing my guitar and singing at a local bar. It's how I feed my creativity where no one knows me, no one knows I'm my dad's son, and no one compares me to him. I have the freedom of anonymity and get to lose myself in my music.

Even with that freedom, there are those lingering words. The ones that haunt me. The ones that eat away at me. The ones that fester in my soul.

"He's no Niccolo Mancini."

The ever-present memory that shoots to the forefront of my mind every time I get on stage. Dad knew how much I loved playing and singing with him. When I was still in college, he'd set up an audition for me with two agents. The day is still so vivid in my mind. I was nervous and excited.

I climbed onto the stage in a small bar just before they opened to the public for the night. Each step on the wooden platform clamored in my head as my nerves shimmied inside me. The staff shuffled about, setting tables with plates, glasses, and silverware. Moving my guitar strap over my head to rest on my shoulder, I stood and stared at the men who were there to watch me, to judge me. As I looked at them, I was struck with memory of being laughed off stage in middle school because I froze from stage fright. As much as I tried to push the devastating experience from my thoughts, it was dug in. Still, I played and sang my heart out, giving it all I had in me.

This is my chance to make my dad proud. Maybe my chance to make a career out of my music.

Sitting with arms folded across their chests, the men didn't move. They simply watched with stony faces, one checking his watch a couple times.

When I finished, they were expressionless, void of any emotion. Busy wait staff and bartenders made the only sounds that echoed through the air. My heart sank in my chest. The men thanked me for coming to audition and said they'd be in touch if they wanted to move forward. I already knew they didn't. Every bone in my body embrittled with defeat by the certainty.

As the bar opened for business and a few people filtered in, I politely thanked them for their time and hurried to the bathroom to catch my breath that'd been stuck in my chest. Locked in the stall, I recognized their voices as they entered the bathroom. Paralyzed, I listened.

"Not bad. Not bad," one man said.

"Yeah, but he's no Niccolo Mancini," the other said.

The words flew like a dagger hurled at my chest that cut me open, allowing all the air in my lungs to be sucked out. Words I'd always feared hearing ricocheted off the tile walls, pelting me with a thousand needles. To this day, they're my shackles, reminding me that I'll never be as good as my dad.

So now, my music is my hobby, my escape. Every time I get on stage, it's a challenge to wash away the memories. To push through them and allow myself to enjoy what I love so much. To do it for no one other than me.

I've made some new friends since I've been out here and dated a few women. Trying desperately to make some kind of life for myself.

I guess this is it. This is what being an adult is like.

My life isn't at all how I'd imagined it would be.

I suppose it's time to make new dreams. But a life without Lucia is no dream at all.

God, I miss her. I miss her so much it hurts.

Prisha bursts into the apartment and flings the door shut behind her. "Yes," she cheers, thrusting her arms into a victorious V. "I aced that baby."

Looking over at her from above the back of our worn brown sofa, I try to stifle the finals-week panic that's swimming in my blood and be happy for her. "Prish, that's awesome. I knew you'd crush it."

"Thank you. Thank you," she says as she playfully bows. "Want me to make us a celebratory lunch?"

"No. None for me. My stomach doesn't feel good." It doesn't matter how much I study or how hard I study, finals week always sets me into an irrational panic that I'll fail and my body goes off kilter.

Walking my way, her gaze sweeps over the textbooks and notebooks scattered across my lap, the sofa, and the coffee table.

"You're going to study yourself into an early grave," she says, shaking her head and planting her hands on her hips. "Maybe you should take a break."

"It's finals week, I can't take a break. I know, I'm a stressed-out mess, like always. I don't know when to eat, when to sleep, when to study. And my body is completely out of whack. My period is late. My boobs hurt. Ugh. You'd think by now I'd know how to better manage my stress."

"You should take a break and meditate for just like fifteen minutes. I'm going to make us something to eat and if you haven't meditated, I'm going to force you to stop and eat." She dips her chin and raises her eyebrows as if to say, *"So there."*

She heads to the kitchen, clanging pots and pans. I haven't eaten much today. Maybe that's why I have no energy and feel like crap. No time for meditating, but I'll stop and eat with her when whatever she's making is ready.

I put my head back into my studying. Within minutes, the apartment blooms with the scent of her turmeric chicken coconut curry. Within seconds, I'm running to the bathroom to vomit. Prisha's immediately by my side, holding my hair off my sweat-covered face and rubbing my arm that's wrapped around the cold, porcelain toilet.

"Okay. It's okay," she says, soothing me with her voice and gentle strokes.

I spit a few times into the toilet and flush. Then I grab a tissue and blow remnants of vomit out my nose as my stomach churns. Drained of energy, I rest my back against the tub and hug my knees to my chest. Prisha crosses her legs under her, facing me. Resting her hand on my arms, she gazes at me with concern etched on her face.

"You're so pale. I'm worried about you." Love radiates from her. She's going to be such a great mom someday.

"I'm okay. I'll be okay." I blow a loud exhale. "I'm sure I'm just overdoing it. No surprise there." I push a smile to my lips. "I don't even know what happened. I was studying my notes and then I smelled your chicken curry dish and felt nauseous and ran in here."

"Wait a minute," she says, drawing back her body, her eyes widening. "Did you say your period's late?"

I shrug. "Yeah."

"And your boobs hurt?"

What's she getting at? "Yeah. They always do when I'm about to get my period. Why?"

"And now, something I make like once a week, suddenly has you puking your guts up?"

"Prish, I'm a basket-case. I'm stressed out." My stomach continues to percolate.

"You're *sure* Joe wore a condom?" Her question blindsides me, sending adrenaline whizzing through me.

"What? Yes. Yes, I'm sure. I saw him put it on." I trace my memory frantically, replaying every uncomfortable minute on fast-forward.

Her face twists into a grimace. "Those things aren't a hundred percent reliable."

"I'm not pregnant." I shake my head, a hint of worry sitting at the back of my mind. "I'm just tired." No. There's no way. There's no way I'm pregnant. *God, please don't let me be pregnant.*

I unwrap my arms from my legs. Prisha stands up and holds out her hand to help me up.

"I'll take a break. I'm *not* eating your chicken curry tonight though. I'll have some crackers." Even crackers don't sound appealing. Maybe I have a stomach bug.

"Do you want me to throw it out?"

"No, no. Don't throw it out. You eat it. I'll be fine. I'll try not to puke again." I chuckle weakly and she joins me.

"You sit on the sofa. I'll bring you some crackers and water," she says, heading to the kitchen. "If your period isn't here by tomorrow, I'm getting you a pregnancy test."

"It'll be here. I have one more exam and then I'm done. Then I'll be back to normal. And then we graduate." I try to push excitement into my voice because I'm truly excited for us, but my current state is pathetic…and now I have an even bigger worry. *I'd better not be pregnant.*

⇶ ⇇

Though I didn't vomit again, my stomach was queasy the rest of the night. Prisha's gone before I wake up. She has her last final this morning and then she's meeting up with some friends. My last final is at eleven. I crawl out of bed and go to the bathroom. No period. A zap surges quickly through me. *It's fine. I just need to get through this final.*

Unable to shake the unease in my stomach, I opt for water and crackers for breakfast. I head to my class early so I can get the seat I want, and sit quietly and study. We get two hours to finish. Once I have the exam on my desk, I close my eyes and meditate for a few minutes, attempting to clear my head of distractions. Yeah, that's not possible. Thankfully, I know the material and dive in.

Finishing in an hour and a half, I feel confident about my answers. Before walking home, I stop to use the bathroom. No period. I didn't feel anything during the test, but I wanted to check, just in case. My pantyliner is spotless. I can't stop my thoughts from turning frenzied.

I know Joe wore a condom. I *saw* him put it on. I didn't see anything on me when I went to the bathroom after. If there was a hole in it, wouldn't I have seen his cum on my thighs or something? There's no way this is happening. *Stop it. Breathe.* Nothing has happened. I don't know anything for certain.

On my way home, I stop at the campus store and get a pregnancy test. Walking as fast as I can, I go straight to the bathroom to pee on a stick. With blood pounding at my temples, I read the instructions…three times. I know it's best to do it in the morning, but right now, I'm freaking out. Taking a deep breath, I situate myself above the toilet, stick between my legs, and pee.

Even though the stick has a timer, I set one on my phone. And wait…

Don't check too early. Don't check too late. Breathe in. Breathe out. Don't panic. Hasn't it been three minutes yet? Don't look at it. Wait for the timer.

Both timers go off, the sounds clamoring between my eardrums. My heart pounds so loud, it thunders in my head. Blood courses through my veins, fast and furious. I close my eyes, exhale, then open them and look at the stick…

PREGNANT.

I gasp for air as my knees give out and I drop to the toilet seat. Grabbing the edge of the countertop, I lower myself to the floor as black and white dots fill my vision. My breaths are rapid, in and out of me. The high-pitched ringing blares in my ears. *Oh, God. I'm gonna faint.* Blackness envelopes me.

When I come to from passing out, my skin is coated with sweat and my head is groggy. I lift myself to sit on the floor before standing. Taking the stick off the counter, I hold it in my hand, staring at it.

PREGNANT.

What am I going to do?

8

Lucia

Putting the stick in a plastic bag, I write a note to Prisha and put it next to the stick.

> Prish,
>
> I didn't want to ruin your night. I hope you had a blast. I'm going to see Angelo. Call you later.
> I love you,
>
> Luc

Prisha's my best friend. And she knows that Angelo is too. Despite his notable absence from my life, he's still the one person I trust when I need help and will always go to when life upheaves. Prisha knows basically everything about our relationship. She'll understand that I need to see him right now.

I'm lost.

I'm scared.

I need him.

It's a two-hour drive there and I'll arrive before he even gets off work. As I drive in my chaotic state of mind, thoughts and questions stack one on top of the other in my head. *What am I going to say to him when I see him? I don't even know when he gets off work or what time he'll come home. What if he has plans? Shit, what if he has a girlfriend?*

What if they live together? My stomach sours at that thought. *What am I supposed to do with a baby? What about my teaching job?*

For as long as those three minutes felt, driving to Angelo's condo is an eternity. My thoughts reel with nothing but windshield time and no one to help calm me.

A little after four-thirty, I arrive at his building in Escondido. It's a nice complex, two stories high with trees and grassy patches here and there. I drive around until I find his number and park. Before getting out of the car, I take a moment to try to collect myself in case he's home. I fold my hands in my lap, close my eyes, and take a few deep breaths. Though I still have no idea what I'm going to say to him, I get out of the car, hoping words find their way out of my mouth.

I climb the stairs to the porch of his unit, hold my breath, and knock on the door.

Nothing.

Maybe he's in the bathroom. Let me give him a minute.

I knock again. Nothing.

He's probably not home yet. I plop myself into the cozy chair — hmm…one chair, not two — and gaze at the swimming pool below. No one's in the water, but it ripples with the slight breeze in the air. Glints of sunshine bounce off of tiny peaks as it moves.

I'm still hurt about him walking away from our friendship, and even a little bitter, but I'm willing to let all that go. I pray that he's also willing to leave the past behind us and be the best friend I desperately need right now.

My emotions have been a roller coaster today. I was exhausted after I passed out. Then I was riding high on adrenaline all the way here. Now, I'm just so tired.

⟫⟫⟫ ⟪⟪⟪

"Lucia. Hey, Lucia." Angelo's soft, familiar voice soothes my core as his gentle caress on my arm fills me with the comfort I need.

I push open my eyelids to see his handsome face, the face that's haunted my thoughts for the last two years. My heartbeat ticks up.

"Hey, there you are." I've missed the way he smiles at me. He holds out his hand and I take it. "Come inside."

I stand slowly, a little unsteady on my feet. It never did take much for him to make my head feel like it's spinning. His keys jingle against the metal door as he unlocks it. Leading me inside, he drops the keys and his wallet in a basket on his kitchen counter that's immediately to the left as we walk in.

"Can I get you something to drink?" he asks, grabbing a glass out of the cabinet.

"Yeah, some water would be great. Thank you." I left my apartment in such a hurry that I forgot my water bottle.

He pours water into the glass from a bottle in the fridge and hands it to me. His eyes wander across my face like he's reacquainting himself with my facial features.

"What're you doing here? Are you okay?" There's a slight tilt to his head as his brows knit together. "Is something wrong?" Compassion and concern coat his words. Me showing up on his doorstep after two years of no communication, he knows something's not right.

The burn behind my eyes makes me blink. My jaw vibrates. Words scratch out of my parched throat before I can think. "I'm pregnant," I blurt as my breathing staggers.

Instantly, he wraps me in his arms. Arms that have always provided me comfort and support. Arms I've longed to be back in for two years. I melt into him, sobbing.

He's in no rush to let go. Holding me as I shake, he strokes my hair, gently rocking our melded bodies. No words are exchanged, yet they flow between us. Unspoken apologies. Regret for lost time. From his heart to mine. From my heart to his. Forgiveness.

Once I've calmed myself, I pull back from his chest and wipe the tears from under my eyes. He releases me and takes my hand in his, leading me across the light tan carpet to his sunlit living room.

"Come here," he says, sitting on his sofa.

I sit next to him and he turns his body toward me, resting his arms on his thighs.

"Wanna tell me what happened?" Tension stiffens his posture as he keeps his voice low and tender.

"Please don't be mad at me." Emotions war. Fear and safety battle inside me. He's going to be furious. He's also still my protector. *Which part of him will react?*

Squinting, he shakes his head. "Lucia, I won't be mad."

He sits still, and waits. Once I tell him, I can't take it back. My nervous system rattles and my mouth feels like a desert. Even though I know he won't judge me, I know he's going to be disappointed. He warned me to stay away from Joe. I let him down…in the biggest way possible.

"It — it was Joe." My confession comes out in a crackled whisper as shame strangles my voice.

His fingers curl into his palms as the veins in his arms and neck plump. Nostrils flare as he takes a deep inhale.

"Did he force you?" Vexed words pound between his gritted teeth. "Did he hurt you?" His volume increases as his eyes darken and his fists tighten.

I lean forward, shaking my head and placing my hand on top of his balled fist. "No, no. Angelo, he didn't. I promise he didn't." I squeeze his fist to reassure him. "It was me. It was my decision." Tears threaten as I bow my head, the shame swarming me. "It was stupid. So stupid."

His fists loosen. "What do you mean, it was your decision?"

My stomach twists. "I can't believe how immature this is going to sound." I roll my eyes to the ceiling then return them to his face. "I didn't want to be a virgin anymore and Joe's been really nice to me and Prisha. Since we don't have feelings for each other, I figured I'd just — do it. And I know. I know you told me to stay away from him. And, and I'm sorry. I'm *so* sorry."

His torso rounds forward, shrinking, as his eyes narrow, pulling in his brows. It's like he's physically fighting his thoughts. He takes a breath and straightens. "You don't need to be sorry, Lucia. I'm just surprised that after waiting this long, you'd give something so —

precious —" His shoulders rise to his ears as hurt veils his eyes. "To Joe."

"I know." I slump. The weight of his words is so palpable, I can feel the pressure surround my heart.

His pain and disappointment penetrate the air, crushing me.

"What does he have to say about this?" The irritation exuding from him is a stark contrast to the concern he's infusing into his voice.

I can't tell if he's mad at me or hurt. His incongruent body language and tone have me so confused.

"I haven't told him yet. I haven't told anyone. Well, Prisha knows. But I haven't told my parents. I don't know how I'm going to tell them. I took the test this morning and then came straight here."

"He didn't wear a condom?" Anger sets in his eyes once again.

"No, he did. I made sure he did. It must've broken or had a hole or something."

Thrusting his hands through his hair, he releases a loud sigh.

"You're going to have to tell him and your parents. The sooner, the better."

"I know. They're gonna be so mad at me."

"They might initially, but they'll understand. Your parents are amazing." He pauses, eyes quietly searching mine. "Do you want to keep the baby?" Creases pinch between his brows.

Blood pumps in a frenzy, lighting my veins, pulsing loud in my ears. "I don't — I don't know. I don't know what I want. I don't know what to do. I don't want to get rid of a baby, my baby. I also don't want *Joe's* baby. What if —" My breaths heave out. "What if this is my only chance?" The muscles of my face tighten as tears pool in my lower eyelids. "You know my mom was only able to have me and Nonna was only able to have her." Breaths spew. "What if this baby is all I'll ever get?" Acid rots my stomach.

He holds open his arms. "Shh, shh, shh. Come here, come here," he says, scooting close to me and wrapping me in his arms again. "We have no way of knowing that. Don't think that." His lips are at the top of my head as he holds me against his chest. "Don't think that," he says again, his voice just above a whisper.

I stay in the comfort of his arms for a few minutes, trying to pretend that the reason I'm enveloped in them has vanished. But it hasn't.

He releases me. "We don't have to figure it out right now. It'll be okay." He offers a reassuring nod that does nothing to convince me. "I'm betting you're hungry and tired."

I wipe my eyes. "Mhmm."

Reaching over with his thumb, he sweeps an errant tear from under my eye out to the corner, his gaze following the movement. As he returns his eyes to mine, the corners of his lips curl up.

"Then let's get some food in you. You'll sleep here tonight. Tomorrow, you tell Joe and your parents. Then, we'll figure out the rest."

"We'll" figure the out the rest? He's still trying to take care of me, like he's now part of this mess I've created. It's mine to fix. Mine alone. Somehow, just that small word — we'll — makes me feel less alone.

I nod. "Okay."

For a brief moment, it feels like it's going to be okay.

But it's not...

9

Angelo

That motherfucker! She gave her virginity to *Joe*? That asshole got what should've been mine? It was supposed to be me who got that honor. It should've been *me*. She fucking offered it to me and I pushed her away, fucking up everything. I should've told her how I felt about her. I should've told her that I love her and let her give me what she was asking me to take, what I'd wanted for so long.

Instead, I denied and humiliated her, even though that wasn't my intention. Then I made things worse when I rejected her after I kissed her.

Fuck!

Rage consumes me. I controlled myself when she told me. I'm not violent by nature, but right now, I want to hunt Joe down and beat the fucking shit out of him.

It's not like I expected her to save herself for me after I up and left, not even bothering to call her to try to explain myself. I wanted her to be with guys. Yet, at the same time, I didn't. I wanted her to stay pure, for *me*. And still, I pushed her away. I fucked this up so badly. Of all the fucking guys, *Joe*. And now she's pregnant with his baby. This is a nightmare. My chest felt like it was actually caving in on itself when she told me.

She's here. *I'm* the one she came to. I have to focus on that. Maybe she's forgiven me, though I'm not sure I deserve her forgiveness after my behavior. Maybe this is my chance to earn her forgiveness. I've missed her so much.

"What do you want to eat? I can make something or we can order out."

She holds out one hand like a stop sign and touches her stomach with the other. "No. Please don't make anything. Some smells are making me nauseous and I don't know what they all are. I don't want to have you cook something and then not eat it, or worse, throw up."

I can't stop my face from cringing. "Okay, no problem. Uh, you tell me what you can tolerate and that's what we'll do."

"Honestly, I've been eating crackers because that's all I can seem to keep down. I think I need an actual meal." Her lips twist to the side. They always do when she's contemplating. "Maybe…do you happen to have any oatmeal and bread for toast?"

"I do," I say, standing up.

"Wait, wait." She waves her hand at me. "Um, I — I just showed up here out of the blue and, clearly, I'm kind of all over the place, not really thinking straight. Do you have plans tonight? I mean, it's Friday night, do you have a…a date? Or a…girlfriend or something? I don't want to presume I can just show up here and take over your night."

I chuckle. "No date. And no girlfriend. You're my priority right now," I say, walking toward the kitchen.

"Oh." She sounds surprised. "Okay."

I whip up two bowls of oatmeal and four slices of toast and we catch each other up on our parents, sticking to a safe-to-talk-about subject, while I prepare it.

"You don't have to eat oatmeal for dinner just because of me."

"I thought I'd live dangerously." I wink, handing her the bowls of oatmeal as I grab the plate of toast and walk to my small, round wooden table on the other side of the kitchen. "Seriously, I haven't had breakfast for dinner in a long time. Thought it'd be fun."

"Okay," she says, putting our bowls on the placemats and pulling out a chair. "I like the dark gray upholstery. Very classy-masculine." She scans my open floor plan. "Your place is really nice. You've upgraded from your frat room." Her adorable chuckle rolls out of her.

It's the first time she's genuinely smiled since she's been here.

"Thanks. Upgraded my car too." I nod toward the window facing the pool and parking spaces.

Before she sits, she goes to the window and looks out. "The BMW?" she asks, looking back over her shoulder at me, eyebrows raised.

"Heh. Yeah, I got rid of that old clunker. The Beamer felt like a better fit." Being an accountant may not have been my life's goal, but a small sense of pride fills me knowing that I earn a really good paycheck and can afford the things I want.

"How's your job going?" Walking back over to the table, she sits down. Since she immediately hit me with her pregnancy, we didn't have a chance to talk about much else other than our cautious catchup about our parents.

"It's okay," I say, scooping out a spoonful of oatmeal and blowing the steam. "I mean, it pays well, obviously. I also don't have many expenses with it being just me."

"Do you —" She hesitates. "Like it? Have you made some nice friends?" She picks up a piece of toast and dips it into her oatmeal, scooping some out.

"It's a job. I don't love it, but it's what I'm doing, at least for now."

"But is it what you *want* to be doing?" Her eyes squint the slightest bit. "I never understood why you chose to work as an accountant when you're such an incredibly talented singer and musician." She tilts her head, looking at me with a knowing in her eyes. For as long as I can remember, she's encouraged me to pursue my music. She's been my biggest fan.

I drop my gaze to my bowl of oatmeal. "My music is just a hobby. Something I do to unwind." A small place inside knows I'm lying. I wish it could be more, but that's not a stable lifestyle. Not what I wanted for us. In this moment of keen awareness, I'm not sure there will ever be an *us*. "Besides, you know how I feel about being my dad's son and trying to make it in that industry without his influence or trying to live up to everyone's expectations." I shrug. "This is stable work. I —" I look into her beautiful eyes that are framed by her long lashes. "Want to have a family someday and be able to support them."

"You do?" She blinks a few times, resting her chin on the tops of her fingers. "All these years we've been friends, we never really talked about having families. We always talked about what we wanted to be and do for work."

"Yeah, I want to build a life —" I pause, consumed by her being here. *Will there ever be a chance for us?* "With the right person."

She dips her toast back into her oatmeal and takes a bite. "But, no one yet?" Curiosity alight in her eyes as they capture mine.

I shake my head, longing nags in the pit of my stomach. "Not yet." The emptiness that's ravaged my soul these last couple years begins to fade.

"Mmm." She nods once. "But you've made friends? At work? The gym? You like it here?"

"I have. I play in some pickup games a couple nights a week and I do like it here. I don't know if I'll stay here forever, but for now, this is where my job is. I have no idea what's coming next." I also didn't plan on two years of my life passing by in the blink of an eye.

She sighs. "Neither do I. I can't believe I've gotten myself into this situation." Her eyes cast down. "I'm going to have to figure out what to do about my job. School starts in August and I'll probably be about three months pregnant. I'll have to take maternity leave right in the middle of the school year. I'm not sure how they're going to feel about that. I hope they'll still want me."

"Hey, I'm sure they will. Tell them what's going on and I'm sure you can work something out. They'd be crazy not to keep you."

She presses her lips together, uncertainty washing her face.

Finishing our breakfast-dinner, we load the dishwasher.

"Want some tea? And maybe a movie?" I ask.

"That sounds nice."

"Let's get comfortable first. I'll go change and get you some sweats to put on. Go ahead and find something on Netflix." I head to my bedroom and get changed. Then I lay out a pair of sweatpants, a T-shirt, and socks on my bed for her. "Room's all yours," I say as I exit my room. "I'll make the tea."

She comes out wearing my clothes, looking adorable, and settles in on the sofa. Two mugs of hot tea in my hands, I join her, catching the image on the screen. "*Red*, huh?" It was one of our long-standing summer vacation movies.

With a side-smile and mischief dancing in her eyes, she's a tempting mix of cute and sexy.

I hand her a mug and set mine on the coffee table then hit the button to play the movie. We laugh at the same spots as always. As pathetic as it sounds, this is the most fun I've had since I've been here. And Lucia finally seems like herself. By the time the movie ends, the sun's gone down. Warm, muted light cascades over the room from my lamps.

Bending her knee up to rest on the sofa, she shifts her body to face me. "Why did you walk away from our friendship?" she asks, heartache flooding every syllable of her soft voice.

While I should've anticipated the question, as it's a fair question and she deserves an explanation, I wasn't ready for it. But it's time I answer it…though I can't fully confess.

I take a deep breath and exhale. Words don't come right away and I gaze down to my hands, my thumbs fumbling around each other. Then I look into her eyes, giving her my full attention.

"I'm so sorry." I pause. Shame crawls up my body. "What I did was unforgivable. I crossed a line I shouldn't have. I — had too many shots of tequila and I guess I got sentimental or something and felt like everything was changing. I didn't know when we were going to see each other again and I think in my head I was saying goodbye. I — I don't know." I shake my head, guilt pricking my skin. "It was immature and wrong and I'm really sorry."

Her eyes roam my face as she sits silent. Listening.

"I wanted to call you…so many times. I was worried I'd ruined our friendship. I wanted to give you some space. And then days passed. I'd go to call you. To apologize." My heart thumps in my ears. "But I didn't know what to say. And then months passed. I felt like such an asshole at that point. And so, I — never called. Then years were gone. I didn't think there was any way to get you back in my life. Back to being my best friend."

She takes a deep breath. The silence that hangs in the air is excruciating.

"You ripped my heart out." She holds her hand to her heart as her eyes narrow and her brows pull tightly together with the hurt she's carried these last two years. The words strangle in her throat as they pierce my soul. She's the only person who can make me feel with such intensity. And right now, guilt, pain, and remorse torment me.

I swallow hard, choking down the lump that's practically suffocating me. My chest is so tight it hurts. "I know." I drop my head then lift it to meet her gaze. "I'm so sorry. I know I can't sit here and say I'm sorry and expect you to just forgive me and move on like nothing happened. And I know I may not deserve your forgiveness. But I hope that I can somehow earn my way back to being your friend."

"Ang," she says, tenderness in her voice. "We've been best friends since before I can even remember." She shakes her head, gently. "You can't get rid of me that easily." Her delicate smile melts me. Though she didn't come out and say it, I think I might be forgiven. "Will you sing for me?"

My heart warms at her request. "Always." I grab my guitar from the corner of the living room and sit back on the sofa. For the next half-hour or so, I sing to her, weaving in some new songs I'd written. The way she looks at me when she watches me sing, it's like oxygen, giving me life. I haven't felt anything like this since the last time I saw her. It's intense, intimate, addicting. I feel it all over my body. Lucia Cipriani does something to me. Always has. Always will.

When she yawns, I know it's time for both of us to get some sleep.

"Come on," I say, getting up and leading her to my bedroom. I turn on the bathroom light and step in. "I know you didn't pack a bag so I got out a toothbrush and washcloth for you." I gesture to the items on the sink counter.

"Thank you."

I walk back to the bedroom doorway and she follows me, then leans against the doorframe. Warm light caresses her skin as she looks up at me with her doe-eyes. Those eyes. They melt me every time I look into them. Standing there in my too-big-for-her clothes, she's just as painfully sexy as when she had on her lacy black bra and panties with my dress shirt falling off her shoulder.

"Why *did* you kiss me that night? Tell me it was more than just the alcohol," she murmurs. The sadness blanketing her expression reminds me of the pain ravaging her face after I pulled away from our kiss and ordered her to go inside the house.

Heat spreads through my chest, a wildfire raging. A magnifying urge to kiss her again, feel her lips burn against mine, begs my lips. *How the fuck am I supposed to answer this?*

At the mention of our kiss, I can't stop my gaze from sweeping to her lips, desperate to taste her again. I force my eyes back to hers, raising my hand to hold her jaw. Dragging my thumb across her cheek, desire amplifies. Being this close to her is unbearable.

10

Lucia

The touch of his hand on my cheek sends heat through my core. My breath lodges in my chest. I want his lips on mine again. I want to feel his passion grip me again. I want him to tell me he feels what I feel and that the powerful connection that ignites between us every time we're close is *real.* That he wants more than just my friendship. That he wants all of me and for us to build a life together.

But I think I've destroyed any chance of that ever happening now that I'm carrying Joe's baby inside me. Melancholy drapes my shoulders, tugging down.

"Why, doesn't matter anymore. What matters is you're here. And we're friends again…I hope." His eyes search mine as he waits for my forgiveness and affirmation of our friendship.

"Forever," I say, my voice just above a whisper. My body floods with a mixture of gratitude and yearning.

A faint smile tugs his lips as his gaze holds mine. "Good night, Dandelion Girl." His utterance is low, nostalgic. He hasn't called me that since we were kids. Butterflies dance in my stomach.

Cupping my shoulders in his large hands, he bows his head and kisses my forehead. My heart plummets with the friend-zone life-sentence. Without looking at me, he turns and walks down the hall, his steps leaden.

"Why, doesn't matter anymore?" What does that even mean? How can it not matter? It absolutely matters — at least it does to me. But I

guess it doesn't matter to him.

Closing the door, I walk toward his bed, my eyes drawn to a picture on his bookshelf. It's the picture I gave him for his college graduation. *He still has it. It's in his bedroom where he said he'd put it.* I run my thumb along the side of the frame, my mind filling with memories of making that go-kart and the day of the race. He was so proud of us.

Taking off his sweats and socks, I climb into his bed, wearing his T-shirt. Watching him and listening to him sing always overwhelms me with emotion. I fall into his all-consuming trance and want to stay there forever. He sings from his soul and there was something tonight, I can't place it, but something in the way he looked at me that settled deep in my heart. I lie here, surrounded by him, immersed in a temporary escape.

It's not long before my thoughts are jolted back to reality. Sleep evades me for hours as my brain runs through the conversations I need to have with Joe, my parents, and the principal of the school where I'm supposed to start my teaching job. Finally, in the very early hours of the morning, my brain turns off.

⟫⟫⟫ ⟪⟪⟪

The scent of coffee wakes me. For a second, it smells delicious, until…

I jump out of Angelo's bed and bolt to the bathroom, barely getting the toilet lid up before vomiting. I grip the bowl, heaving with such force, when my hair is pulled from tangling around my face and falling into the bowl. Angelo rubs my back in small circles as he holds my hair.

After a few more heaves, the vomiting stops. I sit on the floor, catching my breath. He takes the chocolate-brown towel off the hook on the back of the door and puts it over my bare legs. There was no time for me to put his sweatpants on before running in here. Then he opens a narrow closet door and gets a fresh washcloth, soaking it in the sink. Squeezing it out, he sits in front of me on the floor and wipes my face with the warm cloth. Then he picks up a few strands of my hair and wraps the towel around them, dragging them through to get the vomit off.

"I didn't get to you fast enough." He offers a compassionate smile as his tender eyes try to console me.

"Thank you." I push the words out. Vomiting is exhausting. "It's the coffee."

"What's the coffee?" His brows pinch together.

"I smelled the coffee and the nausea hit me."

His eyes widen. "Oh, my God. I'm so sorry. I didn't know."

"It's okay. Neither did I." I try to smile. "It seems many of the smells I typically love are now wreaking havoc on me."

"That sucks."

"It does."

"You okay now?"

"Yeah, I'm good."

"I'll let you get cleaned up."

He leaves the bathroom and I take my non-vomit washcloth from last night, rut it under the warm water, and wipe off my face. Then I brush my teeth and put on my clothes from yesterday. I'll shower when I get back to my apartment.

When I come out of his bedroom, he's sitting on the sofa with no coffee mug in his hand. I peek into the kitchen and the coffee pot is empty.

"You didn't have to throw out your coffee."

"Ah, it's okay. Stuff's no good for me anyway." He winks. "I can get one when I go out."

"Okay." Purse in my hands, I walk over to him. He stands and faces me with his broad shoulders. "Thank you, for — everything."

"I'm always here." The earnestness in his eyes matches the warmth of his voice.

Wrapping my arms around his neck, I ease at the feel of his arms caging me. *I want to stay here forever.*

He releases me and takes a step back. "You heading back home then?" There's a sort of melancholy to his voice.

"Yeah, I have some tough conversations to have." My stomach coils as nausea teases.

"Let me know how things go. And call me if you need to talk, vent, cry, anything."

"I will." It's so good to have him back.

Not sure when I'll see him next, I hug him one last time, cherishing our embrace, not wanting to let go.

Sitting in my car before I leave, I text Joe, letting him know I need to talk to him. We set plans to see each other that afternoon.

On the long drive home, voices chatter in my head once again. So many different scenarios of how the conversations could go. Anxiety rattles every corner of my body. I have no idea how anyone is going to react.

I call Prisha as I drive, partially to fill her in and partially to quiet the chaos in my head. Windshield time leaves a lot of space for all the noise and panicked thoughts to live in my mind.

"Hey, I've been worried about you. I mean, I know you were with Angelo and I wanted to give you some space. I've just been thinking about you. Are you okay? I know, stupid question. I know you're not okay. What's going on?"

"I didn't mean to worry you. I just had to go see him. No, I'm so not okay. I'm freaking out. I'm scared. I think I just fucked up my entire life." My grip on the steering wheel involuntarily tightens.

"I want you to take a breath. We're going to figure this out, okay? I promise."

"I don't know, Prish. This is big. I can't undo this. It's not, picking the wrong job and then being able to find a new one. This changes my entire life."

"I know. So, we'll figure it out as we go. Did you tell Joe yet?"

"No. I texted him and we're meeting up as soon as I'm back. Well, after I shower. Then I'm going to go home and tell my parents. They're both in town right now."

"Okay, good."

"I'll have to tell the principal at Canyon. She probably won't even want me anymore. I'd have to take maternity leave in the middle of the school year."

"One thing at a time. You don't need to call her right now and you have no idea what she'll say. Today, deal with Joe and your parents."

I blow out a huge puff of air. "Okay. You're right."

"Get back here. Meet with Joe. Do you want me to come with you?"

"No, no. I'll be okay on my own."

"Okay. If you change your mind —"

"I'll tell you. I'll be home soon."

On the rest of my drive, I focus on what I'll say to Joe and what my options are. He could say he wants to marry me. *Ugh, I don't want to marry Joe. He'd never say that.* He could say he doesn't want to marry me, but he's willing to support me and the baby. *Somehow, I can't see him saying that either. Would I even want that?* He could say he wants nothing to do with me or the baby. *This is likely what he'll say.* And, if that's the case, I can either figure out how to be a single mom or put the baby up for adoption. *Put my baby up for adoption? I don't think I could do that.*

My thoughts clatter chaotically as I stare out the windshield.

11

—

Lucia

I get to the kitchen of the frat house before Joe arrives. Palms wet and nerves jittery.

The creak of the warped wooden front door announces his arrival, sending adrenaline powering through me, my muscles practically seizing.

We've barely spoken or seen each other since the night we had sex. Just a quick wave as we pass one another on campus.

He strolls through the kitchen doorway with that cocky stride, clearly having no idea what's about to hit him in the face. Swinging his leg over the stool next to me at the island, he winks. Acid percolates in my stomach.

"What's going on?" Getting straight to it, he nods with a cocksure side-smile and a sweep of his eyes down to my chest.

I look him dead in the eyes when he returns them to mine. There's no point in beating around the bush. "I'm pregnant."

A red hue creeps up his neck, along his face, and up to his forehead as his jaw drops. "Fuck." The word scrapes through his teeth. "You're sure it's mine?" His brows knit together tightly, creasing down to the bridge of his nose.

"Yes, I'm sure," I say quietly, squeezing my palms together. "You're the only one I've been with."

He shakes his head, blowing a puff of air. "But we used a condom." While I expected anger from him, blame even, he's as confused as I am.

74

"I know. Those things aren't a hundred percent reliable." *Un-fucking-fortunately.*

Elbows on the island, he leans forward, putting his head in his hands. He closes his eyes, the muscles in his jaw pulse out. Then he lifts his head and looks at me. "What the fuck am I supposed to *do* about this?" He's asking himself, not me. "I mean, you're a great girl, but — this — I can't —"

I'd already made up my mind before I got here. "I don't need you to do anything." My vocal cords tremble.

"I'll give you half the money and I'll drive you there —"

"No." I shake my head. "I'm not having an abortion. I'm — keeping the baby." My heart hammers against my ribs. "I'll figure things out. I don't need anything from you. I just — wanted to let you know. I owe you that." I swallow hard, twisting my folded hands.

"What do you mean, you're *keeping* it? You can't keep it." His voice begins to raise as he gets off the stool and paces. "I can't have a kid out there in the world right now. We're too young for this. Our lives are just starting." His arms form a W as his fingers spread and his eyebrows arch toward his forehead. "You need to get rid of it."

Acid bubbles in my stomach. "I'm not getting rid of my baby," I state firmly. Tears burn behind my eyes as my body temperature rises.

"Look, I didn't sign up for this." Neck jetting forward, he shakes his head. "I don't want *any* part of it." Leaning toward me, he crosses his arms then sends them flying to his sides. His face swells with a crimson hue. This is what I was expecting.

"I don't need you to be. I'll figure this out on my own." Heat rages in my chest as I raise my own voice.

Someone walks through the front door and the smell of coffee wafts into my nose, sending me running to the sink to vomit.

As the vile fluid hurls out of me, he sputters behind me in disgust, "Jesus."

Not sure he'll still be here when I'm done, I rinse off my mouth and nose, drying them with a cheap, rough paper towel.

When I turn around, he's standing there, staring at me. Slowly moving his head back and forth, he then looks me up and down, disdain painting his expression. Without another word, he turns and walks out the kitchen door.

I've never felt so alone.

Leaving the frat house, I choke back tears. *I expected this. I'm going to be okay. I'm going to figure this out. I don't know how yet, but I will.*

Every muscle in my body is tense as I walk back to my apartment and drive to my parents' house. I know they'll support me in whatever I decide to do. Still, I feel like a huge disappointment to them. Especially my dad. I love my mom with all my heart. She's strong, fierce, and the most incredible role model. With my dad, there's this special bond between us. It's tough to explain.

When I was little and even into my teens, he took me on daddy-daughter dates. I didn't realize it at the time, but he was teaching me how I deserved to be treated by men. He taught me how to value and respect myself. He wanted so much for me and my life. Telling him is going to crush me. I can't help but feel like I'm letting him down. My heart droops as I force down the lump lodged in my throat.

When I walk in the door, Mom's in the kitchen making tea. Thank goodness it's not coffee. She comes over and gives me a hug. The warm, neutral colors of home attempt to provide me solace.

"Hi, honey." Sweeping a finger down the side of my face, she catches a strand of hair and tucks it behind my ear. Her eyes study my face. "You look exhausted. Want some tea with me?"

"Yeah, tea sounds nice. I'm wiped out." Physically and emotionally. Though I don't feel like having this conversation, I may as well get it over with. "Dad home?"

"He's in his studio, playing some music."

"Okay. Be right back." I head to his studio, nerves starting to hum.

He's on his keyboard, playing and singing. I've always been enamored of his talent. I think it's one of the things that made Mom fall in love with him.

"Hey, Dad." He looks up and a smile spreads his cheeks as he stands up to embrace me.

"There's my girl." Standing back and taking in my disheveled appearance, he holds my shoulders in his hands. "Tough week, huh?"

"Very tough." I blow a stream of air and bug out my eyes. "Do you have a minute? I want to talk to you and Mom about something." My nerves increase to a vibration.

"Of course," he says, getting up and throwing his arm around my shoulder as we walk back to the kitchen. With each step, another knot ties itself in the rope coiling in my stomach.

Mom has tea ready for me and sets it on the island. I pull back the stool where she set my tea and angle it out so I can face both of them, every movement occurring in slow motion. Mom sits next to me while Dad stays standing.

"What did you want to talk to us about?" Dad asks.

My breath stalls in my chest, nerves escalating to a tremor. *Just spit it out. Breathe.* "I — I'm pregnant." All the air evacuates my chest.

Silence hovers as they stare at me.

Dad walks over to me and squats down, putting his hand on my thigh and looking me square in the eyes, comfort radiating in his gaze. "Are *you* okay? Were you hurt?"

"Yeah, I'm okay. I mean, I'm not entirely okay, but I will be. No, I wasn't hurt."

"Do you want to tell us what happened?" Mom asks calmly, putting down her tea and leaning toward me.

I sigh, shame caving my chest. "It was stupid and immature. It was my choice, no one pressured me to do it. I wanted to. Everyone else had done it. So, I gave up waiting for the one guy I'd been saving myself for and just…picked a guy I was sort of friends with. We used a condom and…apparently it was faulty." The words sputter out of me so fast. By the time I'm done, my face is tight, my lower lip is quivering, and there's a tingling behind my nostrils. I look back and forth between them. "I'm *so* sorry." I drop my head, no longer able to hold myself together, and let the tears fall.

Dad is by my side, clutching my head to his chest. Mom joins his embrace. They let me cry, blanketing me with their physical and emotional support.

Once my sobs have tempered, they release me. Mom sits back on her stool and Dad sits on one, facing me.

"Does the father know?" Dad asks.

"Yeah. I actually just came from telling him." Gravity pulls my shoulders. "He wants me to get rid of it. He wants nothing to do with me or the baby."

"What do *you* want?" Mom asks, sipping her tea, gentleness coating her words.

I run my hands down my thighs and back up. "I want to keep the baby." As the words leave my lips, the tightness in my chest eases. I know it's the right thing to do. "I told him I don't need anything from him. I know, right now, I have no idea what I'm going to do or how I'm going to handle it all, but I will." I look at each of them. "And I don't expect you to take care of me either. I don't want to be a burden to you. There are a ton of single, working moms out there who are able to manage it successfully. This may not have been what I wanted for my life, but I'm going to figure it out." Fear and uncertainty may be residing in me at the moment, but determination is in my DNA.

"Lucia." Mom touches my arm. "You could never be a burden to us." I know she says it with sincerity.

"Look," Dad says. "We don't need to figure anything out tonight. You've had a long week and this is a lot to take in. You're staying home tonight?"

"Yeah, I want to."

"Good. Then tonight we'll have some family time together and you can try to relax," he says.

"That sounds really nice." I smile at him then turn my attention to Mom. "Will you help me find an OB/GYN? All I did was take a pregnancy test yesterday and kind of freaked out. I should probably have a test done by a doctor and then set up some kind of plan."

"Of course I will. We can go to your appointment together, okay? I know you're independent and you'll figure this out on your terms. You also don't have to do it alone. We can help and we're here to support you."

"I know." My throat tightens. I pull in my lips as tears well in my lower lids. "I'm so sorry I disappointed you both." The words struggle to get out. "You've given me everything and done so much for me and I'm sorry I've let you down and messed things up." I give in to the heaviness of my head and let it drop forward. Tears dribble out, falling into my lap.

Dad stands in front of me, lifting my chin in his hand. He shakes his head slowly. "You could never disappoint us. We've always taught you how to make the best of even the worst situations in life and we're confident you're going to do exactly that. Okay, this isn't what you planned, but you are fierce, tenacious, and resilient and we're very proud of the woman you've become. We know you're going to make this work and you're going to be the best mom you can be to this child."

God blessed me with the most incredible parents. Their love and support loosen the tightness in my chest and temper the electricity zapping my nerves.

"Thank you, Dad." I wrap my arms around his waist and he holds my head to his mid-chest. Then I tilt my head up, giving him a grateful smile. We release and I stand up, going to hug Mom. "I have a couple calls to make. Then we can have some family time?"

"Sure," Mom says.

I call Prisha and let her know I'll be staying home tonight and then I'll be back at our place Sunday night for our last evening together in our apartment. Our parents are helping us move out on Monday. We've been there for three great years together. I'm going to miss seeing her every day. Thankfully, she's staying in the area so we'll still get to see each other often.

My next call is to Angelo. I told him I'd let him know how things went. He picks up right away.

"Hey. How'd it go?"

I sigh. "With Joe, it went pretty much how I thought it'd go."

"What'd he say?"

"He wants me to have an abortion. When I told him I'm keeping the baby, he basically said he wants nothing to do with any of it and left."

"Fucking asshole." Anger rakes his words.

"You know what? It's okay," I say, beginning to settle with the fact that I'll be a single mom. I'm terrified and clueless right now, but I'll get a plan together and learn what I need to. "I'm not sure how involved I would've wanted him to be anyway. Maybe this is for the best."

"Still, he's a coward for not stepping up and sharing in the responsibility with you. He just left? Walked away? What the fuck?" he seethes.

"Ang, it's okay. I'm moving my things back home on Monday and then my parents will go on their second honeymoon. I'll have some time to think and figure things out while they're away."

"Wait. You're going to be there alone? No." The last word comes out like a command. He pauses then softens. "How about you come here? Stay with me. I mean, you'll need someone to hold your hair out of the toilet when you're puking." He chuckles. "If — if you want." He morphs from my dominating protector to the timid little boy from my childhood in seconds.

I'm stunned. He's so sweet to offer, but he clearly has no idea what he'd be getting himself into. "Ang, you don't have to do that. I'm not your responsibility. This is my situation to sort out."

"I know you're not. And I know you will. I just — don't think you should be alone right now and I want to be there for you, especially given the circumstances. I have lost friendship-time to make up for." Such a charmer.

I process his words, not able to come up with a response.

"Please?"

"Um." I wrestle with my thoughts. I don't want to be a burden to anyone.

"Please, Lucia." His plea tugs at me.

"Give me a little time to think about it. I'm going to spend some time with my parents tonight. So, I'll think about it and let you know tomorrow, okay?"

"Oh, you're staying there tonight? Okay. Yeah, let me know tomorrow. Have a nice night with them."

"Thanks."

We hang up and I'm still baffled when I join my parents in the living room.

"Honey, are you okay?" Mom asks, grabbing my favorite white fluffy blanket from the arm of the sofa and holding it open for me to sit next to her.

I sit and curl my legs up onto the cushions. "Yeah, um, I just talked to Angelo and he — he wants me to come stay with him while you guys are gone. He said he doesn't think I should be alone."

"Angelo?" Mom's voice raises, as do her eyebrows. "I didn't realize you two were back in touch."

"I went to see him after I found out. He's still my best friend and — I'm sorry I told him before you. I just needed to go see him."

"You don't have to apologize. I'm glad you're back in touch. To be honest, your Aunt Destiny and I were so sad your friendship faded just because he moved a couple hours away." She tucks the blanket around my legs.

For a moment, my mind returns to our kiss and the real reason our friendship ended. I quickly push it from my thoughts…and my heart.

"Do you want to stay with him?" I thought she'd be more surprised by his offer, but there's an undercurrent of encouragement in the way she asks.

I shrug. "I don't know. I have so much to figure out right now that I can't even seem to think. I told him I'd let him know tomorrow."

"Then give it some thought tonight before you go to bed and see how you feel about it when you wake up."

I nod and exhale. "Okay."

Dad joins us and we watch a movie and then have dinner together. It's the most relaxed I've been in weeks. Before I fall asleep, my thoughts go to Angelo and his offer. While part of me is comforted by the thought of staying with my best friend rather than being alone, another part of me worries that it's going to be torture being so close to him. Though I've tried…and tried and tried…to let go of my feelings for him…endlessly lying to myself, pretending I was over him…the truth is…I'm still in love with Angelo.

12

—

Angelo

While I'm used to just walking in the door at my aunt and uncle's house, I decide to ring the bell. It's been a couple years since I've been here and it's also only a little after nine in the morning. I don't want to just barge in since I didn't tell anyone I was coming.

Uncle Enzo answers the door.

"Angelo, hey." He wraps his arms around me, patting me on the back. "It's so great to see you. Come on in."

"I'm sorry to drop in unannounced. I hope it's okay."

"Of course it is. You know you can come over any time. Our home will always be your home." A warm smile lights his face. "Want some coffee?" he asks, walking to the kitchen.

"Coffee? Uh-oh." My insides cringe for Lucia.

"You don't drink it anymore?"

"No, I do. Did Lucia not tell you about her morning sickness and the smell of coffee?"

"Ah. Is that what's going on up there? Your aunt's with her." He offers a reassuring nod.

"Okay, good. I'll skip the coffee, thanks. Maybe you can toss it for today?"

Before I finish the question, he's already pouring it out.

"I remember this stage." He moves his head from side to side. "Your aunt had it for her entire first trimester. Wait until the weird cravings start." His eyebrows shoot to his forehead. He sits on a stool at the kitchen island and I join him. "One of her favorite combinations was mint chocolate chip ice cream and beets." His entire face contorts in disgust followed by a burst of laughter that I join. Once his laughter settles, his expression turns serious. "Lucia told us you want to take care of her while we're gone. Are you sure about this?"

"Yes, I am. With your and Aunt Candi's blessing. And if that's what Lucia wants. She can stay with me the whole summer or until she figures out what she's going to do." I drop my gaze and return it to his eyes, then straighten my posture as a sign of my preparedness for what I'm offering. "I haven't been a very good friend to her these last couple years. I'd like a chance to make up for that."

He leans forward, placing a firm hand on my shoulder. "I've always thought of you as a son. And you've always taken care of Lucia. So yes, you have my blessing. Your aunt and I support any decision she makes." His gaze into my eyes is a mixture of sincerity and compassion.

"Angelo." The sweet voice of Aunt Candi comes from behind us. "How great to see you." She walks over, arms spread wide. I stand and hug her. "It's been a while," she says, releasing me. "How're you doing? How's your job?"

Dragging behind her, Lucia looks as wiped out as she did after she vomited at my place. Big, fluffy socks on her feet, she walks slowly toward us and puts her hand up in a pathetic, "Hi" wave. I offer a compassionate smile.

"I'm good. Yeah, work is all right. I have a great condo and I've met some nice people. You know, nothing exciting, but it's good. Stable job with stable income." I toss the last part out there to confirm I can provide for Lucia.

Uncle Enzo walks over to Lucia and kisses her forehead. Bathrobe wrapped around her, she comes over and sits on the stool he was on.

"Well that all sounds really good." Pride hints on her smile. Since they weren't able to have any more kids after Lucia, I know she thinks of me as a son as well. With her and my mom being best friends, we're like family. "I guess we'll be switching to tea in the mornings for a little while." She rubs her hand gently across Lucia's back. "Can I make some for all of us?"

"That'd be great," I say.

Hair plopped on top of her head with pieces falling around her face, Lucia nods.

"What're you doing here?" Lucia asks. "You didn't tell me you were coming."

"No, I know. I wanted to be here to help with your move tomorrow and if you decide you want to come stay with me, we can head back to my place on Tuesday. I already took a couple days off from work, just in case. Once we have your things back here, you can figure out what you want to bring for however long you want to stay…if you decide to come stay." *Please come.*

Her eyes roam my face as I talk. I used to be able to read her expressions so well. Right now, I can't read anything. Maybe I overstepped by just showing up.

"But there's no pressure." I look over at Aunt Candi. "And obviously I want to make sure you're okay with this too, Aunt Candi."

She looks at Lucia before setting her eyes on me. "We're okay with whatever she decides is best for her. Since she doesn't start her job until August, we'll give you some money for food while she's with you."

"No." I insist, adamant to drive home the fact that I'm sufficiently capable of taking care of their daughter. "You don't need to do that. I'll take care of any expenses." I look at Lucia. "So you'll start your job still?"

"I don't know yet." She shrugs as her lips draw back into an uncertain grimace. "I'm calling the principal on Monday. I hope so though."

"Okay. Well, whatever you decide, just know you're welcome to stay at my place for as long as you want to be there."

Her brows tug together. "Ang, I don't want to disrupt your life because I made a stupid mistake. Where would I even sleep? I don't know about this." She pulls in her lips.

"Lucia, you didn't make a stupid mistake. You couldn't have known this would happen. And my sofa turns into a pull-out so I can sleep there. You won't be disrupting my life," I say it as though she's already decided to come, even though she hasn't. "We'll figure out a routine that works for both of us."

Yes, she's my best friend. Yes, I've missed her. Yes, I want to make up for lost time and my stupidity for not reaching out and apologizing *years* sooner. And maybe…just maybe…this is my chance. My chance with Lucia. Even though it pisses me off that it's Joe's baby she's carrying and not mine, I'll love it like it's my own. Maybe now she's ready for me to be in her life beyond just our friendship. Maybe now I can prove that I'm worthy of her giving us that chance. *Please say yes.*

"Nothing has to be decided today. Just think about it. My parents are out of town so I'm going to stay there tonight and I'll meet you guys here in the morning to at least help with the move, okay?" I shift my gaze to Aunt Candi and Uncle Enzo for their agreement. They both nod.

"Will you stay for breakfast?" Aunt Candi asks.

"I had breakfast before I drove here, but I'll stay for a little while."

Hands folded in her lap, Lucia sits pensive, like she's processing everything, possibly overwhelmed.

"Can I help with breakfast?" I join Aunt Candi on the other side of the island, giving Lucia some space.

⫸⫷

"Good morning." I announce myself as I walk through their front door, ready for a day of moving furniture and boxes. I offered to help pack yesterday, but Lucia and Prisha wanted to spend their last day and night at their apartment together. Uncle Enzo got a small U-Haul that he's already hitched to his Range Rover. I hop in with them and we drive over to the girls' apartment.

"Have you spoken with Lucia?" Aunt Candi asks, shifting her

body in the passenger seat so she can look at me in the back. "Did she make her decision?"

"No, I haven't heard from her." Waiting for Lucia's answer winds tension into every muscle in my body. The anticipation is unnerving.

"Are you sure you want to do this? You know you don't have to. We can even cancel our trip."

"No. I don't want you to do that. I'm sure about this." I bow my head with confidence. "I wouldn't have offered if I wasn't. This has to be a tough time for her. If it were me, I wouldn't want to be alone. I know how strong and independent she is. I also know that underneath her strength and independence, she's scared. I think it'll be good for her to be with someone who she knows cares about her, especially right now. And — I want to be that person for her."

"Okay," she says, her lips spreading into a warm smile. "We know you'll take good care of her. We'll only be a phone call away, and we can get back quickly if the arrangement doesn't work out."

"I know." If Lucia says she'll come, I can't imagine it not working out. I'll do everything I can to help her through this.

The girls' apartment isn't far. They're ready by the time we pull up. Prisha's parents arrive within minutes, their U-Haul in tow. The girls walk us through the apartment, giving us instructions as to what goes in each truck. We get started and my heart rate kicks up when I see two small boxes with "Ang" written on them in black marker. Knowing this isn't the time to ask, I keep moving. With all of us working together and them having everything organized and ready to go, packing up the U-Hauls doesn't take long.

When their place is empty and the U-Hauls are filled, goodbyes are exchanged and we head back to Aunt Candi and Uncle Enzo's house.

"How about a break for lunch before we start unloading?" Uncle Enzo asks as he pulls into their driveway.

"Yes, I'm starving," Lucia blurts out, making us chuckle.

We all get out of the car and Lucia stops, holding onto my arm, causing me to stop too.

"We'll be right there," she says to her parents.

"Okay," Aunt Candi says as they go into the house.

Lucia stands in front of me, looking up at me with dark circles under her eyes. I stare down at her beautiful face.

"I've made my decision and, if you're sure you want me to come, I'd like to stay with you for a while." Expectancy glints in her eyes.

My hopeful heart thumps in my chest.

Maybe…

13

Lucia

Though I'm glad I won't be alone these next few weeks while my parents are gone, I'm not completely confident in my decision. I'm happy to have Angelo back in my life, but my situation really changes the dynamic of our relationship.

He still doesn't know how I feel about him…the crush that just won't fade…my heart that's longed for him my entire life. The only thing he knows is that I drunkenly ambushed him and asked him to take my virginity. And he made it clear that our tequila-kiss was just that; a passionate kiss, given and taken under the influence of tequila, nothing more.

Now, I'm going to be under the same roof with him…just the two of us…for a few weeks. Given the fact that I'm now pregnant with another man's baby, it certainly doesn't seem like the time to confess my true feelings for him. I'm going to have to keep them stuffed away…forever.

Angelo's at my parents' house by eight-thirty. We all eat breakfast together then pack up my car with my things. I've mostly brought clothes, shoes, towels, books, and a few other items I'd take on vacation. I tell my parents to enjoy their second honeymoon and Angelo and I head out to his place. My mind continues to reel on the drive there. Everything still feels so uncertain.

We arrive and unload my car together, and he brings my things to his bedroom.

"You can make this your home base. I got those plastic drawers for your clothes as a temporary dresser since mine is filled with my clothes." He points to a stack of three clear-plastic drawers next to his dresser. "And I made some space in my closet in case you have things you want to hang."

I drop my bags on the floor and peek into his walk-in closet. There are ten new-looking hangers in an open space that's about a foot and a half wide.

"It's not the most quality stuff, but I thought it would do for now."

He went out and got things for me before he even knew my answer? My heart warms at his thoughtfulness and desire to make me feel welcomed. One of the many reasons I love him. *Even though I shouldn't.* He thought it would do "for now?" *What does that mean?*

"If you're up for it, we can hit the grocery store and then hang here for the rest of the day so you can unpack and settle in a little. What do you think?"

Still somewhat dumbfounded, I look back at him, standing there with my bags at his feet as he gives up his bedroom to me and allows me to invade his home for a few weeks. "Okay, that sounds good."

"Great. I'll drive." He turns to walk out the bedroom door.

"Ang?"

When he turns back to face me, my heart thumps at how handsome he is in his worn jeans and old, gray UCLA T-shirt. "Yeah?"

"I'll do my best to be invisible. I don't want to disrupt your life." I can't shake the awkwardness in the air.

His steps toward me are slow, deliberate. I draw in a breath, holding it. When he reaches me, he takes my hands in his, bowing his face above mine.

"I don't want you to be invisible. I asked you to come here so I could take care of you." Gently squeezing my hands, he hushes his voice. "I *want* you to disrupt my life, Dandelion Girl. I've missed you." Leaning down, he presses his lips to my forehead, sending a warm wave over me. "Come on, let's go."

Does he have any idea how he tugs at my heart? How am I supposed to banish my feelings for him?

Going up and down the aisles of the grocery store is comfortable, familiar. We discuss meals for the week and I guess at what might not send me running to the bathroom to vomit. We stock up on oatmeal, bread, and tea.

When we get back, he offers to put away the groceries so I can unpack my things. Taking my time, I put away my clothes in the plastic drawers and hang a few things in the closet. This feels so strange.

I hadn't really looked around much when I was here the other day. Everything is tidy, minimalist, and has a masculine touch. One of his guitars sits in a stand in the corner of his room. Tasteful guitar art decorates his walls, displaying his love of music. I wander the room, soaking in his essence. He's definitely upgraded his style since college.

When I go back out, he's finishing putting away the groceries. I lift myself to sit on the countertop.

"Too early for dinner?" he asks, putting a box of spaghetti into the pantry.

"No. I could eat." I'm constantly hungry. It's going to be weird experiencing this baby growing inside me.

"What do you feel like?"

"I realize I inherited my mom's pathetic cooking skills, but I don't expect you to cook me dinner every night while I'm here. In fact, maybe I'll try to cook dinner for *you* a few nights." I swagger my head, trying to appear confident.

He laughs. "I don't want my kitchen burnt to a crisp."

"Hey," I rebut playfully and join his laughter, knowing he has every right to fear that possibility.

"It's not a problem. I have to cook for myself anyway. So, what do you want?"

"Mmm. Can you make those cheesy eggs my dad taught you how to cook? The ones you make on Saturday mornings when we're on vacation?"

He smiles. "Toast?"

I raise my eyebrows and nod.

"I'm liking this breakfast-for-dinner trend." He grins as he goes to a cabinet and takes out a bowl.

"Can I help?"

"You can scramble the eggs. *I'll* cook them." He points to his chest with a playful glint in his eyes.

"Deal." There's a lightness in my chest. Being with him brings me such comfort.

I get the eggs and milk from the fridge as he gets out a frying pan and spatula.

"What're your typical days like? You know, so I know what to expect from your schedule." I crack an egg into the bowl.

"I hit the gym in the mornings before work. I'll make sure to keep my gym bag out here so I don't disturb you." Opening a drawer, he gets out a whisk.

"Are you sure about this? I'm totally fine sleeping out here. I feel bad taking over your bedroom." Cracking another egg, I look over at him.

"Then I'd definitely wake you up early every morning with you being such a light sleeper. You don't want to be woken up at five AM when you're on vacation. No, this works out better. Then by the time I get back, you'll probably be up. We can eat, I can shower, and then you'll have the place to yourself. I'm usually home around six and eat dinner while I watch a little TV. Then I read some before I go to bed, which is usually around nine or ten."

"Okay, I'll make sure I do my things around your schedule." I crack the next egg, accidentally dropping two small pieces of shell into the bowl.

Looking into the bowl, he bursts into laughter as he crosses his arms over his chest. "This is the easy part."

"Shoot." I stick my finger into the bowl, trying to fish out the pieces of shell. Every time I think I have a piece in my fingers, it sneaks out because of the slipperiness of the egg whites.

"Ready for me to take over?" He holds his hands out toward the bowl, quirking a devilish smile.

"No," I insist. "I'm not helpless in the kitchen. Just hold on. I'll get them out." Patiently, I manage to move each small piece to the side of the bowl, pressing it against the surface and dragging it out. "How many should I put in here?" I ask, triumph riding my tone.

Amusement plasters his face. "Put in three more," he says, getting plates out of a cabinet.

I crack the rest of the eggs and pick up the whisk, moving it vigorously from left to right in the bowl. Feeling his eyes on me, I don't look up. I stay focused on my task.

"Um, whatcha doin' there?" When I look over at him, he points his chin toward my workspace with a quirk in his smile.

Dropping my shoulders in defeat, I surmise I'm somehow doing this wrong. A huge smile spreads across his cheeks.

"I'm stirring the eggs," I say with confidence.

"Well, you're doing *something*." His shoulders move up and down as he chuckles and moves his body behind me. His chest inches from my back, he puts his hand around mine on the whisk. Warmth drizzles through me. "Loosen your death-grip a little," he teases. I do as he says. "Instead of having your hand do the work, let it flow loosely from your wrist. You kind of want to make oval shapes." He moves my hand in his as he explains. His mouth close to my ear, his breath sends warm whispers down my neck. I focus on keeping my breathing steady. "Let me put some milk in." When he steps away to get the milk, the heat from his chest leaves my back and I feel the loss immediately, releasing the breath I'd been holding.

Standing next to me, he pours in some milk. "You did good. I'll finish it up." His arm muscles flex as he whisks the mixture together like a professional cook on TV. The movement has heat spiking up my spine. "Hey." He looks over at me and I quickly shift my gaze from his taut muscles. "How'd you make out with your job? What'd they say?"

"She was so nice. She said she was impressed with my resume and my interviews and still wants me to start in the fall. She said we'll get a sub for the time I'll need to be out. I don't think I'll take the full leave. My mom's not traveling as much as she used to and she'd probably love to help out. Then I'll get day care for the days when she can't."

"That's great. I know you were worried you weren't going to have a job."

"I was. I'm so grateful she still wants to hire me."

He finishes whisking the egg mixture and pours it into the pan he had heating. Mild sizzling floats into the air. When the eggs are still runny, he shreds in some sharp cheddar cheese. So far, nothing is making my stomach churn. Thank goodness because I'm hungry. It's a quick meal to make and we sit at his small dining table to eat.

"I have a cool rooftop deck. Wanna go up after dinner? We can bring a blanket and watch the clouds until the stars come out."

Nostalgia weaves through me. "Just like we used to when we were kids." Almost every evening when we were on vacation, we'd lay blankets on the sand and watch clouds drift by with Bella. When we'd see one that resembled an animal or an object, we'd call out and point to it. He often challenged my declarations of what they were.

"Yeah." His smile is somehow sexy, like the sinfully hot man he's turned into, and also adorable, like the little boy who stole my heart so many years ago.

I nod with a smile. "I'd like that."

We finish up dinner and do the dishes. After grabbing a blanket from the black industrial blanket-rack in the living room, Angelo leads me down the hallway between the kitchen and his bedroom. He opens a door at the end of it and I follow him up the stairs to his private rooftop deck. Laying the blanket on the ground, he takes pillows from the small outdoor sofa and sets them on the blanket. Then he gets a few pieces of wood from a black, iron holder in the corner and puts them in the fire pit.

"Grab me some of the smaller pieces? And the lighter?" he asks.

I bring the items over to him and he lights the small pieces of wood, then touches the flame to the wicks of four tiki torches that are dotted around the cozy space.

"It's nice up here," I say, getting comfortable on one of the pillows.

"Yeah. This is one of my favorite things about this place. I spend a lot of my downtime up here. You know, writing music, reading."

He joins me on the blanket and opens his Calm app, choosing "Starry Night." Setting his phone on the blanket above the pillows, he lies down and gazes at the sky. I fluff my pillow and lie next to him. The celestial music swirls in the air surrounding us as we lie quietly, breathing. My situation has me uneasy and anxious, and this serenity feels nice.

As my eardrums absorb the music, my mind wanders to the many nights we'd spend watching the clouds together as kids. He'd always put himself between me and Bella on the blanket. I'd keep my arms down by my sides, hoping he'd take my hand in his. A few times, when our fingers would brush, I swear he'd linger before pulling away. Those brief touches always made me feel funny inside though I was too young to understand what it meant.

Now, lying next to him as a grown woman, I still want that little boy to reach out and hold my hand. It seems silly, but I can't help it. And the way I feel being this close to him, I completely understand that funny feeling inside me…it's full-on desire.

You'd think that him having walked out of my life two years ago and hurting me so badly would make me want him less, but the more I'm around him, the tougher it is to convince myself that I'm not still deeply in love with him. It doesn't help that my body turns into a raging inferno making me want him more each time we're together.

"Look at that one." He points to the cluster of clouds above us. "It looks like an elephant. See the trunk?" Leaning toward me a little, he traces the air with his finger, curling the elephant's trunk.

"I see it." Comfort settles in my bones as I gaze at the puff of clouds.

We watch the clouds move over us as the crackle of the fire mixes with the soothing sounds of harp and piano.

"Oooo, that one," I say. "It's a duck. Can you see it?" I point and look over at him.

He's not watching the clouds, he's looking at me. A burst of heat brushes up my neck.

Turning his face up, he smiles. "A duck? It's a genie's lantern." He playfully chides. Still questioning the shapes I deem the clouds.

"A lantern? No, it's not a lantern. If it was a lantern, the duck's head would be in the middle. It's clearly a duck."

He chuckles. "Okay, okay, I concede. It's a duck."

"Clearly." My word strikes confidence and victory.

Time passes as clouds wisp by, moving through the sky. *Why does this feel so good?*

"There's a bunny." I point at a puffy cloud structure with a body and ears that slightly resemble a bunny if you tilt your head the right way and squint a little.

"A bunny." He says it matter-of-fact, not challenging my declaration. "I'll be right back." Getting up, he goes down the stairs.

When he comes back, he sits cross-legged next to me. I sit up and face him, curiosity tugging at me when I see a gift in his hands.

"Here." He hands me a rectangular, wrapped present. "I'm sorry I don't have a card. I've had this for a long time and intended to give it to you for your graduation. With all that's been going on, I completely forgot."

"It feels like a book. What is it?" A twinge of excitement shimmies through me.

"Open it." He gestures to the package.

I rip open the seams to expose the book inside and my heart freefalls with delight and sentimentality. I gasp, clutching my chest and holding the book in my hand. "The Velveteen Rabbit," I say softly over the pebble in my throat.

He shrugs. "I know you were heartbroken when you lost yours. I saw it in this dingy bookshop and thought of you. It's old, but it looks like it's in pretty good condition. It's not signed by the author, but there's a note in there. Looks like it was to a grandson from his grandparents. I know you like that kind of thing."

Touched and overwhelmed, emotion steals my words. I climb into his lap, wrapping my legs behind him and curling my arms around his neck, nuzzling my head into the crook between his neck and shoulder.

How can I not love this man? He knows me better than anyone.

My parents had given me The Velveteen Rabbit book when I was a little girl. I loved that book so much and brought it with me everywhere. One summer vacation, I somehow lost it and was devastated to the point of tears. This is the most thoughtful gift I've ever received. My heart melts into a puddle.

Drawing my body back from his I force words through my constricting throat. "Thank you so much for this. I love it," I manage to push out. Taking a breath, I unwrap myself from him and sit across from him again. I pick up the book and flip through it, joy skipping inside me. It's old and worn, but in very good condition. It had to be expensive. "Ang, I hope you didn't pay a lot for this. I mean, it's beautiful and I love it. It's just, this is a first edition. Do you know how rare this is?"

"I do now." He winks. "The price doesn't mean anything. Seeing how happy it's made you makes it worth it." He lies back down, adjusting his head on the pillow. His nonchalance reveals that he doesn't understand the depth of impact his gift has on me.

Still in awe, I flip through a few more pages, filled with nostalgia and reminiscing about how much I loved the story of the little rabbit. I lie down next to Angelo and we talk for hours, looking up at the sky until the sun fades and the moon and stars join us.

"Remember how you used to catch fireflies in a jar? And your dad would poke holes in the lid so they could breathe? Somehow, you always managed to get me to help you and we'd run around scooping them out of the air." He chuckles, staring up at the starry night.

"You were always better at catching them than me." Unbidden, I release a tiny laugh. He'd always do the crazy things I'd ask him to do.

"And those dandelions." He blows air through his nose. "I could never *not* make a wish. You insisted I make a wish every time. So, I'd make the same wish as always and then you'd let me blow the fuzz off."

When I look over at him, the smile on his face makes me smile. "You always made the same wish? You never told me that."

"Yup. Same wish. Every time." His eyes are cast up to the sky.

"What'd you wish for?"

He turns on his side to face me, propping his head in his hand. "What? I can't tell you that. You know the rules. If you tell anyone, it won't come true." The corners of his lips pull up into a sexy smile.

"What? That's when we were kids. I can't believe you won't tell me."

"Hey, I don't make the rules." He shrugs a shoulder with a mischievous grin on his face.

"So, has it come true?" What could he have wished for and why won't he tell me?

Pulling in his lips, he shakes his head. "Nope. Not yet."

"Would I know what it is?"

The corners of his lips drop down. "I don't know." His grin turns playfully smug.

Curiosity eats at me. We must've made thousands of wishes over the years. He made the same one *every* time? *What did he wish for? Why won't he tell me?* Ah, his music. It has to be that. I hope his wish comes true.

His smile fades as his brown eyes shift back and forth between mine. "I know you're going through a lot right now. And I know you have some decisions to make about how you're going to move forward. I want you to know I'm — I'm here — for you, for all of it. You know, if you need me. You don't have to do this alone." He lays his hand gently on my stomach.

My heart sighs as I wrestle with my feelings, fighting the words I want to say. "Ang, I can't ask you to help me with this. It's not your responsibility."

"I know that. And you're not asking. I'm offering. You made me watch so many of those sappy movies where the guy best friend steps in to do the right thing. Well, that's all I'm offering. Who knows," he says, moving his hand in small circles on my stomach, "maybe I'd be an okay stepdad."

I place my hand on top of his. "You're going to be a great dad someday." I pause. "I've missed you. I've missed our friendship so much." *So much that I've carried the pain of losing you every day.*

"Me too." Removing his hand from my stomach, he lies on his back.

It's not long before I'm tired. We douse all the flames and head downstairs.

"Let me grab my gym bag and I'll be out of your way."

Together, we go to his bedroom. He walks over to the nightstand next to his bed and switches on the small lamp that dusts the room with warm, muted light. I sit on his bed and he grabs clothes out of his dresser, putting them in his black bag. Scooting into his closet, he comes back out with a baseball hat on…backward. There's something so hot about the way he looks when he wears it like that.

"You shouldn't hear me in the morning," he says, walking toward the bedroom door. "I'll be up and out."

I follow him and he stops in the doorway, turning to face me. "I'm glad you're here, Dandelion Girl," he hushes, lingering.

Thump-thump, thump-thump. While my heart pounds beneath my ribs, my eyes defiantly sweep to his lips. *Kiss me, Angelo. Please.*

14

Angelo

Looking down into those beautiful eyes, it took everything in me not to pick her up, wrap her legs around my waist, and ravage her right there in the doorway last night. I was desperate to taste her lips again, to feel her body pressed against mine. Desire coiled through me.

What the fuck have I done to myself?

I *will* control myself. She needs a friend right now. Someone who cares about her. Someone she trusts and can rely on. She doesn't need the guy who's been fantasizing about her for the last eleven years. The guy whose heart and balls she's owned since we were kids.

I'm going to be the man she needs. This is my chance. What I've been waiting so many years for. A chance to take care of her in the way she deserves to be taken care of. A chance to show her my undying love. To support her in every way and be her partner for the rest of our lives. I've been waiting for her to be ready for me. Even though her situation changes what I've always envisioned for us, I'm done waiting. I have to take this chance. Because I'm ready to be hers forever…always have been.

I hit the gym, *hard*. Trying to get out my pent-up sexual frustration. It's pointless. Every time I lay on the bench and press the weights up, I see her straddled across my lap, her seductive eyes gazing down at me. Every slam into the punching bag is a desirous thrust between her thighs, a fantasy I've played over and over in my head. Trying to ignore my need for her is becoming increasingly difficult.

The second I walk in my front door, that frustration does the tango with my dick. The refrigerator door is open and Lucia's bent over, looking in. Her pink pajama shorts hit just below her tight ass, giving me a delicious view of her sinfully long legs. *Fuck me.*

"Good morning," I say, hoping my voice sounds casual and not like a twelve-year-old boy who just woke up from a wet dream starring her.

She straightens herself and turns toward me, her nipples greeting me from behind her matching pink pajama tank. *Jesus.* My dick stirs. "Good morning. How was your workout?"

"Good workout." I nod, heading for the bathroom. These gym shorts aren't going to do anything to hide the hard-on that's about to join our conversation.

"You want breakfast?"

"Yeah. I'll be right back." I duck into the bathroom, hoping that taking a leak will shut down my dick so I can eat a quick breakfast with her. I throw on a pair of jeans and go back out to the kitchen.

"I'm making oatmeal, toast, and tea," she says in a sing-song voice, then chuckles. "I'm a little scared to try anything else right now. Want some?"

"Yeah. Sounds good." I grab bowls from the cabinet and set them on the counter next to the stove.

While her cooking skills are seriously awful, which is adorable, she's conquered oatmeal and toast. She spoons oatmeal into the bowls while I butter the toast. We bring everything to the table and sit down to eat.

Puckering her lips, she blows on a spoonful of oatmeal. "Okay, I don't understand. It's not tax season, so then what do you do at work all day?"

"Heh. True, it's not tax season, but there are still tax returns to do. Mainly we work on extensions for corporations. There's also different types of audits we perform for companies and schools, that kind of thing."

"Oh." She picks up her toast and dips it into her oatmeal. "I always wondered how accountants made so much money when they only work three and half months out of the year." She smiles before putting the oatmeal-coated corner of toast into her mouth.

It's impossible to stop myself from glancing at that beautiful mouth of hers. I chuckle at her thought process. "Trust me, there's plenty to do beyond April. I'm actually working on a really complicated return right now and I'm trying to find a large discrepancy in the numbers I'm seeing. It takes a lot of meticulous research and digging."

"If there's one thing I know about you, you'll figure it out with precision and determination." The way she states it so matter-of-fact makes me swell with pride.

"Yup, I'll find it. There's a ton of data to sift through, but I'll find it." I take a sip of tea. "What're you going to do today?" I ask, glancing at her and trying not to let my eyes wander down to her nipples.

"Since it's officially my last summer before real adulthood —" She pauses as reality seeps in, tinging her words. "— and a baby to care for, I thought I'd lay by the pool and read. Just relax and be lazy after all the craziness of these last few weeks."

My thoughts immediately catapult to her in a bikini. Long, tanned, luscious legs, hourglass curves through her waist, and hard nipples protruding from her perfect breasts, taunting me from behind triangular pieces of fabric. The older we've gotten and the more she's filled out her bikinis, the harder it's been to conceal my erections. *Fuck me. Put a potato sack over her and refocus.*

I clear my throat. "That sounds like the perfect way to spend the day."

"Technically I'll have summers off, but I think I'll tutor a little bit. I know the baby'll keep me busy, but I think I'd like to do something to keep my skills and brain fresh. Plus, my salary's not much so the extra money will be nice." She tilts her head.

Though *I* want to be the one taking care of her financially… and in *every* other way…I admire her independence. Always have. It's damn sexy.

"I think I'll find a bookstore tomorrow and check out books

on pregnancy, having a baby, you know, *What to Expect When You're Expecting* types of books." Her eyebrows lift as somberness washes her face.

"And if *I* know anything about *you*, you're going to be so on top of things when this little baby arrives." I smile, trying to offer some kind of consolation.

"I hope so. I mean, this is something I wanted and knew I'd prepare for someday." Her eyes drop to her half-eaten bowl of oatmeal. "Just, not now, and — not his." Her voice lowers as sadness drapes her, a weighted cape, penetrating the room and seeping into me. She shakes her head the slightest bit, not looking up at me. I witness the reality eat at her.

An ache gnaws at my core. I'm helpless. I can't fix this for her. I can't change it. I can't make it go away. Guilt rails into my chest. *Should I have taken her virginity? Is that how I could've protected her? The way I was supposed to protect her. Would she not be in this situation if I'd just done as she'd asked?* My mind races, thoughts spiraling out of control. *It wasn't the right time. It was too soon. She wasn't ready for me. I know she wasn't. But now, here we fucking are. She's in my condo, back in my life, with some asshole's baby inside her, and me, wanting to profess my lifelong love to her and be her knight in shining armor.* What a fucking shitshow.

She lifts her head and looks at me, regret painting her expression. "I'm — I'm sorry. This isn't yours to deal with or have to listen to," she says, scooping another spoonful of oatmeal.

"Hey, I'm here for all of it." I reach out, putting my hand on her forearm. She stares down into the bowl. "You know you can tell me anything, right?"

Silence takes over the room.

"Lucia." She looks at me, eyes filled with hesitation. "You can always tell me anything. No filters. That's not how our friendship works. We tell each other everything and anything, remember?" I gulp down the guilt of my secret, lifelong love.

She nods her head, a hint of unease still present in her eyes, her posture.

I gesture between us. "This? What we have? It's rare, special. There's no shame, no judgment, and no place for being embarrassed. We don't hide things from each other." I shake my head. "We're safe. Here. Together. Always."

"And forever?" Her misty doe-eyes pierce my heart. I know she knows the answer and I know fear and uncertainty have shaken her sense of confidence and trust in herself.

In that moment of her vulnerability, I inwardly vow to help her rebuild those qualities in herself. I lean in toward her. "And forever." The magnitude of the word permeates the air. I nod, keeping my gaze on her eyes so she can absorb my sincerity...my promise. Turning my body to face her, I spread my legs a little. "Come here," I say, opening my arms in invitation.

She gets up from her seat and sits on my thigh, wrapping her arms around my neck and resting her head against mine. Enveloping her in my arms, I revel in being her safe place. We sit in the quiet.

Once she releases me and returns to her seat to finish her oatmeal, I head to the shower then go to work. I'm already looking forward to coming home to Lucia. Throughout the day, I can't keep my thoughts from wandering to her.

When I get home, I change and make dinner for us. We chat about our days then head up to the rooftop deck to spend the rest of the evening stargazing. Our mutual yawns tell us it's time to go to bed so we call it a night and head back downstairs. I pack my gym bag for the morning and go out to the living room, desperately wanting to kiss her goodnight.

Finally falling asleep, I'm startled awake by a scream coming from my bedroom. Adrenaline races through me, springing me up. I run to the room. Flip on the light switch. Rush to the bed.

In the muted light of the small lamp on the nightstand, Lucia's skin glistens with sweat. Breaths heave out of her. Her gaze is disoriented. I immediately get into the bed with her, curling my arm under her body and pulling her onto my chest. She wraps her arm around my waist with indomitable force, clutching on for life.

"Hey, hey," I say, wiping the wet hair from her forehead. "It's okay. It's okay. It was just a dream. You're okay. You're okay." Keeping my voice calm, I stroke her hair.

We lie quietly while she catches her breath.

"Wanna tell me about it?" I ask after her breathing becomes normal and she loosens her grip.

"It was so awful. I was walking through the desert, all alone. And my feet were kind of below the sand. It was so heavy. I had to keep pulling them out to move forward. As I was walking, the sand started to spiral into this huge funnel that flowed into some sort of sinkhole. I couldn't feel my feet under me anymore. All I could do was watch it suck me in and I was screaming for help, but nothing was coming out of my mouth and no one was there." She looks up at me, eyes still holding fright.

"You always did have wild dreams." I give her a small smile, trying to ease her. "It kinda makes sense though, you know? Your life just got flipped on its head. I know you'll figure it out, still it's a lot." I adjust my head so we're a little more eye-to-eye. "Listen to me. *You* are a force of nature. Delicate, yet strong, powerful, fierce, and brave. You're going to do exactly what's best for you and your baby. You're going to look that sinkhole in the eye and spit fire into it."

She releases a weak chuckle, making me feel like I might've helped just a little.

"Thank you, Ang." Curling her head down, she squeezes me. "Will you stay until I fall asleep?"

"Yeah, I can do that." I kiss the top of her head. "Your pajamas are soaked. Want a T-shirt?"

"Okay," she says, lifting from my chest.

I get out of bed and grab a T-shirt from my dresser, tossing it to her. "Be right out." I go into the bathroom to pee and get my head on straight. *This is going to be tough.* I didn't see her for two years. Now in two days, I swear I'm ten times deeper in love with her. It's also becoming harder to shove away my magnifying attraction to her. *She needs me right now. I can do this for her.*

I open the bathroom door and call out before exiting. "You ready?"

"Yup." The sweet sound of her voice erects the hairs on the back of my neck.

I get back into bed and turn out the light. She rolls herself into my side, resting her head on my chest once again and draping her arm across my stomach. Warm air from her nostrils sweeps down my chest.

Sweet Jesus.

15

Lucia

Being wrapped around Angelo calms my nerves. He's my safety. Always has been. As my desire for him compounds with every minute we're together, right now, I let myself be swallowed by the comfort of his embrace. I don't know what's ahead of me, but for now, all I'm going to do is be present, existing only in this moment.

When I wake up, I vomit immediately. He's at the gym and I rest a little before making my oatmeal, toast, and tea. After he leaves for work, I shower and head out to do some shopping and get a few books. By my third bout of vomiting in public bathrooms, grateful to have made it to the toilets, I'm ready to go back to Angelo's.

Completely exhausted, I want to relax by the pool, but it's probably best for me to be close to a toilet. I snuggle up on the sofa and start reading one of the books I got. It talks about having a support system. I'm lucky to be surrounded by people who love me. The one person I haven't yet told is Nonno. My heart sinks in my chest. Of all the people I've worried about disappointing, Nonno is the one I've been worried about the most. Probably why I haven't called him yet. While I'm not sure he'd say it to my face, I know his heart will hold disapproval. I may as well do it. I take in a deep breath and let it out as I grab my phone.

"Hi, Nonno."

"Lucia!" The joy in his weathered voice makes me smile. "How are you? Are you enjoying your summer so far?"

A small lump begins swelling in my throat as the confession draws near. "I'm good. Yeah, it's been quiet so far. How're you doing?"

His sweet, scraggly chuckle makes me smile. "Oh, you know. My wrist aches every time rain's coming. My knees don't work like they used to. And my friends are starting to die. Other than that, I'm good." He usually ends on a positive note. Mom says he softened when I was born.

I swallow over the lump that's growing a little larger. "Nonno, I have some news to share with you."

"About your new job?" His voice lifts. He's so excited I'm going to be a teacher.

I shake my head and shift my position on the sofa. "No. Not about that. Um —" *Just say it.* "Nonno, I'm going to have a baby." I vainly try to infuse happiness into my voice, and fail.

"A baby?" He chuckles. "You can't have a baby. You're not even married. *You're* a baby. What are you talking about? Are you getting a puppy?"

His confusion and disbelief tug at me. "No, I'm not getting a puppy. I — I made a bad decision that turned into a big mistake." I swallow as tears fill my eyes. "And, and now I'm pregnant."

"Mmm." It's the only sound he makes.

"I'm sorry, Nonno." When I blink, tears dribble down my face.

"No," he says gently. "I don't need your apology."

"But I know you're disappointed in me. It's certainly not what I planned for myself."

"I'm not disappointed in you, Lucia. I hurt for you. It's different. I don't hear pleasure in your voice as there should be when you're expecting a baby. This is what hurts me." He pauses. "And the father?"

My heartbeat ticks up. "I'm afraid he wants nothing to do with me or the baby."

"Mmm." There it is again. The nonjudgmental sound that's cloaked with silent disapproval.

"Does Angelo know?"

I choke down another swallow as I gaze up at the ceiling,

muscles tight under my skin.

"Yes, he knows. I'm staying with him while Mom and Dad are on their trip. He's taking care of me."

"He's a good man." I envision that nod of respect he has when he speaks about Angelo.

"Yes, he is."

"What does he have to say about this?"

"You know him. He's compassionate and supportive of me and my decisions. He's my best friend." I shrug.

"Mmm." It's the same sound, yet he manages to impart different secret meanings behind it that I try to decode. He's a man of few words, great depth, and insightful wisdom. "He's a good person to have in your life, yes?"

"Yes."

"And you care for him?" He's trying to sound innocent in his line of questioning, but he can't hide the insinuation behind his words.

"I do. Very much." I've never told Nonno how I feel about Angelo. He's keenly perceptive.

"Then it's good you're there with him." He lays it out.

"It is. I've been suffering from morning sickness all the time and he's been so helpful."

"Your mother was very sick with you. I'm sorry to hear this. I hope it passes soon."

"Thank you. Me too." I pause. "Nonno?"

"Yes."

"How did you know Nonna was the one for you?"

"Mmm." A sweet chuckle follows the sound and I know his eyes are twinkling like they always do when he speaks of her. "People complicate it these days. Really, it's not so complicated. I knew it the first time I held her hand in mine. It fit like no one else's ever had. And my whole body felt warm." His soft sigh comes through the phone. "When it happens, your heart will know. It will tell you. It's really that simple."

How I wish it was that simple. I do love how he looks at life in an unembellished way.

"Maybe once your sickness is gone, you can come up for a visit before summer is over."

"I'd love that, Nonno."

"Okay, we'll plan it when you're feeling better."

When we hang up, I go back to reading my book and try to push the tension from my body. I wake to the sound of Angelo making dinner. We chat about our days, catching each other up on what we did. Then we watch a little TV together and go to bed... separately. I can't deny that I loved falling asleep in his arms last night when he stayed with me after my nightmare. I want to fall asleep in his arms for the rest of my life. But I know that can't happen.

I spend the next day reading more and doing some research online. I know a lot of motherhood will be learned in the moment, but I want to be as prepared as I can be. I'm also going to make dinner for Angelo tonight. He's been taking such good care of me, I want to thank him somehow, even though my cooking may feel more like penance to him than gratitude.

I start cooking and try my best to time it so it's ready soon after he comes home from work. The thing I didn't anticipate, and really should've by now, was more vomiting. I love lasagna. I love everything about lasagna. How can it now be something that sends my body into a violent hurling of acidic liquid? Each time, I drag myself off the floor, wash off my face, brush my teeth, and try to persevere. Determination pushes me...until exhaustion keeps me clutching the toilet.

Angelo

When I walk in, I put my keys and wallet in the basket on the kitchen counter. Surveying the countertop, I see cooked noodles spread out on parchment paper, a cheese mixture in a bowl with bits splattered around, and a pot of sauce on the stove. It looks like Lucia's making lasagna...or trying to anyway. I could go for a homemade lasagna. Then I hear her, a weak moan coming from the bathroom. Rounding the corner, I find her hunched over the toilet.

Crouching down, I scoop up her limpish body. "I take it we're adding lasagna to the list of things not to eat?" I ask, walking toward the bed.

"Oh, God. Don't even say the word." At least she still has her humor about her.

"What happened?" I place her on the bed and sit next to her.

"I wanted to make you dinner. To thank you for taking care of me." Her expression is adorably pathetic and I can't hold back my chuckle. "All I ended up doing is making a huge mess for you to clean up because I don't think I can finish making it."

"How about we do this? I'm going to clean up in there while you stay here and watch TV for a little while. I'll open the windows to air out the smell. Then you can come out to the living room while I make something a little milder for us. Sound good?"

The corners of her lips curl down as she looks up at me with tired eyes from under her lashes. "Okay." One side of her mouth twists up. "I'm sorry."

"I don't accept your apology," I say, standing up. "I offered to take care of you. I want to take care of you."

"Well, I'm sure you didn't quite sign up for *this*."

Leaning down, I kiss the top of her head. "This, and whatever else you can throw at me, Dandelion Girl." I wink and head to the kitchen.

No sense in throwing everything away, so I pack it up in airtight containers and put it in the fridge. Maybe I'll make it when she's out of the house and bring it in to work for lunches. Then I whip up some scrambled eggs and toast and let her know when they're ready.

As we eat, she tells me about her day and how sick she was. She looks and sounds so tired. There's not much I can do to help with her morning, well her all-day-long, sickness, but what I can do is draw her a soothing bath with the bubble bath she has on the shelf in the closet with her other toiletries. I don't know if she's taken a bath here yet and I'm hoping the smell of it will be okay for her. I know how much she loves bubble baths. Hopefully it'll help her feel better.

I go out to the living room and squat down in front of her where she's watching TV from the sofa.

"How about a nice, relaxing bubble bath? Got one ready for ya."

She doesn't say anything. She just looks at me. Eyes moving back and forth between mine. Like she's trying to figure out a puzzle.

Then she says softly, "How'd I get so lucky to have you as my best friend?"

"Heh." I shrug. *Friend. I never knew a word could feel so heavy.* "I don't know. I guess it was just meant to be." I stand. "Come on. Before it gets cold."

Rising wearily, she follows me to the bathroom. Before I leave, she curls herself into my chest.

"Thank you, Angelo."

"You're welcome," I say as she releases me. "I hope it helps. Call out if you need anything."

"Okay. I will." She tucks a stray hair behind her ear as she looks up at me with a grayish color under her eyes.

My body battles itself. My heart aches for what she's going through and all my dick can do is think about her naked body soaking in bubbles in my tub.

16

Lucia

As I lie in the tub, surrounded by silky bubbles, my heart and my body are at war. Angelo is the kindest, most thoughtful, loving man I know outside of my dad. He makes me feel special, important, safe, and cared for. And, I don't know if it's my hormones making everything particularly fervid, but every time I'm near him, desire scorches me.

My entire life, all I've truly wanted was to be with Angelo. To have a family and build a life together. Now, because of my own stupidity, I'm with him for a few weeks that are tainted by the situation I created. Once I return home and start my teaching job, we'll be hours apart, which really doesn't even matter because he's firmly established that he only sees me as his best friend and nothing more. Each day is simultaneously the most wonderful and the most heartbreaking.

Carrying Joe's baby, fearing this might be my only chance at motherhood, round-the-clock morning sickness, and living under the same roof as the love of my life while not being able to tell him is…all…pure…torture.

⇉⇇

The next few days are uneventful. Angelo often goes to an open mic night at a local place on Fridays and he invited me to join him tonight. I love listening to him sing and play his guitar. I hope my stomach cooperates. He usually eats dinner there, but we play it safe and eat at home before we go.

It's a cute place. Casual. Clean. Different bands and celebrity memorabilia decorate the walls that emit a creative vibe. With his guitar in one hand, he takes my hand in his other as he walks us to the bar. That's the moment I feel it. Undeniable. Just like Nonno said. Angelo has never held my hand before. It's just not something we do. People who are dating and in love hold hands. Warmth spreads to every corner, every crevice of my body. Overwhelming me. The way he slid his hand effortlessly into mine was so natural, like we've been holding hands for fifty years. They fit like they were made only for each other.

As soon as we sit on a couple bar stools, a bartender sees us and comes over with his smile broadening as he approaches us. His physique is like a wrestler. Massive upper body about ready to burst through his tight T-shirt, with a sleeve of tattoos covering both arms.

"Hey man," he says, stretching out an open hand across the bar toward Angelo. "It's good to see you. Wasn't sure you were coming tonight. You're late."

Angelo grabs his hand and smiles back. "Yeah, yeah. We ate dinner at my place before coming over. Chad, this is Lucia." He looks over at me.

Chad turns his attention to me as his eyes widen and brows rise a touch. "Nice to meet you, Lucia." He extends his hand to shake mine.

"And you," I say, extending my hand to him, hoping he doesn't crush it. Intimidating in appearance, his handshake is gentle.

"What can I get you?"

"Do you have bottled water?" I ask.

"Absolutely," he says, turning his attention back to Angelo. "Liquid courage?" He tilts his head with a knowing in his eyes. Something shared between them.

Angelo chuckles. "Sure."

Chad heads off to get our drinks and we sit on our stools at the end of the bar.

"Liquid courage?"

"Heh. Yeah. I usually down a shot of tequila to calm my nerves before I go up."

"Tequila, huh?" Our kiss…the one that left me breathless… blazed into my thoughts the instant he said the word.

He bows his head slightly, looking up at me. "Just one shot," he says coyly. *Is our kiss flashing through his thoughts too?* The corner of his lip curls up.

Chad returns with our drinks, setting them on cocktail napkins. "Lookin' forward to your jam tonight." He gives Angelo a nod before turning to tend to other customers.

"You guys are friends?"

He tosses the shot into his mouth and swallows. "Yeah, I guess so." He shrugs. "I mean, we've never hung out or anything, but he's usually here when I come in and we talk. He's a good guy," he says, getting up from his stool. "I'm gonna go sign in. I'll be right back."

He walks over to a stand near the stage and signs a sheet of paper. On his way back he shakes hands with a few guys and nods at others.

"Busy night tonight," he says, sitting back on his stool. "There's a few people ahead of me. You okay to drive my car back if I have a beer while we wait?"

"Of course."

He motions to Chad who nods and holds up a finger to give him a minute. We sit and listen to each performer. Some of them are really pretty good, but none are as good as Angelo.

Just as he's finishing his second beer, Angelo's name is called. His eyebrows shoot up his forehead and he looks at me with a bashful smile before standing.

"It's show time," he says, as he gets out his guitar then heads to the stage.

Several people clap and whistle while he situates himself.

Once settled, he takes the microphone that's still in its stand into his hand. "Hey, it's great to see you all tonight." A few hoots and cheers come from the small crowd. "Tonight," he says, adjusting the height of the microphone stand. "I have a friend here with me." He looks at me and that sexy half-smile lights his face, sending butterflies fluttering inside me. "She's someone I've known my whole life. Someone who doesn't know how much she's inspired me through the years. This one's for her." He strums the guitar.

My pulse spikes as goose bumps prickle my skin. That felt… intimate. A secret confession?

When he starts playing the song, I know it immediately. "Tequila." He strums the strings of his guitar and my skin tingles as if his fingers are touching every inch of me. When the words leave his lips, it's like he's whispering them into my ear. My heart pounds in my chest. There's no tequila near me, yet its scent fills my nose, seducing me, intoxicating my thoughts. Strangely, I have no urge to vomit. No, the urge I have is for his lips to be on mine again. They burn at the memory of our tequila-kiss.

His heart drapes over his words like lace as he sings them, sending them directly to me. Everything about him invades me as I'm entrapped in his unknowing spell.

He finishes the song and the crowd erupts with applause. After two more masterfully sung tunes, he comes back to me. My heart is pounding so hard in my chest, it feels like it's shaking the entire room.

As he sits back on his stool, he holds up his thumb and pointer finger, about the size of a shot glass apart, to Chad who lifts his chin in acknowledgment.

When he sits, I'm speechless. All I can do is stare at him in awe.

His bashfulness returns, washing over him. "What?"

I shake my head. "That was incredible. You're amazing. I just…I can't believe you choose to be an accountant when you could be singing. You're *so* good, Angelo."

"She's not wrong, man. You crushed it as usual," Chad says, placing a shot on the small white napkin. "Sure you want this?" he asks, a friendly, protective nature rides his question.

"I'm good. She's driving," he says, picking up the shot glass.

Chad smiles at me, likely having heard what Angelo said on stage.

"I thought you only have one?" I question, not caring how much he drinks.

"Usually, yeah." He downs the shot. "Felt a little vulnerable up there tonight, I guess. Don't know what's wrong with me."

"Well, you were great." *Vulnerable? Because I'm here? Was there something more behind his words than friendship? I know I was fantasizing what I was feeling. But…is there something more?*

"Hey, you wanna head home? I'm kinda tired. It was a long week and I have to go in tomorrow to work on that complicated project I was telling you about. I don't usually go in on Saturdays when it's not tax season, but my boss and I are going to try to dissect where I think the issue is."

"Okay. Let's go." *It's good to see he has somewhere to go to destress from his job with people who truly seem to like him.*

We wave to Chad who returns our gesture. Angelo's quiet on the way home. Tells me where to turn, but not much else. *Something's going on with him, but I have no idea what.*

"Thanks for driving," he says as we walk in the door. "I'll just brush my teeth and be out of your way," he says as he goes to the bathroom.

I change into my pajamas then curl up on the sofa and turn on the TV. When Angelo comes out, he's in gym shorts and a T-shirt, and joins me on the sofa. His cologne drifts into my nose. *I've love the way he smells.*

"You sing there every week?" I ask.

"Pretty much. The people are nice. No one's booed me off the stage yet." He chuckles.

"No one would. I don't know if I'll ever understand why you choose accounting over singing and playing. You're so natural up there, talking to the crowd and everything."

"Yeah, well, that's not a very stable lifestyle. You never know when your next gig will come along. My dad was able to create that stability with his talent and connections. I'm just…not as good." He shrugs.

"But, Ang, you *are*." *Is he being humble? Or does he seriously believe that about himself? How can he not see his talent?*

He rubs the back of his neck. "You gonna stay out here a little longer?" he asks, his eyes sweeping across my shoulders.

What's going on with him? Something's up. Maybe I should

leave him alone.

"Oh, um, I can...go...if, you want to go to sleep." My words hesitate, uncertain.

"I..." No words follow. His mouth remains slightly open as his eyes flit between mine.

He obviously wants to me leave. I get up and walk to the bedroom.

"Luc, wait." He's immediately behind me at the doorway.

Turning to face him, I lean against the doorframe, looking up at him. My heart thumps.

"I...I'm sorry." He extends his arm, placing his hand on the wall near my head. "I think I'm just tired. Probably shouldn't have had that second shot." His gaze drops to my chest. "I should —" He shifts his eyes quickly to the living room then returns them to mine. "I should probably...go." As his eyes lower to my lips, he releases a frustrated sigh, then looks back into my eyes. "You shouldn't look at me like that," he says, boring his tortured gaze into my eyes as he breathes.

The pounding in my heart is relentless. It's too much. The air between us is electric. It can't be denied. There *is* something more between us. I'm not making it up. I'm not fantasizing it. It's lighting the room ablaze. I took a chance once and he stomped on my heart. Do I dare put myself out there again and open myself up to getting hurt *again*?

Desire speaks over my wounded heart. "Touch me," I say, barely able to breathe.

Keeping his eyes on mine, he moves his head back and forth, heaving breaths. "If I touch you —" His breath is loud and hot on my face. "I won't be able to stop. I'll want to kiss you and —" Another loud breath. "Taste you. I'm going to want every inch of you." Words I never thought I'd hear from Angelo Mancini. Words I've been desperate for him to say to me for as long as I can remember.

Every nerve ending tingles with pins and needles... anticipating. "Please." I exhale. "Touch me."

17

—

Angelo

Her invitation unleashes years of pent-up desire. I've pushed it away for so long. Denied it because the timing was wrong. Because she wasn't ready. But right now, I'm out of my fucking mind. Tequila. Lust. Her.

She takes my hand and places it on the soft fabric of the tank top covering her breast. My dick springs to life. A growl churns in my throat.

Her deep breaths push her breast harder into my hand as she lifts her chin. Those succulent lips I've longed to taste again are begging. With my free hand, I cup her beautiful face. Her body ignites mine. Her doe-eyes steal my heart that's always been hers.

Tequila eradicates my resistance as passion takes over. Moving my hand to the back of her head, I tangle my fingers through her hair and lower my lips to hers, claiming them. The touch of her lips on mine has me greedy, needing more of her. I want more of her mouth on mine, more of her hands on my body, more of her sounds to swallow. I want all of Lucia.

Squeezing her breast, I slide my tongue into her mouth. At her whimper, I tug her deeper into my kiss, moving my other hand from her breast down to her lower back. I press my hard-on into her stomach, thirsting to be inside her.

She weaves her hands under my arms and up my back, digging her nails into my shirt. I leave her lips, hungry to taste her skin I've only ever been able to admire from afar. Before moving another muscle, I look deep into her eyes.

"I'm gonna need you to tell me when to stop." I move both hands to cup her face. "I won't do anything you're not ready for," I say, shaking my head slightly.

She's shaking hers back. "Don't stop." She breathes as lines crease between her brows. "I don't want you to stop."

Air hurls out of me. I put my lips on the silky-soft skin of her neck, just below her ear. She tilts her head, exposing her long neck to me. I kiss, I suck, I drag my tongue down, indulging in the taste of her. She's like fucking honey, melting on my tongue. I slide the strap of her tank top off of her shoulder. Golden-tanned skin, waiting for me.

As I trail my lips across her collarbone, her faint whimpers fill my ears, inciting my pulse. The way her body moves in response to my actions is so damn sexy. After planting soft kisses on her shoulder, I'm desperate for her breast. I slide the strap farther down, causing the fabric to roll off her breast. Fucking beautiful. Teardrop-shaped with a rock-hard nipple I want in my mouth. Lifting her breast, I cover her nipple with my mouth, circling it with my tongue. She gasps and flinches, grabbing the back of my head as she arches into me.

I circle and suck, squeezing her luscious breast. I need the other. Now. Still sucking, I move the other strap of her tank top down, fully exposing her. Standing upright, I step back, taking in her beauty. She doesn't move. She stands in the dim light. Sultry innocence.

"Come back," she says, breathy, then lifts her tank top over her head.

Simply stunning.

She reaches out and grabs the hem of my shirt, pulling it up. Throwing my hand over my back, I grab it and rip it off over my head and toss it on the floor.

Stepping closer to her, I lower my face to her other breast. Just as sweet. I love how she tugs my head into her. Circling her nipple with my tongue, I can't get enough. I want more. I need more.

When I leave her breast and look at her, her head is dropped back and her eyes are closed.

"Look at me, Lucia."

She lifts her head and the moment our eyes meet, I slide two fingers between her legs, under the fabric of her short pajama shorts, and between her folds. She gasps, clenching her thighs around my fingers and jerking my face toward hers. *Damn, she's wet.* I groan against her parted lips.

"I'm sorry. I'm sorry." I say feverishly, looking into her eyes.

"No. No. It's — it's okay. I, you, it just surprised me."

"It's okay?"

"Yes, it's okay." She nods.

I weave my hand through her hair to hold her head and plunge my tongue deep into her mouth as I gently slide my fingers back between her wet lips and up inside. Her moan travels down my throat, driving me. Her body responds as her pelvis tilts into my hand and she tightens her grip around my neck. Sliding my fingers out, I massage her nub, causing her to jump and tighten.

Given her reactions, I'm guessing she only had sex with Joe the one time. And I'm not asking for clarification on that. I push that asshole from my thoughts. Lucia is mine. This moment is ours. Every touch seems so new to her and I fucking love it.

Keeping my mouth on hers, I slide my fingers in and out of her, stroking her nub just to hear her sounds. In my fantasies, I never heard the sounds she made. Every whimper, every pleasure-filled moan at my touch drives me fucking wild.

My dick is rock-hard and I'm losing control. I lift her up and she wraps her legs around my waist and her arms around my neck. Grabbing her hips, I pull her into me. Still with her hands around my neck, she leans back, pushing herself against my dick, intensifying the heat where our bodies meet.

Sliding my hands up her back, I lean her toward me for our eyes to meet. "I need to be inside you."

Her response is rapid nods accompanied by heavy breaths.

With her wrapped around me, I walk hastily to the bed. Moonlight streams through the window, lighting my way. I climb onto the bed with her beneath me. After kissing her, I sit back and tug the hem of her pajama shorts. She lifts her butt for me to take them off. As she moves her legs together in front of me, I slide the shorts up and off of her.

Then she returns her legs to straddle mine as I kneel in front of her. Though I've seen most of her body in those tiny bikinis she wears, seeing her completely naked is an entirely different experience. She's a goddess.

I scoot off the bed, drop my gym shorts to the ground, and kneel between her knees again. Her skin glows in the moonlight and she watches me take her in. Toned arms. Full, perfect breasts. Flat stomach. A thin line of tidy hair leading to waiting lips. I can't believe this is happening. Leaning forward, I hover above her with my hands by her shoulders.

"You're so beautiful, Luc," I say, staring into her eyes. Her slightly parted lips seduce me.

She moves her hands to my mid-back and pulls gently. "Kiss me?" she asks softly.

I lower my lips to hers, obliging her request, selfishly. I want to take my time, to savor her, but desire is shrieking through me. My dick perched at her entrance, I'm about to lose my shit. My kiss turns aggressive as I try to hold back from plunging into her sweet body.

That's when she shifts her hands to my ass and tugs. *Fuck! I'm going to come before I even get inside her.* Greed dominates and I give in. I don't even go down on her. I can't think. I just slide my dick between her wet lips. *Holy fuck.*

Her loud gasp fills the room as she digs her nails into me.

A quick panic shoots through me. "I'm sorry. Did I hurt you?"

She shakes her head as frantic breaths powder my face. Her tug on my ass urges me. She's so tight around my dick. I can't hold back a groan. I slide out and back in then out again, barely able to enjoy the sensation because I need more. Wrapping her legs around mine, she lifts herself, scooping me in deeper.

Knowing she's new at this, I want to give her a good experience.

But desire has control of my body. The way she feels, it's too much, it's too good. I can't fucking stop. Her sounds, her tugging. The way our bodies move perfectly together. I plunge deeper and deeper letting her feel every inch of me as I savor every slick inch of her. With every plunge, she moans with pleasure. My mind is crazed. This is Lucia. I'm with Lucia. I'm in fucking heaven.

I plow harder and faster, lost to a frenzy I can't control. The wave of euphoria builds. I want to slow down. I do. But I can't. I want to make her come. *Fuck!*

"Lucia." I pant, looking into her eyes. "I can't last. I'm sorry." I thrust into her, causing a loud whimper. "You feel too good." I thrust again.

A devilish smile lifts her lips. "Then keep going."

Sweat beading on my forehead, I drive into her. Hot pressure intensifies deep inside me. I can't stop it. My panting is louder, faster. "Shit. I'm gonna come." Before the last word leaves my mouth, my body tightens and all the muscles in my dick contract as I spill into her, letting out thunderous groans.

Each contraction fills me with an ecstasy I've never experienced. I'm addicted. To her. To feeling this way. To the happiness in my heart because she's here with me.

Once my orgasm starts to fade off and my muscles loosen, I collapse on top of her. She wraps her arms and legs around me. Nothing in this world could feel better. Nothing. I bury my face into her hair that's splayed out on the pillow. Her sweet coconut smell drifts into my nose. We stay like this for a few minutes, breathing, holding each other.

Then she unwraps from me. "I'll be right back. I need to pee."

"Okay." I pull out and roll onto my back, still basking in the pleasure of what just happened.

When she comes back, she wipes me off with a warm washcloth.

"Thank you." Always the caretaker, my Lucia.

She smiles and goes back to the bathroom. I get up and grab our clothes then put on my sleeping-boxers. Laying her pajamas at the edge of the bed, I get back in, hoping I can sleep with her tonight. When she returns to me, I'm under the covers, propped on my side. She slips back into her pajamas and gets into bed, scooching close to me.

"Can I stay here tonight?" I ask, kissing her forehead.

She looks up at me with those beautiful eyes, the moonlight glowing in them. "I'd like that."

I ease down into the bed, resting on my back. She curls into me. This…is…perfect.

"I'm sorry it was so fast. This was — unexpected."

"It was." She pauses. "Please don't apologize. It felt really good. I like the way you feel inside me."

If my dick wasn't so exhausted, it probably would've sprung into action at her admission.

I chuckle. "I kinda like the way it feels inside you too." I don't know if it's leftover tequila or after-sex insanity, but I end up confessing to her. "You have no idea how long I've wanted to do that."

She uncurls from me and shifts onto her elbow so we're face-to-face. "You have?" It's not pleasure in her tone. It's surprise and confusion, bordering on irritation as evidenced by the furrow between her brows that's being highlighted by the moonlight. "But you've only ever seen me as a friend, like a little sister. So, why *did* this happen?" She sits up. "Is this —" a frustrated sigh flies out of her. "Is this because you had a few drinks?" Annoyance seeps into her tone. "Is this like when you kissed me two years ago?" Her voice increases in volume. "Something you regret but it doesn't matter because in a week I'll be gone and you won't have to think about it again?" Annoyance escalates to anger. "I'm so stupid." She shakes her head.

I sit up quickly. "Luc, no."

"Well, I can leave tomorrow and save you an uncomfortable week!"

I don't think I've ever heard such rage in her voice. This is more than hurt, this is pure, unmitigated anger. I should've kept my fucking mouth shut.

She rushes out of the bed.

"Lucia, wait." I'm on my feet.

"No." She turns, pushing me back down. "Don't come out there. You stay in here. In *your* bed. I'll leave tomorrow."

She storms out of the bedroom, slamming the door behind her.

What the fuck just happened? I need to fix this.

18

—

Lucia

I don't know if it's my pregnancy hormones making me irrational, but my emotions just swung wildly from pure bliss to completely enraged. And embarrassed. *Is this normal? This can't be normal.*

I'm so mad for letting myself be vulnerable with him again. And *again*, I'm going to be left in the dirt.

Everything felt so good. So right. In synch. Connected. Physical desire merged with lifelong love. *Didn't it? Was I making it up in the heat of a steamy moment? What is wrong with me?* This pregnancy-brain is a bunch of bullshit. I need ice cream.

All my clothes and my purse are in his bedroom and I'm *not* going in there. I get lucky and his gym bag is in the living room. Digging through it, I find his gym shorts. I don't care if they're clean or dirty, I throw them on over my pajama shorts. Opening the coat closet, I grab his lightweight jacket and slide my feet into my flipflops. I take ten dollars from his wallet, which I'll replace before I leave tomorrow, and grab my car keys from the basket.

The night air is a little cooler than I expected. I scurry to my car and drive to the 7-Eleven for a pint of Ben & Jerry's Dirt Cake. I saw a small park on my way, so I drive back to it and sit in my car in the parking lot to eat my ice cream and think.

The think-and-eat-ice-cream session doesn't help much. My emotions are a complete whirlwind of confusion. I'm mad at myself. I'm mad at Angelo. I'm hurt. I love him. I'm sad. The sex was incredible, not that I have much to compare sex to, but it was with Angelo and it was…*amazing*.

Maybe I shouldn't have come to him. I should definitely leave tomorrow. I'll be fine by myself until Mom and Dad get back. It'll be less awkward for both of us. Done. Settled.

When I open the door to his condo, he darts up from the sofa and hurries over to me, eyes frantic.

Taking my shoulders in his large hands, he looms over me. "Are you okay? Where were you? I was worried sick about you." Concern, bordering fear, coats his words.

Stunned by his panic, I hold up the empty pint of ice cream. "I went to get ice cream." I shrug, my shoulders still in his clutch.

"Heh." It's sort of a laugh but riddled with frustration. Releasing my shoulders, he takes a step back. "I'm in here freaking out." He throws his arms up. "And you're out getting —" He shakes his hand at the pint. "Ice cream!"

"Why are you freaking out?"

"Why am I freaking out?" His hands fly to the sides of his head as words propel out of his mouth. "I'm freaking out because we made love, you got really upset, making wild and incorrect accusations, then stormed out of the bedroom. I gave you some time to simmer down, and when I came out to check on you, you were *gone*. Your car was gone. Your phone is here. I knew you were upset. I didn't know where you were. And I couldn't reach you. So, yes, I was freaking out. Jesus, don't do that to me again, okay?" He steps in to embrace me.

Keys in one hand, pint of ice cream in the other, confusion swirling through me, I open my arms to let him into me. It seems like my pregnancy hormones jumped into *him*.

He holds my head to his chest with one hand, wrapping the other arm around my back. With my ear pressed against him, I hear his heart thundering. He releases a loud sigh. Stepping back, he cups my face in his hands and shakes his head. Then he takes my keys and empty pint. Dropping the keys in the basket, he opens the lid of the container, confirming it's empty. The corner of his mouth rises as he briefly looks at me, amused that I'd eaten the entire contents, no doubt, then goes to the built-into-the-cabinets trash can and tosses in the container.

Returning to me, he stands in front of me and takes my hands in his. Warmth oozes through my body.

"I'm sorry you're upset. None of your accusations were correct. For some reason, I feel like you're still going to be mad at me. You know I can't take it when you're mad at me. Please don't be mad at me."

I'm so baffled right now. "Ang, we're always going to be connected. By our parents and by our past. We've been friends forever and, unless you decide to drastically change who you are at your core, we'll always have some kind of friendship, whether we have sex or not. But I still don't know what changed. Why did you suddenly want to have sex with me? Was it curiosity? I have no idea. And, I'm sure you know this already, but I'm not a friends-with-benefits kind of girl." My heartbeat ticks up in my chest as I swallow down a lump. This isn't the time to confess my persisting love.

He spreads his legs a little, lowering himself to my eye-level. "No, I know you're not," he says, squeezing my hands.

I remove my hands from his, folding my arms across my chest. Still a little frazzled, I mollify my hormone-driven, possibly irrational anger. "Then, what *was* that? And what did you mean when you said I have no idea how long you've wanted to do that? I need an honest answer."

Moving his body upright again, he clasps his hands around his neck, then drops them to his sides. His eyes move back and forth between mine like he's mustering the will to speak. Then he steps in closer to me, holding my jaw in his hand and running his thumb gently across my cheek.

"A long time." His hushed confession sweeps down my spine.

"But I don't understand. Since when? You don't —" I shrug. "See me that way. You made that perfectly clear. *Several* times."

He brushes a hand through his hair. "I don't know exactly when it happened. I can't pinpoint the precise moment. It just, I don't know. It happened over time, I guess. But I didn't do anything about it because —"

How long has he felt something and *not* bothered to tell me? After I've quietly crushed on him my entire life. I interrupt him, frustration devastating me. "Because why? Tell me why," I plead softly.

"Because." He moves his eyes from mine, looking slightly above my head, searching for words. "Because we're friends. Because I was afraid to ruin that. Because I didn't know how you felt. Or how you'd feel if I told you. Because even if you did feel the same way, you were too young. The timing wasn't right." His energy heightens in intensity as the delivery of his words quickens. "And because if you weren't feeling what I feel, I'd be fucking crushed and embarrassed. Because I didn't know what our parents would think." His head and body jerk a little, including a slight hand gesture, with each statement. "Because I love you and I didn't want to risk losing you. Because not having you in my life is the *worst fucking feeling*." His last three words come out in staccato as he steps in closer to me. Taking my head in both of his hands, he claims my mouth with dominant passion, igniting the air.

I'm speechless. Dizzy. Shocked. The second he said the words, "I love you," pins and needles sprung out all over my skin. And now his masterful tongue is weakening my knees and making my heart race.

Abruptly, he stops kissing me, touching his forehead to mine, catching his breath. Briefly closing his eyes, he opens them. Our eyes inches apart, our noses touching. His next words enter my mouth as he speaks them into my open lips. "Luc, not a day passes that I don't think about you."

"You…love me?" I ask, my shaking voice barely above a whisper as if saying the words any louder would make them not be what I thought I heard him say in the midst of his hurtling confession.

His forehead still pressed against mine, he nods deliberately, washing away my doubts and filling me with an elation that intoxicates me.

Adrenaline flashes through my body as I suck air into my lungs. I squeeze my eyes, processing. He loves me. *Angelo loves me.* How I've longed to hear those words from him. I never thought I would.

He draws back his head to look at me. "Please don't leave tomorrow. Stay with me."

Still trying to process everything that's happened in the last few hours, I don't say anything.

Putting his hands on my hips, he gently tugs me, moving my hips back and forth alternately. "Stay with me, Dandelion Girl, so I can kiss you some more." That wickedly-sexy half-smile accompanies his playful tone.

I can't keep the smile from my face, or my heart.

Taking my hand in his, securing that perfect fit, he turns off the kitchen light and walks toward the bedroom.

"Come on."

Angelo loves me.

19

Angelo

Finally having made love to Lucia after all these years has me feeling every possible emotion all at once. It's overwhelming in the best way. And confessing my love to her, I know more than ever that I don't want a life without her in it.

Wanting to prove I can last long enough to give her so much pleasure, it was extremely difficult to simply hold her as she fell asleep on me. *That* was also the *best* feeling. And waking up to her spooned into my body was something I've thought about for years. Unfortunately, she had to run to the bathroom to vomit before I could kiss her good morning.

When I leave for the office, I regret agreeing to go in to work on this project with my boss. The day is never-ending. My mind is distracted as I replay every detail of making love to her last night. The way her lips felt when I kissed her, needy and desperate like she'd been waiting to kiss me just as long as I'd been waiting to kiss her again. The way her skin heated where our bodies were pressed together. Fuck, the way it felt sliding inside her for the first time with her eyes locked on mine. *Un-fucking-believable.* It was so intense. A connection I've never experienced before. She's ruined me for any other woman, which is fine by me because Lucia's the only woman I've ever truly wanted and she'll forever be the only woman for me. All I want to do is get back home to her.

Lucia

Waking up nestled into Angelo's body was just as perfect as I'd always dreamed it would be. Too bad it was ruined by my having to run to the bathroom. I hope this morning sickness doesn't last much longer. It's exhausting.

We didn't talk about what happened last night before he left for work. I was tired from vomiting and felt gross so I got back into bed and stayed there until he left. As I laid in bed, everything from last night replayed in my head.

I'd seen him shirtless my entire life, but I'd never seen him look at me the way he did after he ripped his shirt off over his head. His eyes devoured me like he wanted to own every inch of my body. I'd spent many restless nights picturing him above me, thrusting himself between my thighs, our sweaty bodies moving together. None of my fantasies could've prepared me for the actual experience.

Every kiss, every touch, every thrust, he stole my breath away. He's always owned my heart and now he owns my body.

I'm still dumbfounded by his confession. He didn't exactly tell me how long he's had feelings for me beyond our friendship, but I'm thinking it might go as far back as his last year at college. His reaction to me asking him to take my virginity makes more sense now. Even though I was twenty, he thought I was too young and he was trying to protect me.

While I'm beyond happy that Angelo loves me, I'm even more furious with myself about the situation I've created. The man I've been in love with my entire life actually loves me…and I'm pregnant with another man's baby. Ecstasy collides with despair, twisting inside me. Anguish gnaws at my joy.

And, what does any of this even mean? He's here with his job, living his life. I'm going back home in a week to start my new job at the end of summer and have Joe's baby that I'll be raising as a single mother. The ache in my heart overwhelms me.

I have no concrete answers to anything except that I'm leaving, so whatever's happening now, ends once I'm gone. I can't change that. I think the best thing I can do for myself is to enjoy the time I have left here with him.

The ache expands, consuming me.

Knowing I need to eat something, I drag myself out of bed and make the usual. After my shower, I feel a little better. Not in the mood to read any of my books, I peruse Angelo's bookshelf. He's grown quite a collection over the last couple of years. There's a section with books about guitars and memoirs of different musicians. A section about cars, of course, including a funny one about go-karts.

The bottom row houses some older-looking books. Tucked into a row of thriller and crime fiction novels, which look to be about fifteen years old, is a tattered poetry book. *Huh, poetry. That's unexpected. How have I never seen this before?* I pull it out and snuggle into my spot on the sofa.

Opening the cover, I flip through the first few pages. Reading each poem, I enjoy the childlike and whimsical aura they offer. Page by page, I read them. When I turn the next page, tiny pieces of dandelion fluff fall into my lap. The empty stem is flat and curved, lying on top of a folded piece of worn, five-by-seven lined paper that's wedged into the gutter between the pages. Older generations used to put greeting cards, letters, money, flowers, and other mementos into their books. I love finding old things like this inside books. Careful not to rip the paper, I open it. The writing is that of a child…

Dear Lucia,

Thank you for helping me build my go-kart. That was nice of you. Your a good friend.

Angelo

P.S. I'm gonna marry you some day dandelion girl.

Adrenaline swarms me, bolting through my body over and over, looping relentlessly. Goosebumps blanket my skin. My thoughts race frantically. *Angelo wrote this? His go-kart? But we built it when we were kids. He wrote this* that *long ago? What?!*

I need to get out of my head. I gather the pieces of dandelion fluff and put them back between the pages. Setting the book and letter on the coffee table, I grab my phone and text Prisha.

Me: Call me when you can. Losing my mind. All is okay. Just need to talk to you.

My phone rings in my hand.

"Hey, how are you? Is the sickness any better yet? What's going on?" She fires questions at me.

"Hi. No, the sickness is still here, with a vengeance. Oh my gosh, I have so much to tell you."

"Tell me."

I fill her in on the highlights. Of course, she has to give me a little dig that she knew Angelo had feelings for me all along. Though her dig was more a claim of victory for knowing rather than an I-told-you-so. She's beside herself with happiness to know that we both feel the same about each other and it's finally out in the open.

"What's crazy is, I just found this letter wedged into an old book and he wrote it when he was like, I don't know, nine or ten years old? Prish, it's kind of a love letter...*to me*."

"No way. How'd you find it? What's it say?"

"It was in this old poetry book I found in his room. Never did I think it was a letter *he'd* written. I wouldn't snoop like that. It looked like an old book he got from a consignment shop or something. I thought it was just a letter some old person stuck in there for safe keeping. And then I read it and it's from *him* to *me*. He thanked me for helping him make his go-kart and he ended it with, 'P.S. I'm gonna marry you some day dandelion girl.'"

Her high-pitched squeal shoots through the phone into my ear. "This means he's loved you since all the way back then. Are you going to tell him you found it?"

"No. I don't want him to think I was snooping, even though I really wasn't. Besides, he never gave it to me so, I'm thinking he doesn't want me to know about it."

"So, what're you going to do?" Her excitement fades a little, fully aware of my predicament.

"Honestly, I don't know. That's why I needed to talk to you. I'm so confused. I mean, right now I'm living in this magical fantasy that I've dreamed about forever, but it's like it's not even real because it all stops when I go back home. He'll be here. I'll be there."

"So that's it? Is that what you really want? Is that what he wants?"

"Well, no, it's not what I want. It's just kind of the way it is. I mean, I start my job at the end of summer and, shit Prish, I'm having a baby, fucking Joe's baby." My heart pounds in my chest as a lump swells in my throat. "And I don't know what he wants. We didn't talk about any of this. It all just happened." Tears build in the wells of my eyes as I choke out my words.

"Oh, Luc. I'm so sorry. I'm sorry you're going through all of this right now. What a time to find out how he's truly felt all these years. Take a breath with me. We'll figure it out." She takes a deep inhale and I follow. She lets it out and I let mine out. "What do *you* want?" Her calmness helps to ease me.

I blow a loud sigh. "I don't know. Spending this time with him and finally knowing how he feels, part of me wants to stay here with him. But I can't do that. I can't just say, 'Hey, how about I move in and give you an instant baby to take care of that's not even yours.' Plus, I have my job. I think the only option is for me to leave next Sunday, as planned. We've rekindled our friendship and we'll stay in touch. That's going to have to be enough."

"You're willing to let go of the love of your life?" The sorrow in her voice sends a dagger into my heart.

Tears spill out. "I don't know what else to do." My voice

squeaks out, the words practically gagging in my throat.

"Okay, here's what I want you to do. I want you to talk to Angelo. We're making decisions kind of on his behalf without his input. Whether it's today, tomorrow — preferably today — just start the conversation and talk to him about how you're feeling. Let him know that you're trying to figure out what to do, and you need his input. Do that, okay?"

I sniffle, wiping the tears from my cheeks. "Okay. I will."

"I think you'll feel a lot better once you talk to him."

"I hope so." I nod.

"I gotta get back to work. Call me tonight if you need me, okay?"

After agreeing to call her, we hang up. Picking up the letter, I gently run my fingers over his childlike writing. I read it a dozen more times, picturing him sitting at that little desk in the corner of his bedroom where he probably wrote it.

Refolding the letter, I put it back between the pages and return the book to his bookshelf. Plopping myself back on the sofa, I run different scenarios through my head of how to start the conversation with him. Nothing feels right.

Trying to distract myself, I turn on the TV. It doesn't help. By the time he walks through the door from work, I'm a bundle of nerves and have no idea what I'm going to say.

"Hey," he says, dropping his keys into the basket. "How was your day? You feeling okay?"

"Hi, uh, yeah, uh, not too bad today. Only happened five times." I stand from the sofa as he walks into the bedroom to set down his laptop bag.

"Jeez," he says, shaking his head as he walks back into the living area. "That's so rough." Walking up to me, he kisses me on the forehead. "Are you hungry at all? I can make us dinner if you're up for eating."

Oh, God. How am I going to start this? Is now the right time? There is *no right time.* "Yeah, I could eat," I stammer out.

"You okay?" He cocks his head to the side, lines creasing between his brows. He's always known when I'm uneasy about something.

"Yeah, I just, um. I'm just a little tired, that's all." My nerves are piqued, my palms dewy.

"I can't even begin to imagine." He steps in closer to me, wrapping his strong arms around me. Planting a kiss on top of my head, he leans back. His eyes wander my face before he lowers his lips to mine, taking me a little by surprise and sending a warm wave through my core.

When he ends our kiss, he leans back again and smiles. "I love being able to do that." Leaning down, he kisses me again.

How am I supposed to focus and start this conversation when he keeps kissing me?

Releasing me, he walks into the kitchen. Trying to rein in my nerves, I follow him.

"Hey, I uh, I wanted to talk to you about something." My stomach churns.

"Yeah? What's that?"

Here we go…

20

—

Angelo

She rubs her palms together, one of her telltale signs that she's squirming inside about something. "I've uh, kind of been thinking today about, well, everything that's happened while I've been here —" Her nervous edge emanates.

"It's been a lot. Good, but a lot, I know."

She chuckles through a breath without smiling. "Yeah."

"I've been thinking too. You know, you don't have to go home when your parents come back. You can stay here with me. I'll take care of you and the baby."

Her torso jolts back as her eyes spring wide and her mouth drops open.

"I'm sorry for the blunt delivery." I hadn't meant to blurt it out that way, but there it is. It's what I want.

She doesn't move. She doesn't speak. Her eyes search my face. I watch her as she processes, the wheels spin in her head.

Finally, she moves. Putting her hand on her forehead, she drops her eyes to the floor, shaking her head. "No. No. I — I can't ask you to do that."

I approach her and lift her chin so I can see her eyes. "You didn't. I offered." I deadpan, letting her know how serious I am about what I just said.

Her eyes oscillate between mine, as her brows pinch together. She shakes her head again. "Why — why would you do that?"

I'm not holding back any longer. "Because I can't think of anything else I want more than to have you here with me. As for the baby, we'll figure that part out, together. And I know —" I shake my head knowing her headstrong nature. "I *know* you, and I know you want to be independent and do this on your own. But you don't have to do it alone. I want you in my life." I close the space between us and run my thumb across her cheek, boring my gaze into her eyes so her soul feels my words. "I need you in my life, Dandelion Girl." Holding her head in my hand, I wrap my free arm around her waist, pulling her close, and lower my head to meet her lips with mine.

A sigh of surrender floats from her throat into mine as she moves her hands up my back. Then she stiffens and pulls away.

"You have to stop kissing me," she says, frustration lacing her tone as she paces.

"I don't want to stop kissing you." I put my hands on her hips to hold her in place.

She looks up at me with those beautiful doe-eyes. "But I can't focus when you're kissing me. And I need to figure this out. I just — I just, I don't know how this would work. You're *here*." She motions to the floor. "My job is back home." Her hand flies outward. "How?" Both hands move to her temples, her fingers pressing in.

I release her hips, giving her space. "There are schools out here. Or I could get a job back home."

"But you like your job. You like it here. And, Ang, that's a *huge* responsibility." She waves her hands in the air as she says, "huge."

"I know it is." I take her shoulders into my hands and look directly into her eyes. "And it's one I'm ready for."

"But this isn't *your* responsibility." Her tone hushes as her brows pinch together.

"I know it's not. And I'm scared, just like you are. I also know that, together, we can figure out anything. That's how I know this is the right thing to do."

"I — I'm not sure about this." She starts pacing again.

"Look, we don't have to decide anything right now. I realize I just dropped this on you. Take some time. Think about it." I move my body in front of her to halt her pacing again. "Just know that I wouldn't be offering this if I didn't understand the magnitude of it…and my commitment to it, and to you. I want this. I want you. I want us." I pause as she stares at me, incredulous. "Think about it?"

Nodding her head, she steps into me and wraps her arms around my torso. "I'll think about it." When she releases me, she looks up, gratitude glimmering in her eyes. "Thank you." Two simple words, spoken so softly, strike me with the power of a sonic boom.

I smile and kiss her forehead. "Now, how about that dinner?"

I make dinner for us and we head up to my rooftop to watch the stars. I pray to God that there will be many more nights of me playing music for her while we gaze at the sky.

When we go down for the night, her tension and uncertainty follow us. I'm not quite sure where I stand as far as sleeping in my bed with her again.

Together, we walk toward the bedroom and I stop at the doorway. Turning to face me, she meets me with quizzical eyes.

"I know you let me stay with you last night. And I realize that doesn't mean you want me sleeping next to you every night. This is all new and you're going through a lot, emotionally, physically. So, I want to do whatever you're comfortable with, okay?"

Stepping closer to me, she slides her hand into mine. "Stay with me?" Her breath ghosts across my lips with electric energy.

Deep satisfaction fuses with joy in my soul.

21

—

Lucia

I'd wanted him to make love to me again. Wanted to feel his touch on my skin. Feel him move inside me. Unfortunately, my stomach had other plans. Instead of his hungry, passionate touch, I was happy to receive his gentle, comforting caress when my stomach finally settled down.

The next few days have kept Angelo later at work than usual and he's been tired. I've spent a lot of time thinking about his offer. Fantasizing about a life with him. The dream I've replayed over and over in my head for as long as I can remember. Then the reality of carrying Joe's baby obliterates the fantasy.

I can't decide what to do. The hopeless romantic in me wants to say, "Yes!" But the practical side of me knows it's not fair to burden him with this responsibility that would, undoubtedly, shift the entire course of his life. And I know he said he loves me, but will he still feel the same when he's helping me raise Joe's baby?

Thankfully, he hasn't pressed me for an answer…yet.

By the time he comes home, I've already eaten dinner and changed into my pajamas.

"Hey," he says, dropping his keys and wallet in the basket, lethargy coloring his tone. "Be right back."

"Okay."

As he walks back in from the bedroom, he's stretching his neck from side to side. Going to the kitchen island, he holds the edge with both hands and twists his body from left to right, making small grunting sounds.

Unwrapping from the blanket on the sofa, I join him in the kitchen. "Long days, huh?"

"Yeah," he says, rubbing his neck and moving it around. "This project is such a mess. Lots of digging and research and things not adding up still. Just hunched over my computer the last few days. I'm all kinked up."

"I could —" I shrug and try to sound nonchalant, "rub your back if you think that'll help." A small surge of desire whirls through me at the thought of touching him again.

His shoulders drop as he tilts his head. "That'd be really nice actually. You sure? How're you feeling today?" Always so thoughtful.

"Yeah, I'm sure. Today's been better than the last couple."

"Okay. Where do you want me?"

Inside me. "I'll have better leverage if you're lying down. Come on." I take his hand and lead him to the bedroom.

Stopping at the bed, I turn to him, looking up into his handsome face. "It'll be better with your shirt off," I say as I move my eyes from his and down to the buttons on his white dress shirt.

He doesn't say anything. His heated gaze follows my path as I unfasten each button on my way down his shirt. When I reach the bottom, I tug the rest of the shirt out from his belted dress pants and unbutton the last couple. His shirt hangs open, baring his chest that's tempting me to touch it. I shift my gaze to his upper torso, too nervous to meet his eyes, and move the shirt off of his broad shoulders, sliding it down his arms. He takes a long, slow inhale that expands his chest. His exhale brushes my face, making me suck in a breath. The shirt gets stuck at his wrists so he takes over. I briefly look up at him as he keeps his eyes on mine and unbuttons both cuffs, dropping the shirt to the floor.

"Anything else you want off?" he asks, staring down at me, the huskiness in his voice shooting a spark straight to my core.

"You should be relaxed." I swallow. "So whatever makes you

feel — comfortable. I have some argan oil that I use for my hair. It'll be a better massage for you with a little oil. Lay face-down for me," I say, leaving him and going to the bathroom to get the bottle.

My heart beats faster in my chest. I've known him my entire life. We've had sex. He's so familiar. Yet, my body reacts as though this is all new. Having seen him, touched him, tasted him — it's fueled my intensifying desire for him. Passion rages inside me.

But right now, he needs TLC so I have to stay focused on that.

When I return, he's in his boxer briefs, lying face-down with his head turned to the side on my pillow and his hands above his head.

I climb onto the bed and straddle him. "I'm going to sit on you, but if that hurts you, let me know and I'll sit to the side, okay?"

"Okay."

Pumping a few drops of oil into my hand, I set the bottle on the nightstand and sit on his butt. Rubbing my hands briskly together to distribute the oil, I then place them on his hard trap muscles. When I start working my thumbs and fingers into him, he releases a low groan.

With slow, methodic strokes, I move my hands up and down his muscular back, and across his expansive shoulders, taking note of the tight spots. After an initial attempt at loosening things, I lift off of him for better leverage and go back to focus on the tighter muscles that line his spine and those that go from his traps up his neck.

My deeper penetration into his muscles elicits more groans and some grunts, all of which are turning me on. Touching him, hearing his noises, it's making me want more. I work my hands down his strong arms, massaging as I travel. Keeping myself lifted off of him, I nudge down the top of his underwear to start my next stroke at the top of his butt. Wrapping my fingers around the sides of his body, I make the stroke long and slow all the way up to the base of his neck.

After several of these long strokes, he speaks.

"You know I'll stay here all night and let you do that, right?" His voice is low and lazy.

I giggle. "Okay," I say, stroking again. "Want me to do your hands?"

"Yeah," he says, moving his arms down by his sides.

"Actually, flip over. The angle will be better." I move my body to his side so he can flip.

"Uh, okay." As he turns over, his bulge looks ready to pop out of his underwear.

My God, he's magnificent. His body is unreal. Even though I've seen most of it thousands of times, knowing I get to touch it now intensifies my ache for more of him.

"You getting back on?" The invitation is saturated with enticement.

Without answering him, I straddle his pelvis and sit. He's so hard. With him between my thighs, pressing against me, it's tough to ignore the hunger churning inside. I take his hand into both of mine and rub circles into his palms.

"Mmm." He groans, putting his resting hand on the side of my thigh. "That feels good."

I take focused breaths. "Many people don't realize how much stress we carry in our hands," I say, circling. After a few more rotations, I take each finger between my curled pointer and middle fingers, pulling lightly as I stroke outward.

My hands are starting to get tired, so I put the hand I'm working on down on the bed and begin rubbing on the other. Slowly, Angelo moves the now-free hand onto my opposite thigh. Once again, I have to focus on steadying my breathing because this entire situation has me ready to rip off his underwear and do things I've only ever dreamed about.

I repeat the sequence from his first hand and set it on the bed when I'm done. He moves it back to rest at the side of my thigh. Not ready to stop touching him, I splay my hands across his abs and move them, slow and determined, upward to his chest, my eyes and my skin indulging in every inch of flesh-to-flesh contact. As my hands reach his nipples, he presses his fingers, hard, into my thighs and tilts his pelvis up into me, letting out a grunt.

When I look into his eyes, I'm met with desire aflame in them.

"The other night, I didn't get to show you how I want to make you feel." His deep tone is like silk across my skin.

"Show me," I say, my voice just above a whisper as my core trembles with anticipation.

Before I can take another breath, he sits up and thrusts one hand through my hair, claiming my lips, and wraps his other arm around my waist, flipping us so I'm lying beneath him. Adrenaline pumps into my blood, racing through my veins.

Still kissing me, he puts his hand on my upper back and lifts me toward him so I'm in his lap with my legs wrapped around his waist. Then he slides his hands under my tank top and moves it up my body and off over my head, tossing it onto the floor.

He looks back and forth between my breasts, scanning every inch of me before sweeping his eyes up to my face. "Jesus, you're beautiful," he says, then returns his gaze to my breasts, taking one in each hand. Lowering his head, he covers my nipple with his mouth, swirling his tongue in circles around it while gently squeezing my other breast. Lifting his mouth from my nipple, he rapidly flicks his tongue across it, shooting a tingle between my legs and causing my back to arch.

I lean back and put my hands on the bed which pushes my pelvis into his hard-on. He groans as he moves his mouth to my other breast, taking my nipple between his teeth. Clamping them gently onto my nipple, he sends an electric zap through my core. I drop my head back as I arch deeper into him with a moan, wallowing in the pleasure.

Abandoning my nipples, he runs his tongue between my breasts and up my chest. I return my body upright, still with my head dropped, and he continues his journey up my neck where he plants feathery kisses all the way up to the tip of my chin. Raising my head to meet his face, I look into his fiery eyes. *My Angelo.*

There's something in this lingering moment as we stare at each other, unflinchingly exposed, physically and emotionally. Wholly present and vulnerable. Joined in heart, body, and soul. It overwhelms me and a tear escapes, trailing down my cheek.

Entranced in this stillness with me, he gently brushes his thumb across my cheek, wiping away the tear as I press my cheek into his palm. Then he closes his lips over mine, teasing my mouth with his masterful tongue as he lays me on my back. Getting off the bed, he takes off his underwear then sits next to me and removes my pajama shorts.

Lying alongside me, he props himself onto one elbow. I put my hand closest to him into the soft hair at the nape of his neck while he moves my other arm over my head, taking hold of my wrist with the hand of the arm propping him up. Once it's there, with a whispered touch, he runs his fingers at an unhurried pace down my arm and traces each breast. He sticks his middle finger in his mouth then pulls it out and circles my nipple with it, causing me to squirm. Lowering his head, he covers my nipple with his mouth, plucking it with his teeth. Then he lifts his mouth and blows on it, the heat from his breath sends a hot wave down the length of my body, making me whimper.

Moving his mouth to my other breast, he trails his fingers lightly down my body. Fingers spread as he moves his hand down my stomach, heat follows his path. Sliding his middle finger between my lips, he curls into my opening as he bites my nipple a little harder. Instinctively, I tug my hand, but he holds my wrist even firmer in his grip. I open my mouth, releasing lusty breaths.

He releases my nipple. "I love how wet you are," he says, gliding two fingers in and out of me. Still holding my wrist, he leans his body toward me and runs the tip of his tongue across my upper lip then my lower lip. Then he dips it into my mouth, but doesn't fully kiss me. Sweeping his tongue across my lips again, he then curls it into my mouth a little deeper, still not completely kissing me. Breaths heave in and out of me with anticipatory desire, begging for his mouth on mine.

He continues tantalizing me then covers my mouth with his, giving me all of his tongue. At the end of each outward stroke of his fingers between my folds, he rubs my nub as he entices me with his commanding kiss.

I pant through my nose as I tug the back of his neck, desperate for more. Changing his rhythm, he spends longer and longer stroking my nub, sending me into a frenzy. I'm starting to understand what all my friends were talking about now when they said how amazing sex is. Not only does this feel incredible, it's with Angelo, and it's so much better than I ever imagined.

Without warning, he breaks our kiss and stops his masterful fingers. His face inches from mine, a devious spark dances in his eyes. Planting a sweet kiss on my lips, he releases my wrist and turns my body diagonal on the bed. Then he moves his body so his face is between my thighs and he looks up at me, that devilish grin of his heightening my anticipation.

Oh, God. My heart pounds and rattles in my chest.

Lowering his head, he tenderly runs his tongue the length of my lips, causing my knees to slam shut, caging his head between my thighs as I gasp.

He stops abruptly. "Woah."

"I'm sorry." I unlock my thighs from around his head.

He rushes his body through my legs, his face hovering over mine. "Did I hurt you?"

"No, I — I." God, I hope my mortification isn't smeared across my face. "I've just never felt…*that*…before." Embarrassment seeps in at my pronounced lack of experience.

"Wait, what? You mean a guy's never gone down on you before?" His eyes squint in disbelief.

"No." I shake my head. "I've been waiting —"

The furrow in his brow awaits the rest of my confession.

"For you."

His eyes fill with the hunger of a voracious, unleashed beast.

"I'm sorry. I — I don't know what I'm doing." With his dick pressed against my pelvis, remembering how to breathe is a challenge.

"Don't be sorry. It's okay." His thirsty gaze and controlled breathing tell me he's ready to devour me. "I do." He pauses. "Do you trust me?"

"Yes," I say, my pulse thumping along the sides of my neck as I breathe my answer.

"I'm gonna need you to relax a little for me, okay? And if

something doesn't feel good, tell me."

I inhale and exhale, feeling completely safe with him. "Okay."

Lowering his face to mine, he sweeps his tongue into my mouth with a dominating kiss that steals the breath from my lungs.

Returning himself between my thighs, he glances up at me and winks as if to prepare me for what he's about to do. Nerves braid together with excitement, blazing through my body.

Propped on his elbows, he gently holds my thighs down, probably not wanting to have his head crushed by them again. He touches the warm tip of his tongue to the bottom of my lips then he flattens it as he moves up in one long, slick stroke to the top. I flinch at the sensation. Going back down, he repeats the movement, barely dipping his tongue in between my lips. I gasp. Down again with the same languid stroke, dipping his tongue a little deeper. My heart raps in my chest.

Back down, his tongue diving deeper. I grasp for breaths before I suffocate. He finishes the stroke with a flick at my nub, causing me to gasp as I grip the sheets. With each stroke that follows, he works his tongue with increasing, passionate aggression. Every whimper out of me is met with his feral hum that vibrates between my thighs.

Keeping his tongue provoking, he moves his hand from my thigh, spreading his fingers across my abdomen and stroking my nub with his thumb, slow at first…then quickening. My breathing grows erratic as tingles cover my skin and my heart thrashes in my ribcage. My whimpers build to moans as he strokes harder…faster. Pressure mounts inside me, amplifying in intensity to the point that I might combust.

"Oh, God. Angelo. Oh, God. Oh, God."

He quickly adjusts his position to sitting on his knees. Still rubbing my nub vigorously with his thumb, he slides the fingers of his other hand inside me, curling them up and stroking what must be my G-spot because…*holy shit!*

"Look at me, Lucia. I want to see your beautiful face when you come for me," he rumbles out, working my body like it's his guitar.

I do as he says just as a sound of pure ecstasy hurls out of me. Pleasure rages in torrents through my body. Sensations I've never felt swarm through me as he rubs and circles. My back arches as I clutch the sheets in my grip, out of my mind. Panting, whimpering, until fireworks explode in my core and between my legs as I scream out. My legs clamp shut around his hands as my muscles contract over and over and over, my body writhing and shaking.

Unaware of when he moved, I feel Angelo curl himself around me as my body starts to calm down. Residual twitches between my legs let me live in the pleasure a little longer as my breathing normalizes. He weaves his arm around my waist and across my stomach, holding me close to him as he plants soft kisses on my cheek.

"Good one, huh?" he asks, whispering against my ear with a lick of pride trickling off his question.

"Are they *all* like that?" My opinion of sex has shifted a hundred and eighty degrees from the little experience I've had with it.

He chuckles lightly. "If *I* have anything to do with it, they will be."

"Mmm. I think I could get used to that." Finally coming down from my euphoric high, it dawns on me that I'm the only one who had an orgasm. I turn my body so I'm lying on my back, looking up at him. "Thank you for that. It was…um…incredible. But, you didn't —"

He shakes his head. "I couldn't control myself the other night. You felt so good. *Too* good. Tonight was all about you. I don't need to come to be satisfied."

He is the most unselfish man. "Oh gosh, you didn't have dinner yet."

"No, I didn't. And I'm hungry." He growls playfully, raising his eyebrows as he tugs on my waist.

"Okay, let's get you some dinner. I'll meet you out there," I say, getting up and going to the bathroom. When I look back at him before entering, he's propped on his side, watching me and smiling, his dick still standing at attention.

22

Angelo

Holy fuck that was good and I didn't even come. Her sounds, the way she moves, the way she breathes, the way she responds to me — it's hot as fuck. I've never had a woman respond the way she does. I've been with my share of women and I've fantasized that each one was Lucia. None of them or the experiences could *ever* compare to my Dandelion Girl. She's beautiful in every way, sensual, passionate, sensitive. It took everything in me not to plow into her.

She still hasn't given me an answer about coming to stay with me long-term. I can't imagine it's something that would scare her, but maybe I'm wrong. It's me. I'm her best friend. She knows I'll take good care of her. And now we've shifted into something that makes our bond even stronger. I wish I knew what she was thinking about all this.

I throw on my gym shorts and go out to the kitchen to make dinner. Lucia comes out soon after. She sits at the kitchen island and watches me as I cook. I stick to plain chicken since the scent doesn't seem to send her sprinting to the bathroom to vomit. Together, we're learning what things she can and can't tolerate. I steam up some broccoli, put it all on a plate, and sit with her to eat.

"How was *your* day?" I ask, cutting a piece of chicken.

"Good. Not very exciting. I read some more of my book. There's so much to know about babies."

I chuckle. "Heh. I'm sure there is. Want some?" I ask, stabbing a piece of chicken and offering it to her.

"No, I'm good, thanks. I ate earlier."

"Okay." I pop the piece in my mouth and go for some broccoli, putting effort into making my next question not sound pressured. "Have you made a decision about staying with me and letting me take care of you?"

Looking down into her lap, she takes a deep breath and lets it out. Then she returns her eyes to mine.

Lucia

There's the question. The one I've been toiling over for days, unsure of what the best decision would be. I can't deny that staying with Angelo would be a dream turned reality. The circumstances, however, make it awkward. Am I willing to let that awkwardness make my decision though? It would be nice to have his support through this upcoming shift in my life. And this newly uncovered mutual passion has taken our relationship to a whole different level. Something stronger, bonded deeper. It's not something I want to let go of. But I need to give him an out. So if he changes his mind, there's no guilt, no feeling bad on his part.

Releasing my exhale, I look back up at him. "If you're sure about this —"

"I am," he says, resting his fork on the plate and shifting his body toward me.

"Then I'd really like to come stay with you." As the words leave my lips, a calm settles within me.

Before I finish the sentence, one side of his mouth lifts followed by the other side. He leans in, takes my face in his hands, and kisses me. When he pulls back, the smile on his lips stretches across his face and there's a glint in his eyes.

He drops a kiss on my forehead then cups my jaw in his hand. "I know we're scared and have no idea what's ahead of us, but we'll figure it all out. I'm just happy you're going to be here with me," he says, picking up his fork and going back to eating his dinner.

"Ang?"

He returns his eyes to me.

"I'm going to need you to promise me something."

He puts down his fork and focuses intently on me. "Anything."

"If, for whatever reason, this doesn't work out, you'll be honest with me and tell me. I'd rather figure out another arrangement than have you resent me. And I promise you, I won't be mad. I don't want to jeopardize our friendship over it. Promise?"

He shakes his head. "I don't see that happening."

"Please. Promise me," I plead. I need to know I won't lose his friendship again.

He looks deep into my eyes like they're holding my heart. "I promise."

"Thank you." A hint of relief quiets my apprehension. "Well, the first thing I need to do is figure out my job situation. I was really looking forward to working at Canyon. I'm sure by now that any teaching jobs around here are already filled. I'll have to start job hunting right away and hope that they'll hire someone who'll need to take maternity leave not long after starting. That part's going to be tricky."

"You'll find something. And if you don't for a while, that's okay. I make enough to support both of us." So typical of his personality: reliable, dependable, generous.

"*And* a child? No, that's not right and I won't have it. I'll work and bring money in. I created this situation." My nerves rattle back up.

"Hey," he says gently. "We're in this together now. Whatever work you find, whenever you find it will be fine. In the meantime, I've got us covered." He puts his hand on the top of my thigh, caressing it and reassuring me.

His dedication is overwhelming and pacifying, setting me a little more at ease. This is all so strange to be thinking about and talking about with him. Us living together, him wanting to take care of me. While it's not exactly how I imagined in my dreams all these years, the idea that we're going to be together has my heart practically skipping.

"Should we —" I pause, looking around the living room. "Live here or should we get a bigger place? I don't want you to feel like I'm crowding you. I mean, I don't have that much to bring, mostly clothes and shoes, that kind of stuff. And at some point, I'll need to get some things to prepare for the baby."

"How about we stay here for a while and see how it feels. We can get you a permanent dresser and I can make more room for you in the closet. If we feel like we need more space once we've been here a while, we'll move. We may want to when the baby comes anyway so you can have a nursery for him…or her. Will you find out what it is?" he asks, then takes a drink of water.

I'm surprised by how into this he is and how curious. While my vomiting reminds me that I'm pregnant, the baby being Joe's somehow doesn't even seem like it's real.

"Um, gosh, I haven't actually thought that far ahead yet."

"What do you want?" His gentle smile holds a hopefulness that my heart struggles to find.

I shrug and tilt my head, considering this option for the first time. "A little girl maybe?" With Mom and Nonna only being able to conceive one child, I worry that might be my fate as well. When I'd thought about my future, I'd hoped to have a girl…with Angelo.

"You're going to be such a great mom." He says it with such certainty. A certainty I wish I felt.

"I'm sure gonna try." I've had amazing mother influences in my life and I hope to be as good a mom as they are.

"You will be," he says with confidence as he finishes his last bite, picks up his plate, and brings it to the sink. "Open mic tomorrow night?" he asks, rinsing his plate.

"Absolutely." I'll listen to him sing anytime.

⚜

I called my parents to let them know about the decision I'd made and they were beyond happy. I wasn't sure how they were going to react, but I'm glad they're good with it. I know there are still a lot of things to decide and figure out and I'm nervous, worried, and scared about it all, but having Angelo by my side makes it feel a lot less daunting.

It's strange. With everything that's happened in the last few days, tonight feels almost like a date. A date with Angelo. I put on the only dress I brought with me, a cute black bodycon with a square neckline and halter ties, the hem falling a touch below my knees. I even put makeup on my eyes and dab on a little lipstick. Keeping my jewelry simple with my favorite diamond stud earrings, I strap on my nude heeled sandals and make dinner for us.

I've watched him cook enough chicken lately that I think I can make it without destroying it. I light some unscented candles I'd bought and put them on the small dining table. He walks in the door when dinner's just about done…I hope.

Dropping his keys and wallet into the basket, he puts his laptop bag on the floor and walks over to me, his mouth slightly open.

"Uh," he says, snaking his arms around my waist while I rest mine along his broad shoulders. "I thought we were going to open mic night."

"We are. I made us dinner first."

"You expect me to eat dinner and go out when you look like *this*?" It's not a question he expects an answer to. He tucks his face into the tender skin of my neck, just below my ear and starts kissing.

It's a spot that weakens me, and he knows it. A warm wave gushes through me. I love the way his lips feel on my skin.

As he plants kisses down my neck, I stretch it up and back, giving him full access. "Angelo," I say, breathy as my pulse picks up.

"Mhm," he mutters, keeping his lips on my neck, traveling down.

I release a loud breath as a tingle pulses between my legs. "Angelo, dinner's going to burn."

"Okay," he murmurs, kissing the tops of my breasts.

I giggle. "No. It really is going to burn," I say, running my hands through his hair.

"It's okay. I'll cook us more," he says, then runs his tongue through my tiny bit of exposed cleavage, causing a gasp to escape from me. "Mmm."

Gripping his head gently, I lift it. He blinks a few times, like he's coming out of a trance.

"It's time to eat and go out." I remind him.

"What? No. You can't expect me to walk in the door with you looking like this and not want you. Do you have any idea what you do to me?" he asks, pressing his hard-on into me.

Though I want to touch him and run my hand up and down his dick, I resist, seriously concerned I might start a fire in the kitchen. "We'll deal with that later. Right now, I have to turn the heat off under the chicken or dinner will be ruined." I release my arms from him.

He grunts in disapproval as he lets me go, then brings his bag to the bedroom.

When he comes back out, I'm putting dinner onto plates. Tucking himself behind me, he wraps his arms around my waist and kisses me on the cheek. "Mmm, it smells good. And you look delicious."

I giggle. "Thank you. Come on, let's eat," I say, turning around and handing him a plate.

As we eat, we talk about the things I'll want to bring from my parents' house. We decide to go there sometime tomorrow and come back here Sunday. Excitement intertwines with nervousness.

After dinner, we head to open mic night. It's not as busy as it was last Friday. Angelo's tenth in line. We sit and listen as we wait for his turn, cheering on every brave soul who gets up on that stage.

When it's time for him to go up, he gives me a quick kiss and a wink, sending butterflies dancing in my stomach. He sings a few cover songs and then…

"I don't usually share my own songs up here, but tonight, I'm going to. I wrote this one for someone special…someone who has my heart and always will." Tingles erupt across my skin. He makes a quick tuning adjustment to his guitar and starts singing.

"You're the girl I've dreamed about.

The only one for me.

You're in every good memory I have.

And when I'm with you, I know I'm right where I belong."

The depth of emotion as he sings hushes the room.

Every word, every syllable, every breath reverberates in my soul. My love for him compounds in my heart as he sings words he wrote solely for me. A lifelong love song…from Angelo to me.

Even the crowd is entranced. When he finishes, they burst into applause louder than for any person who's sung tonight.

He gives a gracious nod to the crowd as he leaves the stage and returns to me, placing a soft kiss on my lips.

With everything that's happened, I can't imagine a life without Angelo. I don't want to. He's the only man I've ever wanted and now I finally get to have him.

"Angelo, that was so beautiful. When did you write it?"

He shrugs as he sits on the stool next to me. "I've been working on it for a while now. Finished it while you've been here." His usual, sexy half-smile is now the shy smile of the little boy I fell in love with.

"I loved it. Thank you." My heart is so full.

He drops his head then lifts it. "Wanna get outta here?"

"Excuse me," says a short man with brown hair who's wearing a white T-shirt, tucked into blue jeans, and a plaid blazer. "What's your name, man?" He extends his hand to Angelo.

Angelo reaches out and shakes it. "Hey, I'm Angelo and this is Lucia."

"Ah, the muse." An acknowledging smile spreads his cheeks as he extends his hand to me.

"Good to meet you both. I'm Nick Taylor and I'm a talent agent. I'm in town for a meeting tomorrow and I stopped in here tonight for a bite to eat. I heard you play and had to come over and introduce myself to you and give you my card," he says, taking a business card out of his blazer pocket and handing it to Angelo. "I don't wanna interrupt your night. Give me a call sometime. I'd like to talk to you about the possibility of going on tour with one of the bands I work with if that's something you'd be interested in." His smile is genuine and warm.

Angelo's eyes open wide as his eyebrows shoot up his forehead and his lips part. "Wow, uh, thanks. This is, uh, this is unexpected," he says, running a hand down the back of his neck.

"You're good, man. My job is to spot talent and you have it. I can't let an opportunity pass me by. I hope to hear from you." He smiles again, offering his hand to Angelo once more. "Enjoy your evening." He nods at me and walks away.

When Angelo turns to me, excitement beams in his eyes as he spreads his arms open then closes his hands around the sides of his head in disbelief. His jaw slightly dropped, his eyes wander my face. I witness him process and interpret his thoughts.

He's just committed to taking care of me and Joe's baby for an indeterminate amount of time. He's professed his love to me. This guy recognized his talent without any influence from his dad, which I know he's ecstatic about. And the opportunity of a lifetime just smacked him in the face out of the blue.

Angelo jumping on this once-in-a-lifetime opportunity *and* taking care of me and a baby *can't* coexist.

My heart constricts behind my ribcage. *How can this be happening?*

I know him well enough to know his insides are ripping apart right now.

"Wanna go home?" I ask, sliding off my stool.

"Yeah, come on." He takes my hand and we go to his car.

We're quiet on the way home. I'm not sure either of us knows what to say. So, I break the silence.

"That was some night."

"Yeah, it was."

"And some opportunity."

"Yeah, crazy, right? Just out of nowhere like that. Wonder if he's even legit."

"You can look him up."

"I might."

"Are you going to call him?" My heart thumps in my chest, awaiting his response.

He looks at me briefly and reaches over, sliding his hand into mine. "I have everything I could ever want," he says with an earnestness that smashes into my heart. Then he lifts my hand to his lips, pressing a soft kiss onto it.

Guilt riots inside me. Maybe I should tell him that I changed my mind. That I want my mom to help me with the baby. I can't let him pass this up. Not for me. I couldn't live with myself knowing I made him miss out on this. I *can't* be the reason.

I'm not going to ruin this night. If this is the last night I have with him, I'm going to make it one we'll never forget.

"I'll be right back," I say as soon as we walk in the door. Going straight to the bedroom, I close the door behind me. Scrolling through my playlists on my phone, I find one with smooth, sexy songs, hit play, and leave it on the nightstand. Then I get some of the non-scented tea light candles and dot them around the room, lighting them as I go. When I'm satisfied with the ambiance, I go back out to the living area.

He's sitting on the sofa, watching TV with the remote in his hand. I walk over and stand in front of him. Bending over, I take the remote, put it on the sofa, and take his hand in mine, gently tugging him to his feet.

Without a word from either of us, I lead us to the bedroom, stopping at the foot of the bed and turning him so his back is facing the bed. He hunches his shoulders as he weaves his hands through my hair and consumes me with a ravenous kiss, probably thinking he's taking control. Not tonight. Tonight, I'm in control. I may not know what I'm doing, but I do know I want him, all of him.

I break our kiss and start unbuckling his belt. In a flash, he strips off his shirt then watches me unbutton and unzip his jeans. As I move them down his legs, he sits on the edge of the bed. Once I have his jeans off, I give him the "come here" sign with my pointer finger. That sexy side-smile quirks up as he stands again.

Keeping our eyes locked, I move the waistband of his boxer briefs over his hard-on and slide them down his legs as I lower to my knees. He takes a loud inhale and exhale. I glide my hand between his knees, moving up to his inner thighs. Turning my hand as I get to his balls, I extend my middle finger between them and stroke upward.

He flinches with an, "Ah."

Wrapping my hand around his dick, I pull up and he releases a loud exhale.

Moving my gaze from his and down to his dick, I put my lips over the head and swirl my tongue around it.

Another, "Ah" as his hands fly to the sides of my head.

Gripping him firmly, I pop his head in and out of my mouth like a lollipop.

His grunts and groans tell me he likes it so I keep going.

A few more repetitions of his head into my mouth and I decide I'm ready to swallow the whole thing. In one swift movement, I release my hand, open my mouth wide, and swallow him until my lips reach his skin.

"Oh fuck." It heaves out of him, breathy, uncontrolled, followed by quick, erratic breaths.

As I move my head back to release him, I follow my lips with my hand, wrapping it around him as I go. When I reach the top, I go back down, slower this time.

A slurping sound comes out of him, then a groan that rumbles in his throat. He presses his fingers into my head, but doesn't pull me into him.

I twist my head on my next journey downward and give him my own moan of pleasure.

"Jesus," he says through gritted teeth.

With my lips around the base of his dick, I look up at him.

He watches me, the eyes of a tiger, ready to pounce.

23

Angelo

Lucia's beautiful mouth is wrapped around my dick, it's a fantasy I've had millions of times. This is far beyond a single one of them. I'm going to have to make her stop because I'm about ready to lose my fucking mind and explode. I admit it would be incredible to watch her take my cum, but I want more, much more. *I want her.*

"Come here," I say, tilting my head upward, motioning for her to stand.

She releases my dick and stands.

I crouch down, wrapping my hands around her outer thighs. Catching the hem of her dress on top of my thumbs and pointer fingers, I work it up her legs, over her hips and narrow waist, and up over her breasts. Lifting it above her head, I drop it to the floor and take in her beauty. Her long, dark hair hangs at the sides of her breasts, black G-string, and heels. She's a fucking wet dream come to life. A goddess molded from a blend of sensuality and eroticism.

I step into her and claim her mouth, trying not to let my volcanic desire turn aggressive. In a quick move, I scoop her up in my arms. Going to the side of the bed, I lay her down and climb on next to her. Peeling her panties down her legs and removing them, I intentionally leave her heels on. She's so fucking sexy. I love learning her body, her sensitive spots. Greed driving me, I slide my hand between her legs.

Immediately, she shakes her head and sits up. "It's my turn tonight. Lay down."

This assertive side of her is a fucking turn-on. She moves toward the center of the bed and I lay on my back.

Positioning herself between my legs, she looks up at me with those doe-eyes as she takes my dick in her hand. She's a visual cocktail of innocence whisked with seduction. Locking her eyes on mine, she lowers her head.

I move my head back and forth slowly. "I'm not gonna last with you doing that," I warn.

The corners of her lips lift just before she opens her mouth and closes it around my dick. *Holy fuck.*

She works my dick so damn good, bobbing and twisting, swallowing me to the back of her throat.

The tingling is building to an intense tightening. *Fuck, I'm not ready.* I need to be inside her. "Luc." I pant. "Luc," I say louder. "Lucia, wait." Louder still as my breathing staccatos.

Letting me fall out of her mouth, she looks up at me, eyes searching my face.

Before she can say anything, I sit up and pull her into my lap. Diving my fingers between her legs, I revel in how wet she is for me. I stick my fingers up inside her and stroke her G-spot as she holds onto my traps and drops her head back, letting out a moan.

"I wanna be inside you." The powerful urgency is relentless.

Raising her head, she lifts onto her knees and slides herself down my dick until I'm deep inside her. Suspended in a moment of time, she gazes into my eyes. Years of unspoken longing are acutely present as we stare at each other. Our bodies fuse together like they're hand-carved with only one possible interconnection. The energy between our hearts thunders as it intertwines, becoming one overwhelming emotion. I've always known I loved Lucia. I never knew it would feel this consuming.

Leaning in, I kiss her and her moan travels straight to my balls. She feels so fucking good as she starts moving from her pelvis to her shoulders like a snake, riding me. Back and forth in a wavelike motion, grinding into me, whimpering.

Then she leans back and grips my ankles with her hands. Nipples pointing up, she gyrates her pelvis, moaning, panting. So *fucking* hot.

She may say she doesn't know what she's doing, but she's showing me how to make love. How sensual, carnal, and intimate it can be.

Laying my fingers on her pelvis, I stick my thumb between her lips and stroke her nub, causing her to gasp. I stroke faster as she drops her head back, pumping herself into me. She's the sexiest woman I've ever seen in my life.

I continue working her as her erotic sounds seduce me, beg me. Her moans get louder, quicker, higher in pitch. Her breaths pant in and out of her rapidly. I match my strokes to her fervid sounds. Finally, a scream of pleasure pummels me as her body hurls forward into me and her walls clench around my dick.

Her high-pitched whimpers dance in my ears as she's draped across me, her arms hanging down my back. I hold her, relishing in every trembling muscle.

Once her trembling subsides, she lifts herself from my chest and kisses me. I don't think I'll ever get used to the fact that I get to be the one receiving her kisses.

"You okay if I finish?" I ask, on the cusp of erupting.

She nods and smiles.

"Get up."

She slides off my hard-on and I get onto my knees. "Put your head down that way, but stay on your knees," I instruct.

Resting on her elbows with her ass in the air, she looks back at me. I put my knees between hers and spread them…wider. Grabbing her hips, I ease myself between her lips. I'm not gonna fucking last. She feels too damn good. Trying to hold out, I pull out slowly and push back in, controlled. Out again. *Fuck!* And in. I can't. *I can't.*

Control vanishes, hunger swarms. Gripping her hips, I plow, hard, fast, deep, slamming into her. The sound of her ass slapping against my skin drives me insane. Thrusting in and out, in and out. Her moans consume the air. My balls tingle, my core tightens. *Boom!* I wail and groan in ecstasy, holding her tightly in place as all my muscles contract and I spill into her. Hot blood rages through me as growling sounds churn out of my mouth.

Residual contractions linger and I drape over her back, planting kisses on her dewy skin.

"Mmm." She reaches up to brush her hand through my hair. "I'll be right back."

I pull out of her and flop onto my back. She scurries to the bathroom as I try to catch my breath. Returning without her heels on, she has a wet washcloth in her hand and kneels next to me. She takes my dick in her hand and tenderly wipes our combined juices off of it.

When she goes back to the bathroom, I put on boxers and get out a pair of her pajamas. Pulling back the covers, I lay her pajamas on the edge of the bed and get in.

She returns to me, her hair a mess, and puts on the pajamas. "Thank you," she says and gets into bed with me, nuzzling her body into mine. Resting her head between my pec and my shoulder, she lays her hand on my chest above my heart. Soft, warm air from her nose drifts across my skin.

I stroke her long hair and kiss the top of her head. "I could stay like this forever, watching time disappear with you in my arms." Nothing could be more perfect.

Moving her hand around my waist, she squeezes and looks up at me. "I always want to remember how this moment feels."

I lift my head and kiss her lips.

⊱⊱⊱⊱ ⊰⊰⊰⊰

We hadn't set an alarm. Our plan was to take our time. I must've needed sleep because I didn't hear her get up and I'm pretty attuned to her morning vomit sessions now.

When I go out to the kitchen, she's already eaten breakfast and showered…and her skin has an ashy tone.

"Good morning," I say, kissing the top of her head as she sits at the kitchen island.

"Good morning."

"Are you feeling okay? Did you get sick this morning? I was sleeping hard and didn't hear you." I sit on the stool next to her.

She shakes her head a little and shrugs. "Yeah, I, I'm okay. I don't feel great, but I'm okay. Got sick so, I showered. I'm surprised I didn't wake you."

Something about her isn't right. I know her too well.

"I was out. Long week, I guess. Then someone exhausted me last night." I wink at her.

She barely acknowledges my attempted flirtation. Something's definitely up.

I get up from my stool and grab a mug out of the cabinet. "I'll have a quick breakfast and shower and then we can go, okay?"

"Okay," she says flatly. "Hey, I looked up that guy from last night. Nick Taylor?" She points at her computer. "He's the real deal. Represents some pretty big names." She glances at me. "You should call him. At least hear what he has to say, you know?"

Her nervous edge reveals she's struggling with something. I stop making my tea and, keeping my eyes on hers, stride toward her. Spinning her to face me, I grab the stool on either side of her thighs, putting my face directly in front of hers.

"If what he has to say has anything to do with me not being around here for you, I'm not interested." I deadpan, hoping to ease whatever it is that's eating at her.

Her eyes shift back and forth between mine. "I — I just don't want to see you pass up what could be the opportunity of a lifetime." Her eyes drop to her lap then return to mine. Conflict swirls like storm in those beautiful eyes. "I…don't want you to…have any regrets." I don't miss the way she winces, ever so slightly, as the words leave her lips.

And there it is. Her worry. Her fear. I wasn't planning to do this today. I've been waiting for the right time. This isn't how I wanted to do it, but I need her to know how committed I am.

"I'll be right back," I say and go to my closet, all the way to the back. *Shit, I can't do this in my underwear.* Taking off my boxers, I throw on a pair of jeans and find the tiny red-velvet box I'd hidden in an old shoebox a few days ago after I bought it. When I snap open the lid, the diamond glints from the light above. I take the ring out and tuck it carefully into my pocket.

As I'm walking back out, I realize I have no idea what I'm going to say. I'd wanted to have a speech prepared. This is so unromantic and not at all how I'd wanted it to go. Fuck it. I know it's going to seem impulsive and catch her off guard. And I know there's a chance she'll say no. But I need her to know I'm in this with her…all the way…no regrets.

I sit back on my stool as nerves entangle with excitement and my heart pounds beneath my ribs. The time has finally come for me to ask Lucia to be mine forever. Heat races through me as my palms become damp.

Taking her hands in mine, I rest them on the tops of my thighs. "Luc, I meant the words I sang in my song last night. I wrote it for you. You've always been the best parts of my past. Every good memory I have, you're in it. I want you to be the best parts of my future too and make new memories together."

Her brows pinch tight as tears form in her lower eyelids.

Her phone rings, jolting both of us from the moment. *Fuck!* She looks at it on the other side of her computer then returns her face to me, her eyes suddenly dark, shaken. "It — It's Joe."

Every muscle in my torso tenses as I grit my teeth with rage. *Are you fucking kidding me?* This can't be good.

"I — I should probably answer it."

"Uh, yeah, sure," I say, releasing her hands and trying to swallow the anger pulsing in my neck.

As she slides the bar on her phone, she gets up from her stool and walks to the stairs that go to the rooftop. "Hello?"

Every minute she's gone, my fury intensifies. My thoughts dart erratically through my mind. From the more benign question of "Is he calling to apologize?" to the malignant question of "Has he changed his mind?" I pace as my mind grinds, my entire body inflamed and anxious.

Finally, she comes down. The skin on her face is ashen once again with an unsettledness embedded in her eyes.

"He — he —" It's all she gets out before her eyes spring open, she tosses her phone onto the island, wraps her arm around her stomach, and runs to the bathroom.

I follow right behind her and hold her hair and rub her back as she vomits violently into the toilet.

When she's done, she looks up at me. "Thank you," she says weakly. "I'll be right out."

I leave her and sit on the sofa…waiting. Waiting to learn what the asshole wanted, irritation smoldering.

She comes out, her movements hesitant, and sits next to me. "He apologized for being a jerk." Her words are slow, cautious. "He said he wants to do the right thing and be part of the baby's life — and mine."

My chest constricts. My blood boils. My body heats to a level of discomfort.

"He said he wants me to stay with him and…figure things out." The look in her eyes screams of confusion and uncertainty.

My chest squeezes tighter. I rub my fingers into my moistening palms as my face grows hot.

"I told him I was planning to stay here, with you. And he said he has rights as the father." Anguish etches her face as deep creases form between her brows.

"What're you going to do?" I ask as calmly as I'm able to, acid seething in my stomach.

She shakes her head vigorously then covers her mouth with her fingers. "I don't — I don't know." Her words come out panicked.

I keep my voice low and controlled. "What do you *want* to do, Luc?" *Please say you'll stay.*

She holds her hands out in surrender as she pulls her shoulders up toward her ears. "I don't think what I want matters anymore." Her posture folds inward. "He *is* the father." There's a defeat in her voice.

"Will you tell me what you want?" *Tell me you want to stay with me.*

Her lower lip quivers as tears pool in her eyes. "It doesn't matter what I want." She sucks in quick breaths. "I fucked up everything." Her breathy words tear at me.

The corners of her mouth draw down as the tears release. I wrap my arms around her and pull her into me. Curling herself into a ball in my lap, she whispers in my ear. "I want *you*." Her whimpered cries turn to sobs as her body trembles in my arms.

All I want to do is keep her, right here, with me, where she belongs.

Once her sobbing abates, she uncurls herself from me. "I have to go home and figure this all out," she says, wiping the tears from her cheeks.

My heart aches in a way I've never experienced. She's slipping away. "Do you want me to come with you?"

"No. There's nothing you can do. I need to see Joe and talk this through."

Heat stirs inside me, anger intensifying. Every time she says his name, my fingers curl into fists.

"I — I'll pack my things." She gets up and goes to the bedroom, her posture listless as the air turns brackish.

I follow her, tension stabbing the back of my neck. Grabbing her bags and setting them on the bed, she starts pulling her clothes out of the plastic drawers. I go to the closet and carry her hanging clothes over to the bed. *Is this really happening? She's leaving me?*

"You don't have to do that." Tears continue streaking quietly down her face.

Sadness grows in my chest as I stay silent and go back to get her shoes.

Her sniffles are tiny needles, pricking the surface of my skin.

She takes her last bag to the bathroom and tosses in her toiletries. With all remnants of Lucia packed into bags, we go to the door. I can barely swallow over the lump swelling in my throat.

We stand, staring at each other. How do I look at the girl I love and know I have to let her go?

"I'm sorry," she chokes out, her breaths choppy. "This isn't what I want, but I don't think I have a choice." A weak smile barely lifts the corners of her mouth as pain paints her face. "Now you can call that agent." She takes in short breaths. "And see what he has to say." She tilts her head, forcing the smile.

"Uh, yeah, maybe." My words are void of emotion. My thoughts are distracted. Nick? Calling him is the last thing on my mind. *I can't fucking believe this is happening right now.*

I open the door and grab two of her bags. She takes the last one and we go down the stairs to her car. Bags in her car, we stand there, so many emotions swirling in the air around us.

I grab her face and crash my lips into hers. She moans against my mouth. A sound that usually kicks my desire into overdrive, now chars my ears. Not knowing when, or if, I'll get to hear it again wrecks me. I kiss her with every bit of love and passion I have. A reminder that no other man will ever kiss her the way I can, will ever make her *feel* the way I can. And no man will ever love her as deeply as I do.

When I release her, she stretches up, wrapping her arms around my neck. "I'll always love you," she whispers into my ear as she squeezes. My heart slams against my ribcage. Every muscle in my body tenses, one by one. I've waited a lifetime to hear those words from her. To hear her say that she loves me. This should feel like the best moment of my life...but it's the worst. Her words pierce my eardrums, sending stabbing, electric shocks blistering down my spine. *Why did that feel like goodbye?*

My heart drops out of my chest, a thin glass ball smashing against a sheet of marble, shattering into a million pieces that bounce up, lacerating my skin.

Before she releases me, she presses her lips into my cheek, searing my flesh as her engagement ring burns a hole into my thigh.

How can such pleasure and such pain come from the same person?

She can't hear the tears hiding behind my eyes, screaming, *"Please don't leave me!"* Knowing she has to do what she feels is best,

I let the words die inside me without ever finding their sound.

When I look into her eyes, conflict interlaces with sorrow, twisting my heart. She tears her eyes from mine as every part of her face falls with hopelessness. Quickly getting into her car, she backs up. With one hand in my pocket, holding her ring, I lift the other to her in a still wave.

I knew she would destroy me someday. But I didn't expect it to be the day I was about to ask her to marry me.

Despair consumes me.

24

Lucia

Torment digs into my bones. Remorse rips at my skin.

As he looked at me through troubled eyes, the pain that scraped across his face jumped into my veins, tearing and scratching as it violently raged through my body, splitting my heart and swallowing me whole.

I'm suffocating.

Even though I'm sitting still, my pulse races. I can't catch my breath that's being robbed by the emotions smothering me. Emotions I'm struggling to ignore because I don't want to feel them. I put down my windows, gasping for air. Tears blur my vision. My entire body tremors. I need Prisha.

I hit her number on my phone and her voice comes through the car speakers.

"Hey. I was wondering when I'd hear from you. How are you?"

I burst into uncontrollable sobs, sputtering unrecognizable words.

"Luc, are you driving?" she asks, panic riding her tone.

"I'm —" I suck in breaths. "I'm coming home." My breaths quaver in and out.

"Luc! Pull the car over, *now*."

I check my mirrors and pull off the road, my arms shaking.

"Are you pulled over?"

"Mhm."

"It's not safe to drive when you're crying like that. What *the fuck* is going on?"

"I messed up everything, Prish. I just wanna come home." I can't control the tears.

"Take a deep breath with me, okay? Let's talk it through."

She inhales deeply. I follow with stilted breaths. She exhales. I exhale in sputters.

"Now, tell me what happened. Why are you coming home?"

I take another breath, trying to collect my thoughts. "Well, I was supposed to come home today and get my things from my parents' house to stay with Angelo."

"Okay."

"And then — and then —" I suck in quick breaths, trying to hold it together. "Joe called."

"*Joe* called?"

"Yes."

"What did *he* want?"

"He apologized and said he wants to be part of the baby's life and mine. He wants me to stay with him and figure things out." My words turn to chaos as I spit them out. "But I don't want to stay with him. I don't want *him* to be the father of my baby. I want Angelo's baby. He loves me. He told me he loves me. And I love him. And everything I ever wanted can finally happen. Only it can't happen because I fucked it all up. And now there's nothing I can do about it. And, and, and —" I'd spewed so many words I can barely breathe. I suck in a few quick breaths. "It's all a mess and I can't fix it." Sobs spill out as a vice-like pressure squeezes my heart.

"Oh, Luc. I'm so sorry." Her compassionate words do nothing to soothe me.

My breaths shake. "You should've seen him when I drove away. He looked like a little boy whose heart had just been crushed for the first time." Angelo's pained face flashes in my mind, stabbing me with agony. "My heart hurts, Prish. It hurts so much." Tears continue down my face.

"I know, honey, I know."

"I don't know what to do. I think I just destroyed Angelo and I don't think he'll ever forgive me. And I don't think that staying with Joe is the best idea."

"Can't you just stay at your parents' until you sort out what you're going to do?"

"Joe said he wants us to try living together to see if we could possibly build a life around the baby. Since we were already friends, he thinks we should at least give it a try."

"Luc, just because that's what he wants, doesn't mean you have to do it. You don't love him. You can co-parent without living together."

"I know that. I *know*. I'm so confused about everything. I'm not thinking straight. And I'm so sorry. I've been a terrible friend. Every time we talk anymore, it's all about me."

"I don't care about that. You're going through something huge right now. Besides, there's not much exciting happening in my life." She chuckles.

"Thank you for always being there for me."

"It's what we do for each other…always."

"I think it'll be good for me to be home by myself. Without Angelo or Joe or my parents."

"When do they get back?"

"Not until tomorrow. I think I'll take a drive up to Nonno's for a few days and try to clear my head."

"That's a really good idea. Plus, he usually has some nuggets of wisdom." She's right about that. Nonno has always given me sound advice or just a shoulder to cry on if I needed it.

I blow out a loud sigh. "Okay, I'm gonna let you go and get myself home. Thank you, Prish. I love you."

"I love you too. You sound in better shape to be driving now. If you need me, call. Anytime."

I drive home, searching my soul. I have a baby with a man I don't love. I think I've destroyed any possibility of ever being with the man I *do* love. I have a responsibility to this baby, regardless of what I want for myself. What's best for my baby has to come first.

Every time Angelo's face appears in my mind, which is often, tears fill my eyes and my heart aches with a profound sorrow that creeps to the depths of my soul, filling it with darkness. After this, our relationship will never be the same. The reality of it sickens me.

When I get home, I unpack my bags, do laundry, and put away my toiletries. I spend most of the night in quiet. Angelo monopolizes my thoughts. Our love out in the open. Our passion connecting us on a deeper level. Living my dream for two short weeks. I fall asleep to the memory of him holding my hand and revel in how right it felt, desperate to feel him again.

First thing the next morning, I call Nonno and we make plans for me to visit him from Monday to Tuesday. My next call is to Joe. We set a time to meet and talk more when I return from Nonno's.

Still having my job at the school, I decide to go shopping and get a couple outfits because most of my clothes are appropriate for college, but a little too casual for a teacher. I get back home about an hour before Mom and Dad.

Greeting them with hugs when they come in, I help bring in their luggage.

"How was it?" I ask, trying to push away my melancholy and sound enthusiastic.

"It was —" Mom's face lights up, "— amazing. We had such a nice time. I'm so glad we planned it. It was just what we needed." She smiles from ear to ear. "And your dad had some romantic tricks up his sleeve." She winks back at him.

Their love is the kind of love I want. The kind of love I might have been able to have with Angelo. The kind of love I may never have now. It's the reality I've created and one I'm going to have to live with regardless of how much it hurts.

"We had a great time." Dad agrees, smiling. "Where's Angelo?"

A spurt of adrenaline rushes through me as I choke down a swallow.

"He's uh, he's not here. He won't be coming. There's been a… change of plans." I can't stop the sadness from pulling down the corners of my mouth.

Mom comes over and hugs me. Dad joins her. Their embrace comforts me.

Once they release me, Dad sits at the kitchen island. "Wanna talk about it?"

Leaving out certain details, I give them a quick summary of what happened over the last couple weeks. Mom's hand goes to her heart and the biggest smile lights her face when I share that Angelo told me he loves me and I reveal that I love him too. Her joy vanishes when I tell them about Joe's phone call and my decision to come back here and try to sort things out with him.

One thing I don't tell them about is the talent agent. That's Angelo's information to share, not mine. There's no need for me to tell them that his opportunity was another factor in my decision to leave him.

"You've always made good decisions," Mom says. "We support you in whatever you choose to do. You're welcome here any time and for as long as you need. I know you want to do what you think is right for the baby." She takes my face in her hands. "Just don't lose *you* in all of this. Make the choice that's right for *you*. That will ultimately be what's right for your baby too." She kisses my forehead.

"We love you," Dad says. "We're here for you."

"Thanks. I love you both."

They go about unpacking and Mom starts laundry while Dad orders dinner, making sure to ask me what he should *not* order that would make me sick.

When dinner arrives, they catch me up on all the wonderful things they experienced on their trip. After dinner, we watch a movie and I pack to go to Nonno's.

⋙ ⋘

Yesterday was so emotional, I'm not surprised I slept late. Nonno and I don't have a set time. I told him I'd call him when

I hit the road, which I do after I vomit, shower, and eat the only breakfast I can seem to keep down these days.

When I arrive, the first thing we do is go to the grocery store. The man always seems to have so little food in his house. We load up the cart with things I can eat and things he can make for himself after I'm gone.

There's a park he likes to go to so we head there after we've put away all the groceries. Taking a walk with him feels like I've stepped back in time. He tells me funny stories about Mom when she was a young girl, talks about the work he used to do, and admits how much he misses Nonna.

Before dinner, I tidy up around his house. Nonna used to do all that. Now, things are a bit messier. His laundry basket is overflowing with short-sleeve, button-down shirts and polyester pants. I throw in a load of dirty clothes then wash the dishes that are piled in the sink. He doesn't mind. Grateful for the love and help, he grabs a towel and dries the dishes after I've washed them.

"I'm hungry," he says, putting away the last pan. "Let's eat."

I chuckle at his blunt cuteness.

"Okay."

I get our meals together and we sit on the gold, blue, and ivory floral-patterned sofa and eat on our dinner trays while we watch TV.

There are more dishes to wash after we eat and then we settle in for a few games of rummy.

"Okay, what's wild?" I ask. "And no cheating." I have to tease him because he wins about ninety-nine percent of the time and I swear he's cheating somehow.

He holds up two fingers and winks at me. Deuces wild. He doesn't shuffle as adeptly as he used to. Dealing the cards, he fumbles a little as time has worn and weathered his hands.

After a few rounds, he stares at me from under his bushy, white eyebrows and purses together his wrinkled lips. "Worry sits on your face. Maybe Nonno can help."

I sigh, quirking my lips, comforted by the fact that he can tell when I'm hurting. "I really messed up, Nonno. And I don't think there's a way to fix it."

"Tsk, tsk, tsk." He waggles a crooked finger at me. "Everything can be fixed."

"I'm not so sure." I look down at my cards, my heart heavy. "I came home to try to sort out the mess I made with a man I don't love."

"The baby's father." It's not a question.

I nod. "And, in doing so, I broke the heart of the man I *do* love."

"Angelo." Again, not a question. A statement of certainty.

I nod.

"I can't go back and change anything. What's done is done and I'm not sure what I should do now. I have to think about what's best for the baby."

"Mmm." He sits back in his seat, puts one arm across his stomach, props the other elbow on it, and rubs his white-scruff-covered chin with his finger as he slowly nods his head. "This decision, you must make it from your heart, not your head. Not what you think is the *right* thing to do, but what your heart desires. Close your eyes." He closes his eyes. "Breathe in silence." He inhales. "Hear your heart." He moves his hand from his chin to his heart.

After a few breaths, he peeks one eye open at me.

"No. Don't watch. Do it," he encourages.

I follow the steps, sitting silently with my hand on my heart. I know what my heart wants. *Angelo.* It's just…not that simple now.

Like he jumped into my head, his hushed words provide insightful wisdom. "Dreams are worth fighting for. Some people are too." He kisses the top of my head. "I'm going to bed. I'll see you in the morning." The shuffle of his slippered feet fades as he walks down the hall to his bedroom.

I put away the cards, wash up for bed, and lie in my mom's old bed with one question lingering in my mind: How do I fight for a man whose heart I just broke?

On my drive home, I resolve that I won't move in with Joe. Prisha's right, there's no reason for it. We can manage co-parenting without doing that.

I hit some traffic on the way back and there's no time to drop off my bags so I go straight to Joe's, nerves rattling. I haven't seen him since I told him about the baby.

I ring his doorbell and shake out my hands, desperately trying to rid myself of the anxiety enveloping me.

When he opens the door, a wall of tension strikes me. "Hey. Come on in." Closing the door behind me, he gives me an awkward hug. "Thanks for coming," he says, walking further into his apartment.

"Yeah. This has all been a lot." I follow him and sit on the edge of a chair across from him. Putting my purse on the chair next to me, I clasp my hands in my lap.

"I know I've been freaked out. I can't imagine what you're going through," he says, offering at least the smallest inkling of compassion.

"Yeah, the morning sickness is…something else," I say, lifting my eyebrows. "And it's pretty much all day long."

"Oh shit. That sounds nasty."

I'm not interested in small talk so I get straight to the reason I'm here. "I've been thinking a lot and, on the phone, you said you wanted me to stay here with you. That's not going to happen. With my morning sickness, even in separate rooms, it'll wake you up. Plus, it's not like we're going to be in a relationship."

"Oh, okay." He drops his head then lifts his eyes. "This is all weird. I guess I was thinking that we're already friends, or I hope we're still friends, and I thought maybe we could try to…date or something?" It comes out as an uncertain question. His face contorts as the words leave his mouth, revealing his utter discomfort with the idea.

"Joe. Just because I'm having your baby, doesn't mean we have to date each other."

"Yeah, I guess. I don't know what I was thinking." He shifts in his seat and rubs a hand over his hair.

"I mean, do you really want to stay home with me every night and deal with my puking all the time?" I chide. "Look, we're young and you like to hang out with your friends and go out. That's not for me and that's not the kind of person I want to be with. We can do this without radically changing both our lives in the process."

"Well, okay. Then *how* do we do this? Should I go to your appointments with you or something? I really do want to take some responsibility in this." It's decent of him to finally want to be accountable in this, but I want him involved as little as possible.

"I mean, you can probably come to an appointment or two, but I don't think I'll need you for much until the baby comes. And we have time to decide what that's going to look like. We'll come up with something that feels fair for both of us in caring for the baby."

"Uh, okay." It's all he says as he sits there with a doltish expression on his face.

"We'll stay in touch. I'll keep you updated on important things and my progress. But me living here with you is not gonna happen." As I say the words, a small sense of relief washes over me.

"Okay." He claps his hands together. "Okay then," he says, following it with an exhale, sounding relieved as well.

"I'll be living at my parents' and I start my teaching job at the end of the summer. You have my number and we'll stay connected." I take my purse and stand up.

"Okay." It's the only word he seems able to even form. He nods his head like it's the conclusion of a business meeting. "And, if you do need my help with something, just, you know, call me," he says, standing up and walking toward the door.

"I will." I follow him, more than ready to leave.

He opens the door and I get in my car and drive home, feeling the slightest bit better about things…at least as far as Joe is concerned.

I don't know what we'll come up with for once the baby's here, but that doesn't need to be decided right now.

The relief provides a temporary escape from my high-tension nervous system, but thoughts of Angelo plague me.

Days come and go. I haven't called him. I can't bring myself to. What do I even say? Every time his face enters my mind, that look of excruciating pain destroys me. How do I say, "I'm sorry for breaking your heart?"

No matter what I'm doing or where I am, my thoughts are of Angelo. He consumes me. I crave his lips on mine. I yearn to feel his touch on my skin again. More than anything, I miss his heart.

25

Angelo

The next several days are a blur. I'm a zombie, going through the motions at work. Even my workouts are shit. My mind tortures me with thoughts of Lucia in Joe's arms, him making love to her…my Lucia. It sickens me. Never in my life have I felt such an intense mix of rage and sadness.

Her leaving ripped my fucking heart out. And the fact that she was going to *Joe* filled me with an anger that rumbled my soul and is stuck there. I can't sleep. My eating is horrible. Everything about life feels pointless.

She's in every room of my condo…and yet she's not. When I go up to my rooftop to play my guitar and try to get lost in my music, her ghost is there, listening to me, watching me. When I go to bed at night, she's not there, but her scent haunts me, lingering on my sheets.

Her laughter echoes in my ears. Her head rests on my chest, charging my heartbeat. Her lips are a memory on mine. Every sunrise, every nightfall, I see her face. She's everywhere and nowhere.

Being with her these last few weeks, our future together was finally becoming real. But now, the vision of the life I'd wanted for us has faded into nothingness.

I never knew my heart could hurt so much.

I'm in a bad place.

I pick up my phone and call Tony.

"Hey, man. What's going on?"

"It's not good. I'm so fucked up right now."

"Shit. Lucia?"

"Yeah. She's gone. Left a few days ago to…I guess to move in with Joe."

"What? No shit."

"I'm out of my fucking mind. Things were going really well and I was about to ask her to marry me when that fucking asshole called."

"It's about time you ask her."

"Well, I didn't get to. I'm ready. I'm ready to start my life with her. I didn't actually plan it. It just sort of almost happened. She's scared. I needed to show her I'm committed and ready to move our relationship beyond friendship. Heh." I scrape a hand through my hair and shake my head. "But I guess that's not gonna happen."

He blows a puff of air. "And now she's with Joe?"

"I guess. He called, she went. His kid's inside her. I don't really know any more than that. She said she loves me. But then she left and I haven't heard from her since. I'm so screwed up." My insides twist in knots.

"How about we meet up for hoops tomorrow after work? We'll grab some beers and talk some more, okay?"

"Yeah, sounds good."

"You're gonna be okay."

We meet up the next day and I fill him in on a few more details, including Nick Taylor approaching me at the bar. By the time we say goodbye, his advice to me is: call Nick and get laid. Not necessarily helpful. And not necessarily a bad idea either. Even thinking about having sex with another woman after making love to Lucia physically turns my stomach.

By Friday night, I still haven't heard from her. She must've talked to Joe by now. Why hasn't she called me? It's not like she has to, I just thought she would've. Shit, this is a lot for her. I guess I need to give her space.

I head to the bar, not in the mood to sing.

When I arrive, I wave to Chad on my way to my usual stool.

He has a shot of tequila waiting for me by the time I sit.

"What's up, man?" He holds his hand up for a handshake. "Where's your girl? She's smokin'." He follows his statement with a whistle and a head-tilt.

"She sure is." I pause, looking down at the shot. "But she's not mine anymore," I say, then toss the liquid down my throat, the burn traveling all the way to my stomach. "Keep 'em comin'," I say as I smack the shot glass onto the small, white cocktail napkin.

"No shit. What happened?" he asks, his tattooed arms outstretched along the bar.

I pull my lower lip up and shake my head. "Not even worth talking about."

"Damn, I'm so sorry." He pours more tequila into my glass. "This one's on me."

"Thanks." I lift the glass toward him and bow my head then toss it back. The burn soothes me on its journey down my throat.

I spend the rest of the night, drowning myself to the point of numbness. And somehow, through the numbness, my heart continues to ache. Nothing will dull this fucking pain.

When I throw my hand up for another shot, Chad comes over, shaking his head.

"Ang, as a bartender and your friend, I can't give you any more. I get it. Love sucks. I had a girl rip my heart out and stomp on it, then throw it in my face. It's a shitty feeling. You drive here?"

"Fuggin' sucks. Yeah, car's in the lot." When I motion toward the parking lot, my movements are in slow motion.

"Can't let you drive, man," he says, his face hazy.

"All getan Uber." I can barely feel my tongue.

"I'm not having some poor Uber driver deal with your drunk ass." His chuckle echoes in my head. "I'm off in five. I'll drive you home. You can Uber back in the morning and get your car or I'll give you a ride back."

"You're a goo-man, Charlie Brown."

He laughs as he walks away.

A few minutes later, he helps me up and we go out to his car. The world whirls in a vortex, with us at its center. My feet drag, cement blocks scraping the pavement beneath me. I have no idea what we talk about on the way to my place, but I know he successfully gets me up to my condo and onto my bed.

As the room spins, Lucia's hologram floats above me. *God, I miss her.*

⚡⚡⚡

Hot sunlight blazes into my bedroom. Squeezing my eyes shut from the blaring light, I move my tongue in and out of my parched mouth, trying to create moisture. When I lift my throbbing head, I squint my eyes open to see I'm still in my clothes from last night and lying on top of the covers. I remember getting shitfaced at the bar. *How did I get home?*

I groan as I force my lethargic body to move, rolling myself up to sit on the edge of the bed. With my head feeling like a fifty-pound boulder on top of my shoulders, I lean forward and stand. As the room tilts, I push my feet to take me to the bathroom. Catching a glimpse of my reflection in the mirror, I look like hell.

Dragging myself to the kitchen, I pour a glass of water and guzzle it down. That's when I see a note from Chad.

Ang,

Bet you're feeling like shit. Call if you need a ride to your car.

Chad

Snippets of last night return to my memory. I haven't been that drunk since probably my sophomore year in college. Deciding to get my ass in gear, I eat breakfast and get showered. I'm a little embarrassed to call Chad so I text to thank him and let him know

I'm grabbing an Uber.

I drone through the day, getting groceries, doing laundry, the usual. My workout is brutal and necessary so I can sweat out all the alcohol. Tonight, I change things up and go to a different bar. I don't typically go out both nights of the weekend and I definitely don't get drunk like that, but I need an escape. Anything to get Lucia out of my head.

After about an hour, a few shots of tequila — only keeping Lucia at the forefront of my thoughts — and a few beers, a woman comes over and starts talking to me. Another couple shots and beers later, we go back to her place. Knowing where this is heading, I have a few more beers, hoping that numbing myself will ease the guilt I'm already feeling by being here…being with someone who's not Lucia.

The woman — I don't even remember her name at this point, total asshole-move on my part — sucks my dick. All I can think about is Lucia as shame and regret pillage me. In my pathetic, drunken head, I somehow thought the distraction might anesthetize my pain. It doesn't. It intensifies it. I stop her before things go any farther and apologize. I shouldn't have let it get as far as it did. Feeling like a dickhead, I leave her and get an Uber home.

The following weeks crash together, mirroring each other. I drink myself into oblivion every weekend, feeling vacant inside. Some sort of twisted self-punishment that does nothing to take away the emptiness in my heart or the pain of losing my Lucia.

26

I still haven't called Angelo. I don't know what to say to him. With both of our feelings finally out in the open and our plans for me to move in with him, things finally started to feel like they were going to be okay. And with one phone call, it all shattered. The pain on his face when I drove away etched a scar on my heart.

Part of me feels like a coward for not reaching out to him. But maybe it's best if I leave him alone and give him some space. Time to heal.

Will he heal? Will I?

Days pass. Weeks. I do my best to enjoy the summer as it'll be my last before my true adult life begins. Tonight, Prisha and I are going to a local place where we're meeting up with some friends.

We're the first to arrive and pull together two high-top tables and some stools, then we order drinks. Within twenty minutes, our friends have arrived and we're getting caught up with each other about what we've been doing since graduation. I sip my virgin piña colada and keep my drama to myself.

There's a tap on my shoulder. When I turn around, Tony's standing there with a smile on his face. It's been a few years since I've seen him. I get up from my stool and give him a hug.

We chat about what we've been up to since we last saw each other, keeping things lighthearted and not talking about Angelo, which gnaws at me.

"Have you talked to Angelo lately? How's he doing?" I finally ask, not sure how much he knows about what happened between us. Guys don't usually share too much when it comes to relationships.

"He's, uh, he's doing okay." Nope, it's too vague an answer. That combined with the way he shifted his eyes when he spoke tells me he knows something.

"Yeah? Good. Okay, that's good to hear." *Is he? Is he really okay? Because I'm not okay.*

He cocks his head and pulls his lips tightly together. "You know —" His eyes drift down then return to mine. "He'd probably be pissed at me for telling you this, but I think it's about time you finally know the truth. I've never understood what the deal is between you two, but you should know, he never wanted to become an accountant." He shakes his head.

He didn't? Then why did he? I'm so confused right now that my questions don't come out.

"He took that job…for you. He wanted to get a traditional, white-collar job that guaranteed he could provide you a stable life someday when you were ready."

My blood cools as my vision becomes hazy. I lean against my stool so I don't fall over.

He reaches out to steady me. "Woah, you okay?"

I blink my eyes, processing. Guilt consumes me. "Yeah, yeah. I'm just…I'm fine. I — I didn't know that," I stammer, trying to get my head around what he just said.

"Didn't think so. Look, it's none of my business whatever's going on with you guys. I just know he would never tell you any of this and I thought you should know the truth."

"Thank you, for telling me." I'm in utter disbelief. Angelo took that stupid job…for *me*?

"He's going to call that agent too. It'll be good for him, y'know?" It's an unspoken warning of protection for his friend as if he's telling me to stop messing up Angelo's life and let him have his dream.

"Oh good. I'm really happy to hear that." My thoughts scatter, chaotic through my head.

"Hey, I'm gonna get back to my friends. It was good to see you." He leans down to hug me.

"Yeah, great to see you too. Take care."

My back still turned toward my group of friends, I sit there, numb, unable to move. My mind starts pulling together pieces of data from a lifetime of memories and information. The conclusion being that Angelo has loved me as long as I've loved him and he set up his entire life, making sacrifices, so we could be together. The realization smashes into my chest, drilling a cavernous abyss into my soul.

Acid churns, lava in the pit of my stomach. Air punches from my lungs as I jump up and run to the bathroom. Rushing into an open stall, I drop to my knees with a thud on the hard surface, barely getting my head over the toilet before the vomit shoots out of me. Prisha's two seconds behind me, holding my hair back from falling into the toilet.

Once the vomiting stops, we get off the floor and I wipe my mouth and nose.

"Want me to take you home?" she asks, swiping a piece of hair from my sweaty face.

Exhausted, I nod. We say goodbye to our friends and I lie, telling them I must've eaten something that's not agreeing with me.

On the way home, I tell Prisha what Tony told me.

"It all makes so much sense, Luc. Are you going to do anything about it?"

I release a puff of air. "What can I do about it? Look at the situation I've created. It's impossible. I've broken his heart and probably our friendship."

She sighs. "You don't know that for sure. I guess at least now you really know everything. God how I wish you'd both told each other how you felt years ago."

My heart sinks. I want to run to him. Right now. I want to

jump into his arms and tell him I'm sorry and that I want to be with him. I can't believe how badly I've messed things up.

When she drops me off, we hug, and I go inside and get ready for bed. Thoughts wrestle in chaos, keeping me from falling asleep. When I finally do drift off, I'm jarred awake by piercing pains in my lower belly. Groggy and dazed from it being the middle of the night, I'm alert enough to know something doesn't feel right.

Did I pee myself? I brush my hand between my legs, meeting a slimy substance with my fingers. *Ew. What the fuck?*

I jolt upright and turn on the lamp sitting on my nightstand with my other hand. Folding back my sheets, shock stuns me. My pajama bottoms are covered in blood. Deep-red blobs coat the sheets beneath me. Panic blazes through my body as breaths heave out of me.

"Mom!" I scream. "Mom!"

I don't move. I can't.

Within seconds, my mom is at my bedside. "Oh, God. Okay. Okay, honey. It's okay. You're going to be okay. I'm here." Sitting next to me, she takes me in her arms and rocks me.

"What's happening to me?" Heavy breaths pant out of me. Fear fists in my chest. "Is this the baby? Is it my baby?"

She releases me, eyes scanning mine as she nods. "I think it might be. Does your stomach hurt?"

"Yes, a lot. Shooting pains."

"Okay. I want you to take these off. I'll get a washcloth. We'll clean you up and call the doctor."

Blood and dark brown blobs are all over my sheets. Mom comes back and starts wiping off my legs.

After several passes, she looks into my eyes. "Think you can stand in the shower and wash off the rest?"

"Yeah," I say, holding out my hand for help up. Weakness clutches me.

She helps me to the bathroom and I take off my bloody pajamas and put them in the sink. Then I get into the shower and wash off my body, mindlessly. Pain jets through my lower abdomen. When I open the shower curtain, I see that Mom's taken my blood-covered pajamas and put a pair of bikini underwear and a pad on the sink for me along with comfy pants and an oversized T-shirt. I go back out to my bedroom to see that she's stripped off the bedding. Looks like the mattress pad saved the mattress from being ruined.

She comes back in with her phone to her ear and a set of sheets in her hand. "Yes, doctor, she's right here. Hold on," she says, handing me the phone.

I explain what happened to the on-call doctor and she believes I probably miscarried the baby. My throat tightens as I grapple for breaths. She tells me to go to the hospital right away. By the time we hang up, Mom's made up my bed and is sitting on the edge of it.

She holds her hand out to me as she stands up. "Come on, I'll take you."

As she drives us to the hospital, the silence is deafening. I'm not even in my body. It's like I'm sitting outside the car, looking in at myself. Reaching over, Mom holds my hand, not pushing me to talk.

The doctor confirms that I lost the baby. It's strange. I'm numb. Detached. Empty.

I don't cry.

I don't scream.

Nothing.

The drive home is just as silent — just as deafening — as we both sit with what happened. Mom walks up to my bedroom with me.

"Want me to stay with you awhile?" she asks.

I nod. "Yeah."

She climbs into the bed and I get in next to her. We sit quietly, our backs resting against the headboard. Apathy spreads through me, overtaking each limb, one by one. Turning my body, I curl into her and she wraps me in her arms.

"Mom?"

"Mhm?"

"What if this was it? My only chance to have a baby. Like you and Nonna."

She strokes my hair. "Honey, we don't know that for certain. We don't know what God's plans are for you."

Overwhelmed by everything, I can't even cry.

Emptiness carves a hollow where my heart used to be.

27

Angelo

What am I doing? This isn't who I am. And this isn't bringing Lucia back to me. After weeks of spiraling and not feeling any better, I decide to get my shit together.

Though I'm not sure I'm ready to tell my parents *everything* that's been going on, my dad's always been a judgment-free sounding board and I sure could use some of his advice right now.

I pick up my phone and call him.

He answers on the second ring. "Hey. I haven't heard from you in a while. How are you?" The joy in his voice comforts me.

"Hey, Dad. Yeah, I'm sorry it's been so long. I've been really busy and the days seem to slip by." I do feel bad I haven't called or been home in a long time. Without a doubt, going home would somehow have led to me seeing Lucia and I haven't been ready to handle that.

"No need to apologize. I know how it can get. It's good to hear your voice. So, your job has been keeping you busy then, huh?"

"It has." I pause. "That's actually part of the reason I'm calling you."

"Okay. How can I help?"

"Well, my life hasn't gone the way I'd hoped. Nothing's necessarily bad and I'm really grateful to you for helping me get my job. It's just not all that fulfilling. It does pay my bills and gives me a good lifestyle, but I took it because of a girl and that might not have been the best idea."

"Mmm, I see. What is it you want to be doing?"

"I love singing and playing my guitar, but I know what a turbulent industry entertainment can be. Were you ever…scared?"

"Heh. Yeah, I was. A lot. It can be a ruthless industry that's not forgiving. But I didn't let that get to me. I had passion and determination. Those, plus a little luck in meeting your mom and being able to meet with your grandma's connections. I'm very fortunate. It wasn't an easy journey and there were a couple of times I did consider giving up. But I didn't. My work is in my soul and I couldn't let it go. I used those difficult times to drive me. After all, anything worthwhile is worth the risk. Regret is for those who let fear deter them from ever taking that chance. I wasn't willing to let fear get to me and risk regretting never trying. I was unwilling to give up. If your talent is something you want to pursue, then you should. I can help you."

"No." It comes out quick. "I mean, I appreciate you wanting to help me, but I — want to do this on my own."

He doesn't push his help on me. "There's not a doubt in my mind that you'll make it happen if that's what you really want. And you know your mom and I will support you."

"Thanks, Dad."

"Of course."

"There's something else I wanted to ask you about."

"Okay."

"Do you remember when I was a kid and you told me that your first love is never your last love?"

He chuckles. "Yes, I do."

"How did you know Mom was your last love? The one."

His laugh is hearty this time. "That's a question many people think about, wonder about. How do you know when you've found the person you're meant to spend the rest of your life with? It can be a scary thing. But it's less complicated than people make it, I think. It truly is a feeling. Something that can't be explained with words. Something you feel deep inside yourself. It's like, somehow your souls are connected and, even if you don't know how to identify it, both of your souls know it and they won't let go until you're together. Do you think you've found this person?"

"I did find her." I swallow hard as my heart weighs down in my chest. "But then I lost her. I guess fate has other plans that I don't know about."

"No, not fate. It's God. God has a plan. It's not ours to know until he reveals it to us. We just have to trust and have faith. No matter the obstacles, if she's the one, your souls will find their way back to each other. That's how it works."

"Mmm." I want to believe him. I do. I just don't think it's possible for me and Lucia at this point. The reality revives that familiar ache in my heart.

"Why do I get the feeling that our talk isn't helping you much?" Love and concern envelop his words.

"It has. I guess I just feel like I've been treading water, waiting for my life to begin, and lately, it feels like I've been drowning instead of even treading."

"One thing I can tell you for sure is that there's no time in life for waiting. If you want something — a job, a girl, whatever it is — go after it and don't stop until you have what you want. Life is short. Waiting gets you nowhere. It's time to live…right now." His encouragement uplifts me.

"Thanks, Dad. This has helped more than you know."

"I hope so. You can call me anytime. And come home for a visit soon. Your mom and I would love to see you."

"Yeah, I will. I promise."

"Angelo?"

"Yeah?"

"I have faith in you." One thing about Dad, no matter what I was doing, he believed in me and he made sure I knew it.

"Thanks. I love you."

"I love you too."

When we hang up, his words penetrate my bones. He's right.

I've been waiting my whole life for Lucia. It's clear now that the life I saw for us isn't going to happen. It's time to stop waiting.

Picking up my phone, I call Nick Taylor.

"Hey, Nick. This is Angelo. I'm not sure if you remember me. We met at Hops and Brews about a month ago?" I say it as a question.

"Hell yeah, I remember you. You can play. And you got pipes. Didn't think I was going to hear from you after all this time. I'm glad you called." His genuine compliment sends a spurt of adrenaline through me.

"Oh great. Yeah, I'm sorry it took me so long. I've had some stuff going on."

"It's all good. One thing I know about this business is it's not for everyone. I have a few bands in mind that I think you'd be great opening for as a starting point. And we'll see how you do from there. Of course, they'd need to hear you play. Are you up for something like this?"

The adrenaline kicks up. Then reality brings me back down. "I absolutely am, but I do have a full-time job. I'm an accountant."

"Hah! An accountant? Okay, I didn't see *that* coming." His hearty chuckle fills my ears.

"Heh, yeah, odd combination of skills I guess." I don't want to pass up this opportunity. Think fast. "That's my stable income so I'd have to figure out how this would all work."

"Sure. Sure. Let's do this. Let me set up some time with you and the two bands I have in mind and then we'll see what we're looking at. That work?"

"Definitely."

He's very accommodating in arranging time for me to play for the bands on the weekend. My excitement — and nerves — build as the weekend gets closer. Both bands are L.A.-based so it'll be a familiar drive in and out.

I still haven't told him who my dad is and I'm not telling my parents about this in case it doesn't work out. I plan to keep to the scheduled auditions then hole up in my hotel room so there's no chance of running into anyone I know.

Friday night after work, I grab my bags and my guitar and hit the road.

Lucia

Mom is such an amazing caretaker. Always there without hovering. She planned a spa day today for the two of us and Aunt Destiny at the Four Seasons. It'll feel nice to be pampered and also to see Aunt Destiny. I haven't seen her since my graduation.

When we arrive at the spa, the scents of lavender and sage drift into my nostrils, immediately calming me. Ribbons of harp music float into my ears. We start our day with lunch in the Eucalyptus Lounge.

Finally feeling like there's no alien in my stomach ready to purge whatever I eat, I order avocado toast. Mom and Aunt Destiny order salads and we each get a glass of wine. Once the waiter leaves, Aunt Destiny looks at me, lips pulled down and compassion in her eyes.

"Your mom told me about you losing the baby. I'm so sorry. How're you doing?" She rests her arms on the table and leans her body toward me.

"Thank you. I'll be okay. It's been a weird couple of months with a rollercoaster of emotions. Right now, I'm just looking forward to getting on with my life and starting my new job."

She nods. "I'm sure. Have you —" She hesitates. "Told Angelo about it?" Gentle love caresses her tone.

Thunk. The question hits my heart, catching me off guard. "No." I shake my head. "And, please don't tell him. I think I've caused him enough upheaval."

She glances at Mom. "You do love him though." It comes out matter-of-fact rather than a question. Like she's known it forever.

More deeply than I ever imagined was possible. I choke down the lump crawling up my throat. "I do," I say, dropping my eyes to my lap then looking back up at her. "That's why I'm not ready to tell him yet. I already turned his world upside down." I shrug. "Please. *Please* don't tell him," I beg.

She reaches over and touches my arm. "Of course, I won't. This is your information. It's not mine to share." Her brows crease together. "I do hope you tell him soon. You've always been so close. I think he'd want to know. He'll find out eventually anyway and this is something that would be best coming directly from you. I'm sure if he knew, he'd be here for you."

That's exactly why I can't tell him yet. "I know he would. I'll tell him. When this is all a little more behind me, I'll tell him." When that time will be, I have no idea. But it would be selfish and unfair of me to do it now. I refuse to be the cause of him not sharing his talent with the world and living the life he deserves. A life he set aside because of me.

"Remember," Mom says, "the best relationships are where both people are willing to apologize and forgive. Now, we don't know the details of what's been going on between you two, but we know things have been unsettled. Your friendship has been something you've relied on your whole life. His friendship has brought you so much laughter and happiness and comfort. I hope you're both able to find your way back to it."

"Thanks, Mom. And you too, Aunt Destiny. I appreciate both of you so much." I hold out my hands to them and they each take one and squeeze as they offer the most loving smiles.

The waiter brings our glasses of wine. When he leaves, Mom raises her glass toward the center of our table, over the small vase of billowy pink and lavender roses.

"To a new chapter," she says and winks at me.

"To a new chapter," Aunt Destiny and I say in unison.

We clink our glasses and sip our wine. I'm so lucky to have strong, loving women in my life.

As I set my glass on the table, I catch the glimpse of a man walking by. Dark hair, broad shoulders. My heart immediately yearns for Angelo. Regardless of what happens in the days going forward, I know he'll always be in my thoughts and will reside in a place inside my heart that *no man* will ever consume.

⟫⟫⟫ ⟪⟪⟪

Mom and Dad are both out of town for work and it's the first time I've been alone all week. Not in the mood to try to make something that resembles dinner, I order from Hana Sushi. When it arrives, I set up a tray table at the sofa and surf the channels for something to watch while I eat. Stumbling onto a marathon of old Grey's Anatomy episodes, I snuggle in for a relaxing night.

A couple episodes in, my palms start to sweat as Dr. Bailey talks about the loss of her baby. I want to change the channel, but I don't. I can't move. I'm frozen as I stare, barely able to blink, and listen to her. She shifts from her typical tough, no-bullshit self to a vulnerable woman trying to work through the pain of her loss.

My heart constricts in my chest as tears well in my eyes. *It's just a show.* My teeth vibrate in my mouth, jackhammering in my head. *I'm fine.* I suck in ragged breaths. *Stop it. Stop watching it.* My body trembles uncontrollably. *Turn it off!* Frantic thoughts thrash through my mind. *It's not happening to me.*

It did happen to me.

I lost my baby.

That might've been it, my one chance.

And now it's gone.

Over.

It's not fair.

Why did it happen?

Did *I* make it happen because I didn't want the baby to be Joe's?

Did I cause my one blessing from God to be destroyed?

My baby is gone.

Angelo is gone.

The two things I wanted most in my life are *gone*.

From a place so deep inside me, a sound I don't recognize

shrieks out, lacerating my vocal cords on its way out of my mouth. It's guttural, raw. A sound rooted in pain, anger, sadness. It tortures my body. Like I'm standing beside myself, I watch, horrified. My mouth open, the terrifying sound is abraded as it erupts out of me again, assaulting every molecule of air in the room. Flames of rage ignite in my core, sending heat blazing through me, spiking my blood pressure. Everything within sight turns white-hot as tears pour out and my body curls into itself, convulsing.

So.

Much.

Pain.

28

Angelo

That familiar feeling…dread…crawls through me as I step onto the stage. All eyes are on me, waiting for me to play, waiting for me to sing…waiting for me to not be good enough.

"He's no Niccolo Mancini." The words plague me. A noose tightening around my neck, strangling my voice. Cords constricting in my palms, crippling my fingers. *Get out of my head.* I take a deep breath and exhale, desperate to blow the words out of my mind, my body, my soul.

"Take your time, Angelo." Nick's calm voice breaks into my self-sabotage. "There's no hurry." I'm sure these guys sense nerves from a mile away.

I clear my throat. "Yeah, okay. I'm ready." With that, I strum my guitar and start singing.

As I play for Nick and each band, they nod their heads and move their bodies to the rhythm, practically dancing in their seats. Glances and smiles dart between them, fueling my energy and excitement.

Both auditions go much better than I'd anticipated and I really like Velvet Reprise. They even play a few songs with me and we click immediately. It's amazing, surreal. They were my second audition and we end the day with dinner and their offer for me to join them as their opening act. Elation sets me on a dopamine high. I did it. I did it on my own, without Dad's name or resources. *I did it.*

Though I'm excited, I'm also nervous that this is just a fantasy that could end before it begins…much like what happened with Lucia.

I let Nick and the band know I'm not ready to give up my accounting job entirely, so I need to sort that out. They understand and give me the time I need. I set up a meeting with my boss first thing Monday morning to discuss the possibility of switching to part-time or working remotely in some capacity. I'm not sure how well that's going to go over in the accounting field, but I'm at least going to ask.

Thankfully, he's willing to let me try it on a six-month probationary-type period. I keep my largest accounts and will go to the office when I'm in town. Nick said that the majority of the gigs will be within the U.S. so that helps.

Stoked out of my mind, I call Nick and give him the good news.

"The fans are gonna love you," he says, his words filling me with pride.

He sets up dates for me to open for Velvet Reprise and I mark them all on my calendar. The only thing I want to do is call Lucia and tell her. Nothing in my life ever feels real until I tell her about it.

But I don't call her. I can't.

Instead, I call my parents and share it with them.

⇶ ⇷

Life moves at a quicker pace. Days turn to weeks. Weeks to months. I'm learning to live half a life without Lucia, aching in places I didn't even know were inside me.

Trying to let her go, I started seeing a woman, Tonya, about five months ago. She's not my Lucia, but she's nice and keeps my mind occupied from my heartache. I think she wants more. I just don't know that I can be what she needs. It's probably time I tell her.

On the tour bus with the band on our way to Nevada, I get a call from Mom.

"Hi, Mom."

"Hi, honey. I have some sad news. Your Aunt Candi's dad

passed away," she says, sadness woven into her words.

My heart sinks. "Nonno? What happened?"

"It was sudden. A heart attack."

"Jeez. I'm so sorry, Mom."

"Yeah, me too. He lived a long life, a good life." She sighs.

"Is — Lucia okay?" She had a special bond with him. She must be devastated. Before everything that's gone on between us, I'd have been the first person she came to when she found out. My heart hurts knowing I'm not that person for her anymore.

"She's okay. You know, sad. The funeral's on Friday. Will you be around? Do you think you can come? I know your Aunt Candi would appreciate you being there."

Without a thought, I answer. "Yes, of course I'll be there." *Shit, it'll be the first time I see or talk to Lucia since she left me.* My soul aches as the memory of her driving away with my heart pops into my head.

"Okay. If you want, you can stay here Thursday night. If that works with your schedule. It'll be good to see you. You haven't been home in a while."

"Yeah, I know. It's been so busy with the band and working."

"I know. Well, we look forward to seeing you."

"Me too. I'll come home Thursday."

We hang up and I let the band know. Thankfully, we don't have a gig next weekend so I'm not leaving them in a lurch. I also email my boss at the firm.

All that taken care of, it sinks in, hard, that I'll not only be seeing Lucia, but I'll also be seeing her with Joe and their baby. Did she have a girl, like she wanted, or a boy? All I hope is that she's happy. When it came to Lucia, there was an understanding between me, Mom, Dad, and even Tony: I didn't want to know anything about Lucia or the baby. They've always respected that.

Mid-week, I call Mom and ask if it's okay if I bring Tonya with me. Maybe having her there will dull the pain of seeing Lucia with Joe, though I highly doubt it will. Mom's fine with it and excited to meet Tonya. *Great…shit.*

On the drive home, Tonya's excited to meet my family and is full of questions. I keep my answers brief and to the point. I haven't quite…okay, at all…told her about Lucia.

Mom and Dad have a delicious dinner ready when we get there. Bella comes over too. As we eat, the four of them talk and get to know each other. Bringing Tonya here was probably a bad idea. As soon as we get back, I need to end things with her. It's only fair. Throughout most of the evening, I sit with my thoughts, anxious about seeing Lucia tomorrow.

Mom, Dad, and Bella go in one car while Tonya and I take mine. When we get to the funeral parlor, there's a line of people waiting to pay their respects. Tension twists in my gut. Stale air carries a subtle odor of chemicals mixed with flowers. We move slowly toward the viewing room, hushed conversations murmuring in the air. People stop just outside the room to look at the poster boards teeming with pictures of Nonno and his life. Quiet sounds of joy seep out as they revel in the memories evoked by the images.

As soon as we cross the threshold into the room, I see her. My Lucia. Beautiful. Poised. Stoic. My heart pounds in my chest as tightness creeps up my spine, gouging at my neck. I must've clenched my hands.

"Ow," Tonya says quietly, releasing her hand from mine. "Are you okay?"

"Yeah, yeah. Sorry. You know, funerals."

"I know," she says and rubs my back, catching my gaze on Lucia.

I scan the room, looking for Joe and the baby. I don't see them. Maybe the baby got fussy and he had to take it out of the room. The closer we get to Lucia, the faster my heart beats.

Reaching Uncle Enzo and Aunt Candi, I hug them, express my condolences, and give them a quick introduction to Tonya.

Lucia stands next to them and clearly heard me introduce

Tonya as my girlfriend. Her gaze shifts quickly between the two of us, her expression impenetrable. I catch her jaw tighten, like she's gritting her teeth inside her closed mouth. The look in her eyes tears at my heart. My mouth goes dry and my breath locks in my lungs. I stare at her, unable to move or speak.

Tension splinters the air.

"Hi, Tonya. I'm Lucia," she says politely. "It's nice to meet you. Thank you for coming." Unnoticeable to anyone else, I know her attempted smile is forced.

"I'm so sorry for your loss," Tonya returns.

"Thank you."

I can't take my eyes off Lucia during their exchange. *Shit, bringing Tonya was definitely a bad idea. What the fuck was I thinking?*

Tonya rubs my back, stirring me from my daze. When I turn back to look at her, her silent perusal slides between me and Lucia. Realizing I need to keep the line moving, I bend down and hug Lucia, her sweet coconut scent awakening my senses and flooding me with a warmth that emanates throughout my body.

I don't want to release her, but I do. "I'm so sorry, Luc."

"Thank you," she says, emotionless, her woeful eyes leveling me.

With Tonya's nudge, we move along and find a seat for the brief service. I still don't see Joe and the baby. Did they decide the baby would be too disruptive? I admit I'm grateful to not have to face the situation just yet. Seeing Lucia again is tough enough.

After the service, we caravan to the cemetery. Lucia's sadness tugs on my heart. As I watch her hand quiver when she places a rose on Nonno's casket, I have to push back tears. The priest closes the burial with an invitation to Aunt Candi and Uncle Enzo's house for food and a celebration of Nonno's life.

Everyone disperses to their cars. Tonya and I walk to mine and as we pass the casket, Lucia pulls one of the white folding chairs next to it. She gracefully sits and places her hand on top of it. Her lips move, then she lowers her head. My heart sinks in my chest. I want so badly to wrap my arms around her and take away her sorrow. When I return my attention to Tonya, the doubt in her eyes riddles me with guilt.

My mind races with scattered thoughts as I drive. Everything from Nonno to Aunt Candi and Uncle Enzo, to Lucia, and to Joe and the baby.

"You don't talk much about your family. They're very nice." Tonya's voice shakes me from my thoughts.

"They are. Yeah, I guess I don't really." Doing so would inevitably lead to Lucia so I've avoided it.

"You seem very close with Nonno's family. But you're not related in any way?"

"Our families have always been close, but no, my Aunt Candi and Uncle Enzo aren't actually related to me. My mom and Aunt Candi have been best friends since way before I was even born so they're kind of an honorary aunt and uncle."

"It was nice to meet Lucia." Suspicion rides her tone. I avoid looking at her. "You've been friends your whole lives then?" She's fishing.

I couldn't stop myself from watching Lucia, at the service, at the burial. Tonya saw me. She senses something or she wouldn't be fishing.

"We have. She's like another little sister." I make my best attempt to squash any further questions from her. "And she and Bella get along great."

"Mmm."

Nothing more is said by either of us as we finish the drive. Unease churns inside me as we approach the house. Surely Joe and the baby will be here since it's a setting where babies can cry and make a fuss without disrupting the serious nature of a funeral.

We're one of the first to arrive. Aunt Candi, Uncle Enzo, and Lucia are buzzing around, helping the caterers. No sign of Joe and the baby.

"Can we help?" I ask, approaching them.

"Actually, I think we're just about ready, but thank you," Uncle Enzo says.

People start filtering in behind us and the house fills with quiet conversations, tearful embraces, and stories of happier times. I still don't see Joe and the baby. When Mom starts talking to Tonya, I excuse myself to find Lucia. She's keeping busy cleaning up plates, napkins, and glasses.

"Hi," I say, matching my voice to the somber occasion that's brought us together.

She must not have noticed me approaching because she startles a little.

"Hi." For a breath, she looks into my eyes, searching. "Thank, thank you so much for coming." Discomfort splices through her words. "It's nice that you came out. We all appreciate it." Her coolness brushes across me like sleet.

"Of course I'd be here for you." *Was there seriously a doubt in her mind that I wouldn't be here for something like* this?

"I heard you called that agent. So, are you playing now?" The corners of her lips lift in a polite, hopeful smile.

Our surface conversation is devoid of the closeness we once shared. Despair is a ghost in my soul. Is it her sadness about Nonno? Is it that Tonya's here? She can't be upset about that, she's with Joe. Or is this what our relationship has become? Polite exchanges. *Fuck.*

"Yeah, I did. I actually have the best of both worlds. I'm still working for the firm part-time so I have some stable income, which is nice. And the touring's been really great," I say with an emptiness. My excitement from the day I'd wanted to call and share all this with her has been tarnished. Time has passed. Heartache lingers.

Her weak smile broadens genuinely. "I'm so happy for you, Ang."

I force a swallow as my face heats. "Where's Joe and your baby?" I swallow again, hard. "I was thinking I'd get to meet him or her." The least I can do is be cordial.

The skin on her face turns pale as her eyes move back and forth between mine rapidly. Finally, she blinks, her despondence rushing the air, emitting from every part of her, slipping beneath my skin. "Ang, I — I lost the baby." Pain lances her words as agony stakes through the center of my chest.

Tingles skate across my skin as my blood feels like it flushes out of my body. *My God. I wasn't here for her.*

Without thinking, I wrap my arms around her, holding her tightly to my chest. Knowing her fear that she may only ever be able to have one child, my soul aches for her. Affection pulsing through my chest, all I want to do is take away her pain. As if my embrace melts her stoicism, she loops her arms around my waist and buries her head into my chest. It feels like I've waited a lifetime to have her in my arms again.

The room around us vanishes, if only for a moment, as we stand body-to-body, heart-to-heart, soul-to-soul, mourning in a different way.

Releasing her, I take her hands in mine. "Why didn't you tell me?" I ask, softly begging to understand why she wouldn't have told me something this big and important.

Her lips pull into a thin line as she shrugs. "I'd already messed up enough things in my life, I wasn't going to mess up yours too. I couldn't let you throw away your future because of me." An edge creeps into her posture as her brows pinch together.

I lower my head, squeezing her hands. "Luc, you're my *best* friend. And I'm yours. We're woven into each other's souls. There's nothing you could ever do to mess up my life." I lie, trying to relieve the guilt her vulnerably is exposing to me. The day she left, she took my heart with her, fucking me up to the point that I didn't even recognize myself. Not a day has passed that I don't think about her. Whether it's the scent of coconut on a random woman walking by me, canisters of oatmeal in the grocery store, or a cloud shaped like a bunny…Lucia lives inside every part of me.

"I couldn't." She shakes her head, a pained smile making my ribs clamp around my aching heart.

I release an exasperated sigh of regret. I'd asked my parents not to tell me anything about Lucia, but I'm surprised they didn't tell me about *this*. I can't imagine what she went through. I'd have been by her side if I'd known. My heart hurts for her.

She moves her eyes from mine and quickly releases her hands from my grip. "Um, it looks like your girlfriend is looking for you. I — I need to clean up a few things." She tucks a stray hair behind her ear and walks away, leaving me standing there, my insides all gnarled up.

Within seconds, Tonya's standing in front of me.

"Everything okay?" she asks.

No, nothing *is okay*. "Yeah, uh, everything's fine." I lie, glancing at Lucia across the room.

"Angelo?" Tonya says, her voice interrupting my preoccupied thoughts.

I return my focus to her.

She swivels her gaze to Lucia then back to me. "At least now I know why you've never wanted to take our relationship further." Despondence draws her weak smile.

"Tonya." Repentance cloaks her name as it leaves my mouth. *Shit.*

She shakes her head. "It's okay. I get it. I want someone to look at me…the way you look at her. I would be foolish to not acknowledge the connection between you. It's what I want, what I deserve, for myself. I don't want to be anyone's second choice. So I'm going to graciously step aside."

"God, Tonya. I'm so sorry. I — I don't know what to say right now." My shoulders slump forward as my stomach turns hard.

She takes my hands in hers. "There's nothing to say. I've enjoyed our time together. And, as much as I'd wanted more from our relationship, deep down, I knew something was missing. So now it's time for me to go find — what you two have." She stretches up, pressing her lips to my cheek and turns to walk away.

"Tonya, wait. I, ugh. What can I do?" *I'm such an asshole. I should've ended things with her sooner. I shouldn't have brought her here.*

"You can stay here with your family and the people you love. I'm going to get an Uber to a car rental place and go home."

"I can — I can drive you." I step toward her.

Her smile is warm. "No. I don't want you to do that. I want you to stay here and follow your heart." She glances at Lucia. "I want to know I did the right thing…for both of us. Goodbye, Angelo."

With that, she turns and leaves. I don't know if I should go after her or let her go. *What a dick I am.* My feelings for Lucia can't be disguised or extinguished. They can't be hidden or vanquished. They've existed since before we were both born and they'll exist long after we're both dead.

And still, I don't know if our love is lost for us in this lifetime.

29

Lucia

People begin leaving, stopping to express their condolences once more on their way out. The day has been exhausting, in so many ways.

Meeting Angelo's girlfriend caught me off guard, *way* off guard. Hurt percolated inside me, increasing to a boil as the day went on. My heart still wants him to be mine. But I messed that up. The best friend in me wants him to be happy.

I busy myself with cleaning up. Anything to take my mind off my anguish and having to look at Angelo and Tonya.

Mindlessly picking up plates in the sunroom, I stack them in my hand. The warm sun beckons my gaze and I look out the tall windows at our back yard, reminiscing. *Nonno pushes me on the swing that hangs from the tree. I giggle as my hair blows behind me, and he laughs that warm, husky laugh of his.*

"I miss you, Nonno," I whisper.

"Lucia?" Angelo's deep voice rumbles through me and I nearly drop the handful of plates I'd collected.

I turn to face him, forcing a smile to my lips. "Are you and Tonya leaving now?"

"No, uh, she left already."

"Oh, I figured you came together."

"We did. And she left," he says flatly.

"Oh." I must be drained from the day because I'm not following.

He approaches me and takes the dishes from my hands, setting them on a nearby table. Shrinking the space between us, he cups my face in his hands and moves his head back and forth slowly, locking his eyes on mine, sucking me into their chasm. Air lodges in my lungs as a rush of heat scatters across my skin.

Bowing his head, he covers my lips with his.

Longing mixes with lost love, pain, remorse, and desire.

Tonya jumps to the front of my mind and I push against Angelo's chest, parting our bodies. "Angelo, we can't. Tonya."

"Tonya's gone. She felt what neither of us can deny. What's always been there between us. And she left." He steps toward me again, taking my hands in his. "I am fiercely in love with you, Lucia. And I have been my entire life. I love how nurturing and generous you are. I love how alarmingly present you are with anyone you come in contact with. I love how funny and smart and compassionate and beautiful you are. I love the way you nibble your lower left lip when you're concentrating. Never the right side, always the left. I love that you prefer chocolate with some kind of fruit instead of just plain." Words tumble out of him, raw and unfiltered as he comes even closer to me.

I'm speechless as I listen, swept up in the wild current of his outpour.

"I know when there's a storm brewing in your eyes. I hear you when your voice is silent. I feel when your heart is heavy. I *know* you. I know everything there is to know about you. And I love all of you. And because of you, I know who I am and what I want. I don't want to live another moment of my life without you in it. I want to exist inside the warmth of your heart every day. And all those crazy dandelion wishes you made me make? *Every* wish I made was to be with you. For you to be mine. My heart was *never* available for anyone else because you've owned it since the day you were born. *You* are my heart, Lucia. It's always been you." His breath hits my lips, knocking the air from my lungs.

Gasping in the wake of his love-filled deluge, I'm flooded with happiness and the purest of love.

"Why did you wait so long to tell me all this?" I ask, as tears spill from my eyes.

He tangles his hands into my hair as he gently brushes his thumbs across my cheeks. "Because. I didn't want to be your first love. I wanted to be your last." The truth in his eyes tears me into pieces.

"You are and will always be my *only* love." *Forever.*

A smile spreads across his cheeks and he kisses me once more. When he releases my lips, he drops to one knee, looking up at me. My heart lurches and pounds.

"I realize this isn't the ideal time or place, but I'm hoping Nonno's looking down on us with his approval because I'm done waiting. I love you with everything in me. Will you marry me, Dandelion Girl, and let me love you for the rest of our lives?"

I sink to the floor with him as tears of joy spill out of me. Overwhelmed with the emotions consuming me, it takes a moment before I can speak.

"Please say yes," he whispers, wiping away the tear that just fell from my eye.

Taking his face in my hands, I say yes repeatedly as I kiss him over and over.

High-pitched squeals come from behind us. When we look over, our moms are in the doorway, clapping their hands and hugging each other. Our dads stand behind them, grinning from ear to ear and shaking their heads at our moms.

We both get up from the floor and our parents walk away, giving us privacy.

Looking down at me, he smashes his lips to mine, kissing me long and hard, intensifying the emotions that are already engulfing me. When he releases me, leaving me breathless as he always does, he stands back a little and shoves a hand in his pocket, rubbing the back of his neck with the other. "This was, uh, not what I was expecting to happen. I'm sorry, but I don't have your ring here. It's back at my condo."

"You — have a ring?" I ask, my thoughts incredulous.

"I've had it for a long time." Bowing his head, he glances back up with his eyes. "I was going to ask you the day you left."

I release a sigh of heartache at his admission. The day I left him. The worst day of my life. Leaving him that day was the hardest thing I've ever done. *That was the day he was going to ask me to marry him?* No wonder there was so much pain on his face.

I throw my arms around him, squeezing him tightly. Knowing that he's felt the same about me as I've felt about him all these years has my heart racing. "I love you, Angelo Mancini," I whisper against his ear.

"I love *you*, Lucia Mancini." Hearing him combine my name with his sends a shiver up my spine and I smile with my face buried into his neck.

For so much of my life, I resented Angelo's need to be my protector. Looking back, I'm so happy he was. I no longer need someone to watch over me. All I need is his love. It's all I'll ever need.

Overcome with emotion, I lift my legs to wrap around his waist and he embraces me in his arms. I've dreamed of a moment like this with him my entire life. And it's nothing short of *perfect*.

30

Angelo

I was terrified of asking Lucia to marry me. The wrong place. The wrong time. And the possibility of her saying no had me incredibly tense. But I couldn't wait any longer. I couldn't let another day go by without her. I *need* her in my life the way I need air to breathe.

When she finally said yes, I thought my heart was going to crack wide open. I almost broke down in tears of happiness. I've never wanted to hear such a simple word so badly in my life. Lucia is mine. She's going to be my wife. I've loved her my entire life and now she'll be mine forever.

We unravel from each other and she settles onto her feet.

I plant my hands on her hips. "Come home with me this weekend. I don't want to be away from you."

A gentle smile lifts her beautiful lips as she laces her fingers behind my neck. "Okay. But I want to stay here tonight with my parents. How about I come tomorrow?"

"Yeah, you should do that. Okay, tomorrow. Then you're all mine."

Her smile broadens. "Yup, all yours." She lifts up onto her toes and kisses me. I'll never get enough of her sweet lips.

My parents and I say our goodbyes to Lucia and her family, leaving them to grieve. I stay with my parents for an early dinner and drive back to my place, excited about all the things I want to do to prepare for Lucia to come tomorrow.

The minute I walk in the door, I get started.

Lucia

I wanted to go with Angelo last night, but it was good I stayed with my parents. It was special time together. After we cleaned up the house, we looked through old photo albums and reminisced, telling stories about Nonna and Nonno.

My sleep was restless after a day of wild emotions. I kept running Angelo's words through my head. It's real. He loves me and I love him. Visceral love spreads through me grounding in my heart.

The drive to him feels like forever. When I pull into the parking spot next to his, he's coming down the stairs toward me, looking so good in his jeans, gray T-shirt, and bare feet. Butterflies dance inside me. I get out of my car and he immediately wraps me in his arms, lifts me off my feet, and kisses me.

"I've been wanting to do that all day," he says with a huge smile, then places me back on my feet. "Come on. I've got the day planned for us." He grabs my bags from the back seat in one hand and takes my hand in the other, and we go up to his condo.

Still holding my hand, he walks us back to his bedroom and puts my bags on the floor near the plastic drawers that are still there. Then he tugs me into the closet with him and turns on the light. Half of it is empty, from the floor to the clothing bar to the shelf.

"Where's all your stuff?" I ask, looking up at him.

The corners of his lips draw down as he shrugs. "I had a bunch of things I don't even wear anymore so I went through it all and brought a couple bags to donation this morning."

I shake my head. "You didn't have to do that."

He pulls me into his arms, his head hovering above mine as he looks at me with his beautiful brown eyes. "Yeah, I did. I wanted to make room for you and your things. I want this to be *our* home. At least until we decide on something a little bigger." His eyes widen as he releases me. "And…" He takes my hand and pulls me into the bathroom then opens the narrow closet door. The bottom two shelves are empty. "For all your lotions and makeup and stuff." His proud smile melts my heart.

I can't help but grin at how adorable this man is. "It's perfect." I lift up to kiss his cheek.

"Are you hungry?"

I nod. "Mhm. I could eat."

"Okay, let's go. There's a place I want to take you. I think you're gonna like it." I don't know what's gotten into him, but he's like an excited little kid. And I love it.

"Okay, I'll be right out."

He leaves the bathroom and I close the door to pee. Looking at the empty shelves, my whole body fills with happiness. When I leave the bathroom and walk toward the door, my eye catches two empty bookshelves that were previously occupied by his books. He's made space for me in every possible way.

He drives us to a cute café where we sit outside under a bright red umbrella. A small glass vase filled with yellow roses and daisies sits on the table. After we place our orders, he asks how my night was with my parents and I share with him some of the stories about Nonna and Nonno.

"So, you're about to be on summer break, right?"

"Yeah, in a couple weeks."

"I want you to move in with me. I mean, I want you to come *now*, but I know you have to finish out your school year. And I don't expect you to just up and leave your job. We'll have to talk about what we're going to do and where we're going to live. And it doesn't even matter to me. All I know is that I want to be with you."

Angelo wants to be with me. It still feels like a dream. "Yeah, we have some decisions to make with our jobs being two hours apart." Though I love my job, I'd leave it in a heartbeat to be with Angelo. I can find another teaching job.

"Come stay with me over the summer and we'll work through it together. This morning I jumped online and checked out some schools in the area and also found some slightly bigger condos. I thought we could drive around and take a look at them to get a feel for what's around here. And if we decide we want to go back closer to home and you want to stay at your school, I can look for a job there. With the band, it doesn't matter where I am. You can even come with me on some gigs if you want."

The waiter brings our food and we thank him.

"I'd love to watch you play." I take a bite of my sandwich. "Mmm, we may have to make this place our Saturday lunch destination. This is delicious."

"I thought you'd like it here." His grin fills with satisfaction.

We finish our lunches and spend the afternoon driving around, looking at schools and condos. Around dinner time, we head back to his place...*our* place.

"Dinner and a movie?" he asks as we climb the stairs.

"Definitely."

"I'll get dinner started. You find a movie for us."

He goes to the kitchen and takes out a large pot, filling it with water and placing it on the stovetop. Then he puts ground beef into a frying pan, turning the heat on low. I flip on the TV and search for movies.

"Lasagna good for you?"

Only one of my favorite meals. "Yes, please. Can I help?"

"Of course you can, just don't burn anything."

We both laugh at the unfortunate reality that I might, and I join him in the kitchen.

"You can work on the cheese mixture. That's safe." He winks then lifts me to sit on the counter, standing between my legs.

Weaving his hands through my hair, he covers my lips with his, sliding his tongue into my mouth. A tiny moan fills my throat and he deepens his kiss in response. I wrap my legs around his waist and he tugs me to the edge of the counter. Pressing his hard-on into me, he moves his lips from mine and travels down my neck with hungry kisses. His neck-kisses make me dizzy with pleasure.

Aggressive sizzling of the ground beef fills the air and he jumps back from me, grabbing the pan and removing it from the burner. Looking back at me, he shakes his head.

"Damn, you're distracting." His lips lift into that sexy side-smile of his that makes me weak.

"Cheeses are in the fridge," he says.

I hop off the counter to get a bowl and the cheeses.

We're making dinner together in our place and everything feels right. Being with Angelo is where I belong, where I've always belonged. He's mine and I'm his.

31

Angelo

After the movie finishes, we clean up the dishes together. My nerves are piqued.

"Should be a nice night for stargazing. You up for it?" *Please say yes.*

Her eyes widen and she nods with a smile. My heart beats a little faster.

"It's supposed to be a little cool tonight. You might want to grab a sweatshirt." I make the suggestion knowing I need to buy myself some time.

"Okay, I'll be right up."

As soon as she's out of sight, I quickly open the cabinet above the refrigerator and grab the small, red-velvet box. Opening it, I take out her ring and put it into my front pocket. Then I get the bottle of champagne from the fridge and dart up the stairs to the rooftop. I'd snuck up earlier when she was in the bathroom and filled the silver bucket with ice. Dropping the bottle into the ice, I light the candles and tiki torches as fast as I can. I hurriedly pull up a playlist I'd made of romantic songs I know she loves. Then I hide behind the door…and wait.

She steps onto the deck and stops, taking in the scene. Blankets laid out with pillows for our heads. Champagne in the bucket with two empty glasses nestled between the pillows. Twenty small glass bottles filled with fluffy dandelions placed around the space. While she's busy looking at everything, I move in behind her.

When she feels me at her back, she turns to face me, covering her mouth with her hands as she breathes in.

Looking down into her misty eyes, I have to swallow the lump in my throat before I can speak.

"Lucia, I've been waiting my whole life to be with you. Life throws us curve balls, that's for sure. But there's one certainty that's always remained a constant for me and that's been that I want to marry you. I love your strength and independence. I love how close our families are. I love that you fill up my heart with all of your love without even knowing you're doing it. I promise to love you for all the days of the rest of our lives."

A tear falls from her eye that I wipe away.

"I know I already asked you and you already said yes, but I wanted to do it better." Pulling her ring out of my jeans pocket, I drop to one knee. "Lucia, will you marry me?" I hold out the ring toward her.

Her face crinkles as tears flow from her eyes and she lowers to join me. Kneeling on both knees, she wraps her arms around my neck, her sweet scent of coconut drifts into my nose. Holding her head against me, I wrap my arm around her as her soft sniffles fill my ears.

"It's still yes, right?"

She chuckles as she releases me and sits back onto her shins. "Yes." She smiles and nods as she swipes tears from under her eyes.

"Here," I say, reaching for her left hand.

She spreads her fingers for me to slide the ring on. Once it's on, she moves her hand around so the candlelight catches the cuts of the diamond.

"Oh, Ang. It's just beautiful." She looks up at me with the biggest smile and happiness floods me.

"*You're* beautiful," I say, winding my arms around her and kissing her.

Though it's been a bumpy road to get here, if I had to do it all over again and live through every ounce of sorrow and excruciating heartache, knowing it would lead me to this moment, right here, right now, I'd do it again in a heartbeat. I'd suffer through the pain, the loneliness, the endless nights of thinking about her, and my wounded heart missing her if it meant that we'd land right where we are in this very moment with her in my arms, wanting to be my wife, and our future together ahead of us. I'd go through it all again because Lucia is worth it. I've been in love with her my entire life and now I get to be her husband and love her for the rest of our lives.

EPILOGUE

——

Lucia

It's been an amazing summer. I finished out the school year at Canyon and Angelo and I got married a month later. We both wanted a small, intimate ceremony with our families and closest friends. My parents hosted our wedding in their back yard and it was like a fairytale. Thousands of twinkling lights hung from trees. Long wooden tables were dressed with rustic table runners of lace and burlap, and clusters of flowers in muted tans and pinks ran the length of them. Uncle Nicco, Dad, and Angelo even played a few songs together for all of us. It was just how I'd always imagined it would be.

Since I've been on summer break, I've joined Angelo on a few of his tours. It's been fun traveling around with him and the band. They're all really great guys, incredibly talented and down-to-earth. When he's not performing, we make the most of our time together experiencing the different towns and cities, and making memories.

He seems to have found a good balance for himself working for the accounting firm part-time and being able to fuel his creative side with his music. Watching him is magical. His talent is raw and pure, just like his dad's. It's in his soul. He lights up from the inside when he's singing and playing his guitar.

We talked through the different options of our jobs and where to live and decided to move back home to be closer to our parents and our friends. I'll continue working at Canyon and it turns out that his boss is fine with him working remotely so he kept his job.

We made sure to get a place with a rooftop deck and when he's home, I get private shows. He's even started to write more of his own songs, which I love. We kept most of the furniture from his condo and went shopping for a few things that we picked out together. Our home is a comfortable mix of both of our styles.

He's away this week for a longer tour and I decided to stay home. Prisha's here for an early birthday celebration and I'm excited to see her. After a day of shopping, we head home for a relaxing night in. She's promised to make my favorite meal of hers and I'm so excited. I haven't had it in a long time and I'm looking forward to it.

As she cooks, I set the table and find a movie for us to watch. The spices of her turmeric chicken coconut curry float through the air, into my nostrils…and wreak all-out havoc on me. I gasp. *I know this feeling.* Panic unleashes in a fury, sending me sprinting to the bathroom.

Vomit spews out as Prisha sits on the floor next to me, holding my hair. When it's over, I look at her. The huge smile on her face makes me laugh.

Her eyes open wide as the muscles in her neck tense. "Do you think?" she asks excitedly.

I shake my head, lifting my shoulders toward my ears. "I — I don't know. Maybe?" I've never been so happy to puke my guts up. This is a *very* different feeling from the last time. I'm a mix of excitement and happiness.

She jumps up. "You stay here and clean yourself up. I'm going to toss the food and go get a pregnancy test. What can I get you to eat?"

I burst into laughter at her giddiness. "Um, okay. We have eggs, I can just make that. But, is that enough for you?"

"Absolutely. You okay?" she confirms.

"Yup, I'm good," I say, getting up from the floor.

"Okay. I shouldn't be long." She squeals on her way out of the bathroom.

Hopefulness swells in my chest as I wash off my face and blow my nose. *Is this real? Can this be happening?*

As I wait for Prisha to return, I guzzle a glass of water and sit on the sofa. My thoughts race. Though excitement pervades, there's an underlying hint of fear that this isn't real or that I might lose the baby if it *is* real.

Prisha blows through the door and dumps the pregnancy test out of the plastic bag onto the kitchen island.

"Come on, come on," she says with animation as she walks over to me, holding out her hand. "Can you pee?"

I stand up and take her hand. "I think so. I downed some water while you were gone."

She sets the box on the bathroom sink and closes the door behind her.

Following the instructions, I pee on the stick. As soon as I'm done, I set the timer on my phone and go out to Prisha.

"I'll make dinner while we wait," she says. "It'll keep us occupied. How do you want your eggs?"

"Good thinking. Scrambled is fine."

I get out the eggs, milk, and cheese. Prisha gets a bowl and whisk. As we move around, neither of us speaks. Nerves bounce between us. She cracks the eggs into the bowl and starts whisking.

My timer dings and we snap our heads toward one another. Clasping our hands, we run to the bathroom to look at the stick.

PREGNANT.

Goose bumps prickle the surface of my skin before we both erupt into joyous screams. She throws her arms around me and we squeeze each other.

"This is a miracle baby," she says softly in my ear, then releases me and touches my stomach as she smiles. Her eyes spring open. "I get to be an honorary aunt, right?"

I chuckle. "Of course you do."

"Yes." She waggles her head and wiggles her body. "Come on, let's eat and celebrate."

"Okay, I'll be right there."

She goes back to the kitchen and I take a picture of the stick before throwing it and the packaging in the trash. I sit quietly on the toilet and wrap my arms around my stomach. Closing my eyes, I say a silent prayer, "Please stay with me."

We eat and she spends the night. Much of our conversation has turned to talking about the baby. When she leaves the next morning, I go to Target and get a onesie® that says, "hi daddy" on it. Then I stop and get the picture of the pregnancy test developed. Angelo will be home tomorrow night and our plan is to celebrate my birthday. But *I'll* have a present for *him*.

⋙ ⋘

When Angelo comes home, he looks exhausted. He drops his bags and guitar case at the door and comes straight over to me. I stand from the sofa and he takes me in his arms, lowering his head into me.

"Mmm, it's so good to be home." He exhales into my hair.

"It's good to have you home," I say as I release him. "I have a present for you." Impatience laces with excitement, humming inside me.

"A present for me? We're supposed to be celebrating *your* birthday. What did you get me?"

I grab the small, wrapped package from the island and bring it to him. "Go ahead. Open it." Anticipation whirs.

"Right now?" Confusion pulls his brows.

"Mhm." I nod, ready to burst.

He rips off the paper and removes the lid then pushes aside the crinkly tissue paper. It takes a second to register. Then he shifts his eyes to me.

Tears well in his lower lids as he drops the box on the coffee table, captures my face in his hands, and kisses me. His kiss still makes my heart race and I have a feeling it always will. Releasing me, he touches his forehead to mine. As tears fall from his eyes, his smile spreads wide on his face. He wraps his arms around me, cradling my head to his chest.

"I love you so much," he says, then lowers to his knees, lifts my shirt, and kisses my stomach. Turning his head to rest on my skin, he closes his eyes and places his hand next to his face. "Hi, baby. I'm your daddy."

The love of my life rests his head on my belly where our baby grows inside me. No dream, no fantasy could ever be this good.

Thank You!

Thanks for reading Someone to Watch Over Me. Your support means so much to me. I hope you loved it!

If you did enjoy Angelo and Lucia's love story, please take a moment to leave your honest review on Amazon, GoodReads, and/ or BookBub. Thank you!

WHAT TO READ NEXT...

Untouchable Zane
https://books2read.com/u/47Npla

AN INVITATION

This is a special invitation for YOU. Yes, you. I know you can join thousands of authors' newsletters and I know that can be overwhelming. The readers who choose to join my free newsletter are friends to me, people who actually want to be with me in my little corner of the world.

Of course, I share updates about my books, and I also share personal stories, tough times, funny times, goats/chickens/bunny pictures, do special giveaways no one else gets, give you the first look at covers and chapters, and more.

So, this is my personal invitation to you to jump into my world and join my free newsletter. When you do, you'll receive free chapters of some of my books and a fun Book BINGO Challenge printable PDF.

HEAD HERE TO JOIN:

https://debbiecromack.com/newsletter/

BROKEN BILLIONAIRE BROTHERS SERIES

WHERE DID THE IDEA FOR THIS BOOK COME FROM?

As I was finishing Kiss Away Your Pain, the love story of Lucia's parents, Candi and Enzo, the idea struck me. Wounded Hearts was going to be a duology until the idea of Nicco and Destiny's son, and Candi and Enzo's daughter falling in love smacked me in the face.

I had no idea what their story was going to be, but I knew it needed to be told. So, I invited them to tell me and then I documented it here for you.

I hope you enjoyed reading Angelo and Lucia's story. Be sure to check out my other books!

MORE BOOKS BY
Debbie Cromack

Standalones
Untouchable Zane

Wounded Hearts Series
Someone Exactly Like Me
Kiss Away Your Pain
Someone to Watch Over Me

ACKNOWLEDGMENTS

My loyal readers and fans who eagerly await my new releases and always share with me your excitement about each upcoming book. Your love of my stories makes me happier than I can even express. Your support is what keeps me writing. I appreciate you so much!

The writing community and my author friends, I'm so grateful for you. Your love, support, guidance, and virtual hugs mean more to me than you could know. Special shoutouts to **A.L. Jackson, Willow Aster, Laura Pavlov, Angela Ford, and C. D'Angelo**. I'm looking forward to hugging you in person one of these days.

Najla and Nada (Qamber Designs & Media), thank you for making my cover beautiful (as always) and for making the interior of my books look fabulous and professional. You're both amazing to work with and I'm so grateful for you!

Susan Staudinger (Stylistic Editing), thank you for your patience, brainstorming, love, and encouragement. Having you in my corner means so much to me. Thank you for helping me grow and learn.

Kat Wyeth (Kat's Literary Services), thank you for trudging through this with me. Not only for making my words make sense, but also for brainstorming with me and holding loving space for me. I'm so lucky to have you on my team.

Ellison Lane (Kat's Literary Services), thank you for seeing all the things my weary eyes grew blind to and making me laugh by pointing them out in your kindhearted way. I appreciate you.

My wonderful beta readers, **Courteney Tunstead and Melissa Johnson**. Thank you for always giving me your open and honest feedback. My craft and my stories only ever improve because of you. THANK YOU!

My ARC and Street teams, bloggers, booktokers, booktubers, and bookstagrammers, thank you so much for your help and support. I could never reach new readers without all of your time and effort. I love seeing the beautiful graphics and posts you create. Thank you for what you do for me and the writing community.

I'd like to send out a special thank you to some of the incredible women in my Slow Burn Sisterhood. You make this wild journey so much more comforting and less isolating by **always** being there for me. Though we've never met, you're sisters of my heart and I'm so grateful that our paths have come together. You are the epitome of who I want to continue to surround myself with because you love, support, care, and encourage without judgement. Someday when we meet, I'm going to hug the stuffing out of you! **KG Fletcher, D. L. Croisette, Gala Russ, Stacey Komosinki, Devin Sloane, Kallyn Jones, and Lily Baines** – thank you for being my constant source of support. I love you.

And **YOU, my new reader**. Thank you for taking a chance on me and reading my book. I hope you loved it!!! Without you, I wouldn't be able to do this work I love so much and bring you more stories to escape into. Thank you!

ABOUT THE AUTHOR

Hi! I'm Debbie and I write contemporary novels that are romantic, sexy, and emotional with a lot of heart and worth-the-wait steam. I've been called the Master of Slow Burn, a title I happily accept.

I write realistic, flawed characters you'd want to get to know in real life. My heroes are virile and also broken. They have huge hearts, respect their women, and have a hidden romantic side. These men don't just fall in love, they fall and never look back. My heroines are often awkward, feisty, and embody everything the hero never knew he needed.

After spending 25+ years in corporate America, being the CEO of an event decorating company, and then an online business coach, I tried my hand at writing romance novels, publishing my debut novel at the age of 50, and have been writing ever since.

I live in an old farmhouse where I care for a dwarf bunny named Nutmeg, two Nigerian dwarf goats named Patches and Tiny, and lots of chickens. I like my book boyfriends how I like my cocoa: hot and yummy! With my knack for decorating, I tend to go all-out for each holiday. And I'm a total sucker for the Hallmark Channel…especially at Christmas.

CONNECT WITH ME

Come connect with me on my **social media accounts.** Here's my Linktree link where you can find **ALL** my links: linktr.ee/Debbie_Cromack_Author